MILLION
PIECES
OF
NEENA
GILL

EMMA SMITH-BARTON

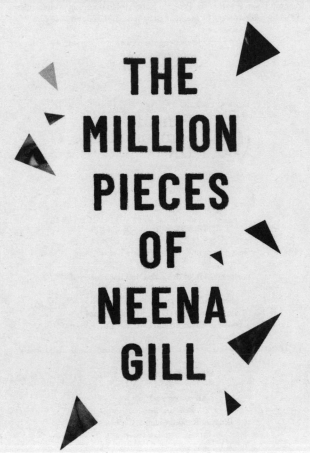

THE MILLION PIECES OF NEENA GILL

PENGUIN BOOKS

PENGUIN BOOKS

UK | USA | Canada | Ireland | Australia
India | New Zealand | South Africa

Penguin Books is part of the Penguin Random House group of companies
whose addresses can be found at global.penguinrandomhouse.com.

www.penguin.co.uk
www.puffin.co.uk
www.ladybird.co.uk

First published 2019

001

Text copyright © Emma Smith-Barton, 2019

The moral right of the author has been asserted

Set in 10.75/15.5 pt Adobe Caslon Pro
Typeset by Jouve (UK), Milton Keynes
Printed and bound in Great Britain by Clays Ltd, Elcograf S.p.A.

A CIP catalogue record for this book is available from the British Library

ISBN: 978-0-241-36331-7

All correspondence to:
Penguin Books
Penguin Random House Children's
80 Strand, London WC2R ORL

For Oli, for everything

Four Years Earlier

The moon is full and bright, and I try to focus on that, try to distract myself, but it's not working. Nothing's working.

We're standing in the middle of the garden, Akash and me. Bare feet on crisp, dry grass. Akash has brought me out here because Mum and Dad are arguing inside. Their voices are getting louder.

I feel sick. I'm breathing fast, as fast as I can, because there's not enough air and I need more. My chest is tight. It hurts. My whole body hurts. I try not to cry.

Akash crouches down next to me. 'Breathe in deep,' he tells me, his voice low and calm. 'Like I showed you, yeah? Deep into your belly.' He presses his hands against his stomach.

I nod. Akash knows all about helping me breathe. He's fourteen and I'm eleven. We've done this before.

I close my eyes, ready to breathe into my belly. But everything – my chest, throat, my whole body – is too tight. Dad's still shouting, but Mum's now quiet. Somehow that's even worse. Pain shoots across my chest, up my arms, my legs. 'I can't!' I tell Akash, my eyes flicking open.

There's a lump in my throat the size of the moon. The moon has fallen out of the sky and down my throat. That's impossible,

I

I know, but this is how it feels. The tears I've been holding back drip down my cheeks.

Akash buries his hands deep into his jeans pockets, his eyes bright. 'You can. Try again. And think of somewhere nice this time. Remember?'

I nod. Dry my cheeks. Yes, somewhere nice. A happy place. I keep my eyes open this time; focus on Akash's wonky smile and straight teeth. I picture the seaside we go to in the summer. See Mum and Dad lying on the beach. I hear waves crashing against rocks. Feel my toes sink into warm sand. Smell salt and doughnuts.

And I breathe. Deep. Into my belly. Eventually, my chest stops hurting. My body feels looser. And, although my chest is still a bit tight, the moon is back in the sky, not in my throat.

'Do you think they're . . . getting a divorce?' I ask, remembering my best friend, Raheela. She cried for months when her dad left. Even in lessons.

'Nah. It's just a disagreement.' Akash shrugs. 'It happens.'

'Really? You're sure?'

He nods. 'Don't worry, OK?'

We sit down on the grass, facing away from the house, looking towards the shed at the back of the garden. Mum and Dad are now quiet. Maybe Akash is right.

'You're very wise,' I tell him, smiling now.

Akash laughs. He drapes his arm round my shoulders and I press my face into his soft, cosy hoody. He smells like he always smells: of deodorant, mints and cigarette smoke. 'Yeah, full of the wisdom, me! What would you do without me, eh?'

I'm staring at my sky-sea. It's my favourite painting in the world. I love how Van Gogh makes the inky sky look like it's water, and the stars and moon have fallen in, making hundreds of golden ripples around them. My brother bought me the framed poster for my birthday. *Starry Night*, it's called. The picture's unbalanced. Unsteady. It's how the world feels when I worry. It's how I feel.

But then is it so surprising that I'm worrying a lot lately?

Mum hasn't left the house for months.

Dad's impossible to be around since everything happened.

And I don't know who my friends are any more. Don't know who I am.

I'm falling into my own sky-sea.

Because my brother disappeared.

It's been ten months.

And I'm shattering into pieces.

2

'Neena?' Mum knocks on my bedroom door and fumbles with the handle. 'You still awake?'

I pull my eyes away from the sky-sea poster above my dressing table and quickly slip into the chair at my desk. All my schoolbooks are out ready for this moment, so I just grab a pen and fix a look of concentration on my face. Furrowed brows. Twisty lips. Totally natural, not staged at all.

'I'm awake,' I call, burying my head in the books. 'Come on in.' I say that last bit under my breath because Mum always barges in after she knocks, like she *really* doesn't get the point of knocking. Not that she'd notice the sarcasm, even if she heard me. She doesn't notice much these days.

'Ach, still studying!' she says, coming into the room.

Laughter and chatter drift in with her. Mum and Dad's friends are over. They're here almost *every* evening now. It's their way of helping, I get that – it's just a bit much. I wish they'd leave us alone. But it does mean I can sneak away without Mum and Dad paying too much attention. Silver lining and all that. And tonight I've got a party to go to. So, double silver lining. They'd never let me go if they actually *knew* I was going . . .

I glance at Mum. She's balancing a tray on her hip. Her long black hair is plaited neatly and pulled to one side, draping over her right shoulder. There's always this transformation when her friends come over: she washes her hair, changes her clothes and wears lipstick and everything. Today it's a berry shade.

I shrug. 'Yeah, still going . . . Got all this homework to do, so . . . It *is* GCSEs . . .'

Mum sighs in this really exaggerated way, like she's the one working. 'You need a break,' she says. 'Are you taking breaks?'

'I'm fine!' I try not to roll my eyes. The moment I actually take a break, she stresses about me not studying. Dad's the same. Can't win. Anyway, if I take a break now, she'll want me to hang out with their friends. Which is *not* happening. At least if they think I'm studying, they'll leave me alone.

'Hmm . . . Well, you *must* be hungry.' She puts the plate of food she's carrying down on my desk. Nudges it towards me.

It's piled high with rice, lamb curry and minty yogurt. A fat leg of tandoori chicken is carefully balanced on top. I don't get hungry much these days, but cooking's pretty much all Mum does since she stopped leaving the house. If I say I'm not hungry, she'll want to know *why*. And *when* did I last eat? *What* exactly did I have? It's easier to always be hungry. 'Mmm. Thanks, Mum.'

She grins. She has a smudge of lipstick on her front tooth.

I pretend to read *Hamlet*, thinking Mum will leave now – usually, she can't wait to get back to her precious crowd in the kitchen. But she hangs around forever, and all I can think of is when she's going to leave so I can get ready for Fi's party. She perches on the edge of my desk and it creaks under her weight. I know it's mean, but I'm worried it'll collapse. I look up at her again.

'You've been . . . very quiet,' she says, fiddling with a loose strand of grey-black hair round her face. 'Everything . . . OK?'

I glare at her. Is she serious? I've been quiet for months! Ten, to be exact. We all have. And is *anything* 'OK'?

'You sleeping at night?' she goes on. 'You look tired.'

I carry on staring at her. She really is unbelievable sometimes. 'So do you,' I say. She has huge dark patches under her eyes. I hear her sometimes, making tea in the kitchen at two in the morning. At least *I* sleep most nights. 'It's not a big deal, Mum.'

Mum frowns and smiles at the same time. Wrinkles crease round her puffy eyes. 'Oh, jaan,' she says, and I'm worried she might cry. She does that a lot lately. Well, since everything happened, which is understandable, but even *more* recently.

She touches my cheek, fingers gently brushing my skin. I smell her perfume, a deep lavender smell, and it's so awkward, the way she's just caressing my cheek and staring, that I flinch and push her hand aside.

Which just makes everything even more awkward.

She snatches her hand back. Looks down at the floor. I turn back to *Hamlet*. I hate these moments that remind us how much easier it used to be to hug and talk. It feels like a lifetime away now, those days when I'd curl up on her bed with hot chocolate and tell her about my day. It's been years.

I grab the leg of chicken and take a bite out of it to make her happy. 'I'm fine,' I tell her. I stick a smile on my face because I am actually. I really am. 'You're right. I'm tired. I'll eat then go to bed.' I give a fake yawn.

Mum nods. Pats my shoulder. 'OK, my jaan. You eat. And sleep well, huh?' She gives me a small, polite smile. 'Goodnight.'

She's itching to get back to her friends now, I can tell. I put down the chicken leg. 'Night, Mum.'

As soon as the door clicks shut again, I go back to my dressing table. But this time I don't look up at my sky-sea. Instead, I pull Akash's yellow-and-purple cap out of the drawer and put it on before looking in the mirror. *Be happy*. That's the last thing my brother ever said to me. My throat goes tight as I remember his words, remember that night, but I quickly gulp down the lump. I'm an expert at that. I've become an expert at loads of stuff I never thought I'd be any good at.

I line my eyes with kohl, swap my blue jeans for black and slip on the silky red vest top I've borrowed from Fi. Then I shove a couple of towels under my duvet so it looks like I'm asleep. I check that my room's tidy: books on shelves; easel stowed in corner; my clothes off the floor and hung up to keep Mum happy. Then I remember the food Mum brought me. *Crap*. I find an old carrier bag in the bottom of my wardrobe and empty the plate into it before tying it up. I'll take it with me and shove it in the bin outside. I do feel bad, but there's no way I can eat right now.

OK, everything's in place. I'm ready. I grab my bag, switch off the lamp and climb out through my bedroom window before pushing it shut. Well, almost shut – I leave a gap so I can open it again later.

It's almost *too* easy. Honestly, one of the few advantages of living in a bungalow is how simple it is to sneak out.

The garden smells of curry, drifting from the kitchen. Not exactly what I want to smell like at the party, especially as I'm hoping Josh will be there. I sling my bag over my shoulder and get away as quickly as I can.

As I hurry round the side of the house, I bung the carrier bag of food in the bin and think about the first time I did this. It was two months after Akash disappeared. I was so scared Mum and Dad would catch me that I was shaking. But there was also this fire burning in my chest. Fi and I were already chatting by then, and when she invited me to her birthday party it was perfect. I could finally find out if she knew any more about what happened to Akash.

In the end, it turned out she knew nothing more than I did about the night he disappeared. But she also wanted to know more. So I kept going to her parties, got better at sneaking out, better at drinking, and Fi and I became friends for real. She gets me . . . like Akash.

I imagine him with me now, my brother. By my side as I make my way up the drive. The bounce in his step. His shiny dark eyes. His black hair gelled sleek and a grin on his face.

He was always happy, wasn't he? And the smell of him: whisky, deodorant, cigarettes and mints, and something deeper, sweeter, that was just *him*.

My throat tightens and again I gulp down the lump. Take in a deep breath. I smile, like he would. I slip off my shoes and speed up – try bouncing like him. It feels good. Like he's me and I'm him. I quietly laugh into the still, warm air. Because that's what he would have done. Everything was an adventure for him. Always.

Moving further from the house, I breathe a little more freely. I wish I could tell Akash – confess that after months of sneaking out myself I finally understand why he did it. Though it *is* different for me. Poor Akash got so much hassle from Dad. With me, they don't suspect a thing. I guess I'm lucky they still think I'm the 'perfect' daughter I once was – studying, sleeping, not up to much else.

I stop walking for a moment. I almost look back at the house but stop myself.

Do they *really* think that? And what would they do if they caught me? I wouldn't be able to go to parties any more. Wouldn't see Fi, or Josh.

And then I think about the art college I've applied to, for after GCSEs: it's basically the only thing I've got going for me. My stomach tightens as I remember how hard it was to persuade Dad to let me apply: months of Mum, Akash and me begging. He finally agreed after Akash disappeared.

A couple of cars speed along the main road, jolting me out of my thoughts. The world spins around me as the worry kicks in: pavement, street lights, houses. What am I doing, standing in the middle of the street? Has anyone seen me? Mum? Dad? Someone they know?

I rush along the main road again, high heels dangling from my hands, head down and eyes focused on the road ahead. I don't look back. Although looking back is definitely one of the things I've become an expert at, this is not one of the times I do it. I don't let myself.

3

Music blasts through Fi's house. I push my way along the crowded hallway, past the family photos of Fi and her parents on the walls, and through the wafts of perfume and aftershave, beer and wine, and smoke that's strong and sweet. I nod some hellos, but I don't actually stop until I reach the small rose-pink kitchen at the back of the house. It's packed, but there's no one I recognize, so I squeeze through and find a bottle of white wine. I pour some into a plastic cup and down it, before topping it up again and looking around to see who else is here.

I'm looking for Josh, I realize. There's no sign of him. My stomach tenses: a mixture of excitement and nerves. But I'm being ridiculous. I don't know if Josh is coming tonight and, even if he is, I have no idea what's going on with us, other than a bit of flirting. I think. I can't even be sure of that. We've known each other for so long that it could be my imagination.

And anyway, even if we have been flirting, nothing can actually happen. No boyfriends: that's Mum and Dad's number one rule. They'd go ballistic.

I mean, if they found out, that is . . .

I drink some more wine and peer into the living room through a gap in the crowd, this time looking for Fi. Normally bright and airy, the room is lit up by just a few candles tonight. But I soon spot Fi's dyed red hair. She's perched on the arm of the forest-green sofa, laughing at something, her head tilted towards the ceiling. When she finally stops laughing, she sees me too. Waves. She slides off the sofa and comes through to the kitchen.

'You made it!' she shouts over the music. 'Yeah!'

She's gorgeous, Fi. Like, seriously stunning. She's wearing a plain white T-shirt, jeans with trainers and a black leather jacket. And she looks like a model. The feathery layers in her shiny, long hair frame her face. Her eyes are clear pale blue. Her skin is glowing. I can totally see why Akash liked her so much; they'd been going out for almost a year. Beautiful *and* totally cool. She holds out her arms and sways into me. I get a waft of vodka as we hug, or I hold her up, it's hard to tell which.

She giggles. 'You need to catch up!'

'On it,' I tell her, downing another glass of wine. My muscles relax as the warmth of the alcohol spreads beneath my skin. At the same time, a flutter of guilt crawls across my chest. It's hard to believe I'd never even tasted alcohol until eight months ago and sometimes I still imagine the look of horror on Mum and Dad's faces if they could see me. No drinking: that's another rule of theirs. All these rules are not just because I'm fifteen – it's also cultural stuff, family stuff – but Mum and Dad have become a lot stricter since everything that happened with Akash.

I try not to think about Mum and Dad now. I push the guilt away. Fi offers me more wine and I let her top up my cup. Akash never worried about my parents. And I mean look at me! I'm living my life. At a party. Having *fun*.

'You curled your hair,' Fi says. 'Looks good! Top suits you too.'

'Thanks, Fi,' I say, feeling proud of myself now. I mean, I know me and Raheela aren't exactly friends any more, but I imagine her standing here instead of me. Ha! No way could she do this. She'd be panicking more than I ever did, I reckon. I've come so far since the first time I came and hid in the corner.

Fi's eyes light up. 'Let's dance!' she shouts, grabbing my arms.

And I can't help it – I dance with her right there in the kitchen. We could go into any room in the huge house, but no. Instead, we dance, surrounded by the kettle and microwave and oven, laughing as we sneak in some ridiculous dance moves. Around us, people join in. A couple of Fi's older friends, who go to college, high-five us as they squeeze past to get drinks. Someone turns off the light and there's cheering as the dancing moves into the living room.

When we finally stop to catch our breath, Fi digs a packet of cigarettes out of her jacket pocket. 'To the garden!' she commands, putting her arm round my shoulders.

I feel energized from the dancing. Light. Happy. A part of me wants to carry on, but fresh air also sounds good. 'OK!' I shout back, grabbing another bottle of wine. She always gets loads in for her parties – her parents are so cool. I tuck it under my arm and follow her out.

It's quieter outside. The usual group of older boys are crowded near the shed at the back, laughing and smoking something stronger than cigarettes. Fi and I sit on the lawn, facing the house, surrounded by daffodils. The whole back wall is covered with Welsh dragon plaques. Fi's parents are so devoted to Wales it makes me laugh, though they spend more time travelling the world than at home.

'You got away OK?' Fi asks, glancing at me.

I shrug. 'Sure. It's not even a big deal now.'

She grins. 'You're becoming *sooo* good at it! Like your brother.'

My skin prickles all over. Has she forgotten how *bad* he was at sneaking out? He was always getting caught. Not that he actually tried to sneak away though: he just went. At least my way isn't upsetting anyone.

Fi must see that I'm irritated. She gently nudges me. 'I just meant that he'd be impressed,' she says.

I nod. He would. I know he would. 'Yeah,' I say, managing a smile.

And then Fi lights a cigarette. Smoke mingles with the air around us and I breathe in the smell. I breathe and breathe, focusing on the fairy lights dangling from the fence, twinkling against the darkness.

The first time I saw Akash smoking, I was ten and he was thirteen. It was the summer holidays. Hot. I'd been doing cartwheels on the lawn and I was standing next to the shed, brushing grass off my skirt, when I smelled cigarette smoke. I looked around, trying to figure out where the smell was coming from, and saw him peering back at me through the shed window. His eyes were wide as he pressed a finger to his lips. He was smirking a bit, that cheeky, lopsided smile of his. Understanding straight away, I nodded and cartwheeled all the way back to the house, our secret buzzing inside me. It was the first of so many.

Fi squeezes my arm and I jolt out of my daze. She blows out a smoke ring the size of a saucer. I gaze in awe as usual.

'What you thinking?' she asks. 'About him?'

I look down at my lap. 'Always.'

'Yeah,' she says. 'I know.'

'Have you . . . got any more clues?' I look at her now. My heart's racing from the hope, the possibility. Fi and I have been trying to figure out what happened to Akash ever since we became friends. We've spoken to everyone who knew him from school, all his friends, but no one saw him that night after Fi's party. But *someone* must know something. And we've promised each other we won't give up.

Fi shakes her head. 'No, I'm sorry, Neens. You?'

I shake my head too.

Fi smiles at me sadly. 'I don't know if I've ever told you this, but he's the one who taught me how to do smoke rings . . .' She blows out another one. It floats up into the air, a perfect circle, and then it spreads, disappears into the air.

There, and then gone.

'Did he?' I say. It doesn't surprise me. 'Yeah, he used to say they're their own kind of art.' I drink some more wine. And then I laugh. My brother could find art in anything. God, I miss that.

Fi nods enthusiastically. 'Art. Yeah. That's it! He said the exact same thing to me.' She leans into me. Rests her head on my shoulder. I rest my head on hers. 'Imagine what he could've done as an artist,' she continues. 'I mean, if your parents hadn't held him back. You know?'

I pull away from Fi. Feel a bit sick. What she's saying is true, but it doesn't seem right coming from her somehow. 'Yeah, I guess. But they always tried their best, you know? And he always did what he wanted anyway . . .' I can't believe I'm defending Mum and Dad.

Fi looks at me hard. 'Sure . . . But all their *rules*, you know? Anyway, you can't let that happen to you, Neens . . .' She's slurring a bit but her eyes are focused. Unflinching.

I peer at the freckles round Fi's nose. 'Yeah,' I say. But it's not as easy as she thinks. Since Akash left me, I've managed to get better at painting, but everything else has become harder.

Fi grabs my arm. She closes her eyes and breathes in deeply. Her cigarette's burning away now, just hanging there between her fingers like she's forgotten about it. She's totally wasted. I down more wine too.

'The thing is . . .' She opens her eyes. 'I know it's a cliché or whatever, but life's fucking short! That's what Akash always said too. You can't let your parents control you . . . You just *can't*. You've got to . . . to . . . follow your heart. It's cheesy but true.'

'I know that!' I tell her. 'Why do you think I'm here?'

She laughs. 'Yeah. Of course you know. I'm sorry. I just . . . I wish things were different. I wish we . . . you know, could find out more about what happened. I just want him to be proud of us both.' She stubs her cigarette out on the grass. 'Do you . . . do you think he is? Proud, I mean.'

I smile at her. 'Yeah.' I don't need to even think about it. I know both Fi and me are doing him proud. 'I don't doubt it for a second.'

Fi smiles too.

This was the last place Fi saw Akash, on the night he disappeared. She was the last person to see him – as far as we know. I look around the garden, half expecting him to jump out on us, like I always do when we're talking about him. It's silly, I know, but I can't help it. And, as always, I'm disappointed when he doesn't. But then I see Josh.

'Oh God, he's here,' I say, not meaning to say it out loud. He's standing in the doorway, peering out into the garden and looking a bit lost. Is he searching for me? No, no. I'm being too hopeful.

'Ahhh. *Josssshhh! Oui!*' Fi grins. 'What exactly is up with you guys?'

I glance at her. 'What? Nothing! And keep your voice down!' I'm suddenly very nervous. Which is ridiculous. It's Josh. Just Josh. He looks over at us and we wave at him. 'Just . . . stay here a minute, will you?' I say quietly to Fi. 'Don't leave me.'

Fi stands up. Grimaces. 'Ahh, I would if I could but I can't – sorry! I've got to . . . go mingle.' She snatches the plastic cup from my hand and knocks back my wine.

'What! No!' I hiss. 'Stay, Fi!'

She shakes her head. 'Just have fun!' Grinning, she waves Josh over. 'Good luck,' she whispers before slipping away.

'What the hell, Fi,' I mumble, clutching the bottle of wine against my chest.

When Fi reaches Josh, she hugs him, and I feel a tiny bit jealous. What's wrong with me? For a moment, I even think he's going to go back inside with Fi, but then he starts walking over to me. I watch him carefully. He's wearing a loose-fitting shirt and looks a bit smarter than usual. His hands are buried deep in the pockets of his jeans and his shoulders are hunched. Why does he look so awkward? He waves to some of the guys smoking at the end of the garden before sitting down next to me.

Oh God. My head's spinning a bit. I shouldn't have had so much wine. But, at the same time, I want some more.

'Oh, hey!' I say, keeping my voice as breezy as I can. It's just Josh. No big deal. Right?

He smiles. 'How's it going?' he mumbles. He's looking at his feet and I can't quite figure out his tone. But I notice he's gelled his hair, the dark strands styled into a sort of wave at the front. Does *that* mean anything?

'Yeah, yeah, I'm . . . good,' I say, desperately trying to think of something witty or funny or just even a bit interesting to say. 'You?'

'Yeah. Good too.'

'Cool.'

'Cool.'

Oh God. Why is he being so weird? Maybe I imagined us flirting. It seems we can't even have a normal conversation. We sit in silence for, like, a hundred years, listening to the music blaring out of the windows and the chatter and laughter of all the people who do know what to say to each other. I actually want to die. But I'm going to kill Fi first. Why did she have to leave us out here alone?

Finally, Josh looks at me. His green eyes are bright. He plays with some of the string bracelets round his wrist. 'Is that wine?' he asks. 'Can I . . . maybe have some?'

'Oh! Yeah. Sure.' Without realizing it, I've unscrewed the cap of the bottle I'm holding. Fi walked off with my cup, so I gulp some down straight from the bottle, trying hard not to spill any. I hand it to Josh. He drinks too.

Then he points up at the sky so abruptly it makes me jump. What's up with him? He's usually so relaxed.

'Sorry,' he says, bringing his arm back down just as fast.

I laugh – one of those stupid forced laughs. Doesn't even sound like a laugh. And Josh's face goes bright red. *Great. Nice one, Neena*. He glances at me and then quickly looks back up at the sky, and I sort of wish I could ask him straight out: DO YOU LIKE ME OR NOT? But I'm too much of a wuss.

Josh clears his throat. 'I was just going to say that . . . it's a good night . . . to see the stars, I mean.' He points up again, slower this time. 'That there is Orion's belt.' His finger draws lines against the black sky, and I don't really know what he's pointing at. All I can see are loads of tiny stars all muddled together.

'Right. Yeah,' I say, taking the wine bottle from his hands. 'I knew that.'

'Oh. You did?'

I swig from the bottle. 'Mmm-hmm. I mean, it's not exactly rocket science, is it? Ha! Get it?' It's a lame joke – the lamest – but I don't care. I'm desperate at this point and it works; he smiles and I'm a bit thrilled.

'You *can* laugh if you want,' I tell him, poking him gently in the ribs.

He grins properly now, his smile wide and a bit goofy, and I get butterflies that burst up from my stomach through to my chest. Maybe he *does* like me. This is what we've been like lately: a bit friendlier than usual, a bit jokier. I grin back at him, a proper, full-on 'I'm so chuffed' grin, which can't be very attractive. I need to calm down.

'Anyway . . .' he continues. 'Over there is the Plough . . .'

'Mmm-hmm. Cool.' I drink more wine. I wish he'd stop looking at the stars and look at me instead. He's obsessed with astronomy. But last week, at another of Fi's parties, he danced with us. And he *never* dances. Am I reading too much into that?

'And there – that's Cassiopeia.'

'Ha! Now you're just making up names . . . Here, have some more wine.'

He turns to face me and, again, his cheeks go red. 'God, you're not making this easy, are you?'

'Huh? Making what easy?' He doesn't take the wine, so I drink some more instead. The redness spreads to the rest of his face and all down his neck. 'Oh! Hang on. Were you . . .?' I get it now. I thought he was just going off on one about the stars because he didn't know what else to talk about. But no, this was *flirting*.

I laugh properly now. It's actually quite funny.

He scratches his neck. 'Look, Neens, I'm not very good at this . . .'

'What? You?' I say, in mock outrage. Josh has had a different girlfriend practically every year since primary school. How can *he* not be good at this? He scratches his neck again. Is he coming out in a rash?

I'm actually enjoying myself now. I thought I was the one who was awful at flirting, but surely even I can do better than that. I shift closer to him. He smells good. Well, of shower gel. But really nice-smelling shower gel.

'Good at what?' I tease. 'Good at talking to girls about stars? Or good at something else . . .' I twist a strand of my hair round my finger. So much for worrying about my parents! Josh stares back at me; his chest is moving up and down fast.

I remember once thinking Josh was flirting with me in science, before we were separated for GCSE and he got put in the top set because he's a total science geek. We were sharing a textbook and, as we leaned towards it, his shoulder pressed against mine, and so did his leg beneath the desk. I couldn't concentrate as I tried to copy a passage from the book. But afterwards he acted like nothing had happened and I thought it was my imagination.

Now he's definitely looking at my lips. 'What about your parents?' he says. 'I always thought . . . with them being so strict and everything . . .'

'Oh God. Please forget my parents!' I lean towards Josh and close my eyes before the moment is lost forever. He presses his lips against mine.

I always thought I'd be stupidly nervous when I had my first kiss. I mean, isn't everyone? But actually, though I am nervous, I'm even more excited to get it out of the way.

Josh's lips are soft with tiny rough bits. He tastes of salty crisps and wine. The sound of the laughter and chatter and music around us fades away. I feel the warmth of his body through his shirt, his heart beating hard and fast, and my body tingles all over. It's sort of similar to the feeling I get when I paint. Free. Light. But there's also something else. Something . . . uncontrollable. And I like that: this good feeling coursing through me, taking over everything else. It's like that day in science, but times a million.

And it's been so long since I've felt something this good that I want more and more of it. I press up against Josh. I can't help it. Then his hands are in my hair, and mine are in his, and we kiss harder. It seems he doesn't want to stop either.

'You said you weren't good at this,' I whisper, when we finally pause for air. 'You lied.'

4

The sun's rising by the time I stumble home. I sip water from the bottle I stowed in my bag before I left for the party, and my head clears a little as I slowly start to sober up. But I'm high on the night, music still playing in my head and a smile plastered to my face as I walk down the drive. Then, as I climb back through the bedroom window and open my curtains, the buzz dies. Dad is sitting on my bed.

'*Shit.*' It comes out before I can stop it.

His arms are crossed, fingers tightly clutching the cardigan he's wearing over his pyjamas. His legs are crossed tightly together and his whole face is frowning: eyebrows, eyes, lips. He's like an angry folded-up giant.

'Shit,' I say again. 'Sorry.' I try to think of some sensible explanation as to why I'm climbing in through my bedroom window at five in the morning. 'I was just . . . I needed to . . . I . . .'

But it's obvious what I've been doing. Dad glances up at Akash's cap and I know we're both thinking about him. Remembering all the nights Akash came home drunk, clumsily tripping over in the corridor, Dad's fist banging on his door as they shouted at each other and Mum screamed at them to stop.

Dad stands up and his face is no longer frowning. It's all screwed up. 'What. Do you think. You're doing?' He's not shouting; instead, there's this pressure in his voice, like he's going to explode.

'I . . . I'm sorry.' I don't know what else to say.

Dad shakes his head. He shakes it and shakes it like it's a moneybox he's trying to get a coin out of. Then he charges over to my dressing table. He looks around for a second and grabs my hairbrush, squeezes it in his hand. It's a bit confusing, to be honest, and, for a weird moment, I think he's going to try to brush his (practically non-existent) hair. Maybe as a sort of lament for his youth or something? But then he growls and hurls it across the room. I jump as it hits the wall above my bed.

'You?' Dad hisses, in his about-to-explode voice.

I stare at him. Wait for the shouting.

But instead Dad sinks down on to my dressing-table stool and stares back at me, like he's seen a ghost. There's something in his eyes that makes it hard for me to look at him. I gaze at my feet instead. It's silent for a long time. I shift from one foot to the other and pull the cap off my head as a wave of guilt rises inside me. It rises and rises until I feel like I'm going to snap.

I can't handle Dad's silence. It reminds me of the days after Akash disappeared, when Dad drank too much and was quiet all the time, as if words were just too much effort. It went on for months and I hated being at home, my stomach constantly hard, like there was a brick lodged there. It wasn't until Mum's friend, Aunty Jasmine, barged in one evening and poured all the booze down the sink that he stopped. 'You'll thank me later,' she'd assured him, pulling on rubber gloves and getting ready to clean the place up. That's when Mum switched from sleeping all the time to cooking and cleaning all day too.

Cold air is drifting in through my bedroom window, making me shiver. I turn round and pull it shut, and it feels like closing something else, officially putting an end to the night. I want to push it open again, but I turn to look at Dad.

'You?' Dad says, and this time it's a whisper.

I suddenly want him to shout at me instead. 'Yes,' I say, clutching Akash's cap against my chest. 'Me.' *Shout at me, shout at me, shout at me.*

But Dad doesn't shout. He rubs his hands over his face. 'Why are *you* doing this?' he says. 'What . . . what's the point of it?'

I almost laugh. 'I don't know, Dad. I don't have the answers to the world's most philosophical questions. What's the point of *anything*?' *Shout at me, shout at me, shout at me.*

He stares at me, silent again. My chest aches. I charge over to the door and open it wide. 'Go to sleep, Dad,' I snap. A year ago, I wouldn't have dared speak to him like this. But everything was different then.

Dad stands up slowly, walks over to me, and out of the room. I think I've finally managed to get rid of him but he turns round before I can shut the door.

'No,' he says. 'You can't do this. Not you.'

I stare up at him. My ears burn with anger. *You couldn't stop Akash*, I say with my eyes. *So what can you do to stop me?*

He must read my thoughts because all the confusion and hurt slowly leaves his face. His eyes go cold and he tugs at his cardigan.

'You're a mess,' he says, shaking his head. His face is filled with so much disgust, I think he actually hates me. 'Look at you!'

Now it's my turn to be silent.

'Be ready for church in the morning,' he says firmly, before turning and walking down the corridor.

'But I've got work!' I call after him.

'Ten o'clock,' he calls back, before disappearing into his room. His door clicks shut.

My chest is tight as I close my bedroom door. Dad's words play in my mind on a loop. *You're a mess. Look at you! You're a mess.*

My chest gets even tighter. I should sit down, do some deep breathing or something, but I'm too worked up. I pace my room, my mind racing. Have I made a mistake by sneaking out? I already hate how much everything's changed with Mum and Dad; how they're stricter than ever and how we hardly ever speak. They never even talk about Akash. Not to me, anyway. Now things will be even worse. Once upon a time, before Akash started sneaking out, we were mostly a happy family. And even then, with everything Akash got up to, it was never me they were angry with. If anything, Akash's behaviour made them even prouder of me. Should I have kept it that way?

But then how can I regret tonight? How can I regret Josh?

I stop pacing. No, I don't regret it. None of it. So what if I sneak out to try and be normal once in a while? Mum and Dad should give it a go sometime.

I sink down on to my bed feeling suddenly exhausted. I look at my phone – it's 5.30 a.m. *Urgh.* I need some sleep and I need something to calm my spinning thoughts.

I pull open my bedside drawer and stare down at the tiny tablets. They're my magic pills. Apparently, they help make me happy, sleepy and hungry all at once. I take one every night since everything that happened with Akash – and I stopped being happy, sleepy or hungry.

I rummage under my bed to find the bottle of whisky I took from Akash's wardrobe after he disappeared. I swallow a pill down with a swig. It's disgusting. Burns my throat. But the smell reminds me of him.

I push the bottle back and climb into bed. I don't bother getting changed into pyjamas. I hug Akash's cap and wish I could talk to him. He'd know exactly what to say to make me feel better.

As I wait for my happy, sleepy tablet to kick in, I close my eyes. I let the bad thoughts come.

If only I'd listened to Akash that night.

If only I'd gone to the party with him.

If only I'd answered the phone later, when he called.

If only. If only. IF ONLY.

I toss and turn as birds start singing outside. The sky turns from orange to bluish white. Then, finally, the pill makes everything hazy and sleep comes.

5

Later that morning, I wake to a lot of angry coughing. Dad's standing next to my bed, dressed in a suit. 'Get up,' he commands as I open my eyes. 'Call in sick at the art centre. We're going to church.' My head's spinning and my lips are ridiculously dry. I open my mouth to protest, but, before I manage to say anything, he says, 'Now.' His voice is barely under control and I have the feeling he'll lose it if I don't do as he says.

I don't feel as brave as I did last night.

'Yes, Dad,' I say sulkily, though every bit of me wants to go back to sleep. I want to press my face into the squishy pillow and ignore real life for now. I want to dream about Josh. I want my head to stop spinning.

Dad storms out of the room. My eyes sting from the morning's brightness. I feel nauseous. But I force myself to sit up and call my boss, Rosie, before the worry kicks in. (What if she doesn't believe me? What if I lose my job?) My voice is so croaky that it's not actually difficult to fake being sick, and Rosie is sympathetic, which is a relief. Once I hang up, I peer across the room, at my sky-sea painting above the dressing table. I wish I *could* go to the art centre and escape everything for a bit. I smile as I remember Akash's face when he gave me the picture. But then I feel sick again. He understood, so perfectly, what I needed. Why did he have to leave?

Suddenly I don't want to be in bed any more. I don't want to think about all this stuff. I drag myself out from under my duvet, stick on the flowery dress I save for church and take in a deep breath to clear my head. If going to church is my only punishment for last night, I reckon I've got off quite lightly.

In the car, I check my phone. I have a message from Fi asking if I got home OK, and three from Josh. My heart races as I scroll through them, glancing at Dad in between to make sure he's not looking. I don't need to worry though: as usual, Dad's eyes are glued to the road. Dad's extra careful about driving. He's careful about most things, always has been, but even more so since everything happened.

6.15:	Amazing night! Sorry about the stars/awkwardness. LOL. See you Monday . . . ☺ J x
9.02:	Sore head? X
9.17:	Oh God, it hurts sooo bad ☹ J x

I look at all the kisses after the messages. They're new. We don't usually add kisses when we message each other. I grin like an idiot, but then I quickly wipe the smile off my face before Dad sees, and message Josh back, trying to play it cool.

> Great night. And oh God, I have KNIVES
> in my head . . .

I also add a kiss, and press send. Then I see that I have a message from Raheela.

> Stop messaging me at stupid times of
> the night. We're not friends any more!

Huh? I didn't message her, did I? Why would I? I'm about to reply to ask what she's on about, but when I scroll up I see that I *did* message her. At 5.30 in the morning.

> Upset. Any chance of a chat? Only you
> get my parents . . .

I stare at the message. Did I really send that? I don't remember doing it. And I don't know why. We haven't spoken properly for months – pretty much since I started hanging out with Fi. I message back to tell her I didn't send her that message. Then I realize that sounds weird because I must have. And so I send another to say I didn't *mean* to.

I sneak another look at Dad. He's got this massive scowl on his face. Is he also thinking about last night? I guess I should mention it, get it over and done with.

'Dad?'

'Hmm?'

'I'm really sorry,' I say, though I'm not sorry I snuck out. I'm not sorry I got drunk. I'm definitely not sorry about Josh. I just wish Dad hadn't caught me.

Dad scoffs. 'What happened last night won't happen again,' he says, his voice robotic, like he's trying to convince both of us. I realize I need to work *a lot* harder if he's going to believe me or trust me again.

'It . . . it was the first time, Dad,' I lie. 'I shouldn't have done it. I won't do it again.' And then, just to make sure there's no doubt, I add: 'I promise.' I feel a bit guilty about that last bit.

I think about Josh and wonder what would happen if Mum and Dad knew about him. A bit of sick shoots up my throat and I taste last night's wine. I'm not sure if it's my hangover or the thought of never kissing Josh again. I can't let that happen.

Dad clears his throat. 'Just think about everything in church today, OK? Think about everything very, very carefully.'

'Yes, Dad.'

'Good.' He glances at me now and I tuck my phone into my bag. 'And I haven't told your mum. This will stay between us.'

'Oh!' I stare at him. '*Kaaaay*,' I add, to hide my shock. I don't want him to change his mind. 'I mean *OK*.'

Mum and Dad are one of those couples who tell each other everything. They weren't always like that, but, a few months after everything happened with Akash, Mum gave up her job. That's when she stopped leaving the house. I think she must have post-traumatic stress or something because she constantly worries something bad will happen. I guess she feels inside is safer. Which I do kind of understand.

Anyway, that's when Mum and Dad started discussing every detail of each other's days. Dad tells Mum exactly what he had for lunch, like if there was lettuce in his chicken sandwich or if the bread was a bit stale. And she'll go on about any phone conversations or visitors she had, what she cooked, what she served with tea. It's seriously boring.

I'm still looking at Dad, trying to understand.

'She's got enough to worry about,' he says, eyes glued to the road again. 'She'll only get upset.'

I nod enthusiastically. 'Yes, yes, good idea!'

Dad's quiet again. He seems to have decided the conversation is over. Suits me fine. I stare out of the window at the quiet streets and houses as my hangover kicks in properly. There's hardly any traffic on the road and I feel totally spaced out. I wish I could go back to bed.

That feeling gets worse when we step inside the church. The colours from the stained-glass windows are too bright for my pounding head. I sit in the middle of a pew, Dad to my left and a row of old ladies in pleated skirts and strappy shoes to my right. I recognize one of them; she has curly white hair that looks like a perfect cloud. Once, when I was younger, she came up to us after the service and asked if we celebrated Christmas. Akash and I laughed and laughed about that. I know we're the only brown family in the church and not many Christian Pakistani families exist, but still . . .

There's a draught carrying the smell of incense, which makes my stomach turn. I lean forward and bury my face in my hands. At least it looks like I'm praying, and I am, just not for what Dad thinks I should pray for. I'm not requesting forgiveness. I'm begging that I'm not sick right here in front of everyone. That my hangover passes sometime in the next thirty seconds. *Please, please, please.* I need a miracle.

The drone of the organ rumbles through the church and everyone stands up. Dad pokes me in the arm and glares at me. I force myself to get up too. Hold on to the pew to steady myself. Everyone sings a hymn about the beauty of the world or something, then we sit back down and the lady vicar, or whatever they're called, starts talking. Her high-pitched voice rings through the church. I zone out again. I feel sleepy. Really sleepy. My eyelids get heavier as the sermon goes on. Then I hear the words *life* and *death* and *forgiveness* and the sleepiness slips away. I remember the day Akash disappeared. My eyes blur and I concentrate on a fly crawling around on the pew in front of me to stop the tears.

It was a Saturday. Three o'clock in the afternoon. None of us had seen or heard from Akash since Friday night. We were gathered in the kitchen, the sun streaming through the patio doors, making us hot and sweaty. All morning, Mum had reassured Dad: 'You know how he is. He'll have his fun and then he'll come back.' But now she was perched on a chair at the end of the dining table, ignoring Dad and calling everyone in her address book.

'Where is he?' Dad kept saying. He was pacing the kitchen, up and down, up and down. I felt dizzy watching him. 'Where THE HELL is he?'

Mum dialled number after number. 'No, it's OK, thank you anyway,' she would say each time, her voice clear and controlled.

I checked my phone for the millionth time. Still nothing. I messaged him again.

> I know you're probably with Fiona, but please come home now. Dad's properly freaking out.

And then I added:

> Just let me know you're OK? Even if you don't want to come back.

Dad stopped pacing. 'Right, that's it. I'm going out to search for him again.'

I stood up. 'I'll come with you.'

But Dad walked out of the kitchen. 'Your mother needs you here,' he called from the hallway and then the front door slammed.

Mum was dialling another number so I slipped into my room and called Akash again. Still his voicemail. Had he switched his phone off? Or had the battery died? Or . . .

I didn't want to think of the worst-case scenario.

Sinking down on to my bed, I replayed the night before in my head again, in case I'd missed something.

Akash had come to my room around eleven and woken me up. 'Come to a party with me,' he'd pleaded, slurring his words. His breath stank of whisky and cigarettes and he was

wearing a white hoody and a yellow-and-purple cap that
seemed too bright for night-time. He looked far too awake.
'You've been so down lately. I'll cheer you up! We can dance!'
Then he'd pranced around my room, waving his hands in the
air in exaggerated Bollywood moves. I laughed a bit, but then
he cupped his hands round his mouth and shouted: 'Oi! Oi!'

I was so worried he'd wake Mum and Dad that I'd snapped,
'Shut up, Akash! And do what you want, but I'm not going.
Let me sleep.'

That was when he put the cap on my head. 'OK, OK!
Just . . .' He sighed. 'You know, try to be happy, Neens. You
deserve that. *Be happy.*'

That was the last time I saw him.

I stared at my phone but still no reply. He'd left the cap
with me. Did that mean anything? Had he planned to stay
away or had he just forgotten it? I had a horrible, heavy,
sinking feeling in my stomach.

I wish I hadn't shouted at him.

I wish I'd gone to the party.

The front door opened and closed. I ran out into the hall
but it was just Dad. He shook his head before I even said
anything. Then there was a loud thud from the kitchen and
Mum's address book landed on the floor by the door. Dad
and I rushed into the kitchen.

'What is it?' Dad asked.

Mum was dialling another number. Her teeth were
clenched. 'Enough,' she said, pressing the phone to her ear.
'No one knows anything. I'm calling the police.'

*

The fly has left the pew and is on my leg. I flick it off but it keeps coming back for more. 'Stupid fly,' I mumble. I reach for a Bible and try to hit it off my knee, but Dad grabs my arm.

'*What are you doing?*' he hisses.

I look round. I'd forgotten I was in church. The old lady next to me glares at me disapprovingly. 'Sorry,' I whisper. 'It was the fly.' But the fly has gone and Dad shakes his head at me. That same disgusted look he had last night. *You're a mess. Look at you!* Everyone stands up for yet another hymn, but I just can't force myself up. I want to go home.

We're leaving the church when I see him. *Someone's got Akash's cap.* I push through the crowd, all the way up the aisle, following the yellow cap with the purple streak. I'm breathless as I grab the guy's arm; grasp the pale skin of his forearm. I peer up at his head as he turns round. Oh. It isn't Akash's cap. This one has a red logo of a tiger on the front. Akash's doesn't have a logo. Just that distinct purple streak through the middle.

The guy tugs his arm out of my grasp, frowning. His soft brown eyes question me. He's about my age. Cute. I die a bit inside.

'I'm sorry,' I say. 'I . . . I thought you were something else. I mean, *someone* else.'

Dad catches up with me. He looks at me, and then at the guy, and I can see him trying to join the dots, getting the wrong idea. 'What's going on?'

I'm all choked up. 'Nothing,' I say. 'I'll see you at the car.' And I rush out of the church before I embarrass myself any more.

All the way home, Dad goes on and on about how I need to think about my behaviour. Pray more. Stay on the 'straight path', not some 'twisted path that leads nowhere'. I'll be going to church with him every Sunday, he tells me. And I need to focus on studying and nothing else now. He'll be checking on me, he warns me.

I try to say all the right things: 'Yes, Dad, of course. It won't happen again.' But all I can think about is how weird it was that I thought that guy had Akash's cap. I mean, *how*? How would he get it? I was wearing it last night. I slept with it in my hands. There's no way he could have it. But it was so similar to Akash's that it was an easy mistake to make, right?

Maybe it was even the same make. If it hadn't been for that red logo . . .

When we pull up in the drive, I start to get out of the car, but Dad grabs hold of my arm.

'Have you been listening, Neena? Do you realize how disappointed I am?'

'Yes,' I say. 'I really am sorry.' But he must not believe me because his eyes go even harder. There's a little twitch at the side of his lip, below his moustache, as he stares and stares at me.

'Art school,' he says finally. 'You really want to go?'

My throat tightens. It's a rhetorical question. Me, Akash and Mum spent a whole year convincing him to let me go, even though he thinks it's not a 'proper' subject.

'What do you mean?' I ask weakly.

Dad nods. 'Hmm. Thought so. Then sort yourself out. No drinking. No sneaking out. No boys – I saw you, Neena.'

'What? But I wasn't . . . I was just asking him something!' I protest, though I know it won't make any difference. He's clearly made up his mind.

'I don't want excuses. Sort yourself out. Otherwise . . . no art college. You won't be going!'

'You can't do that, Dad! I –'

But Dad is already out of the car. He slams the door. The conversation is over.

My hands are shaking as I set up my canvas and paints in my bedroom. I'm dizzy. Fuming. I can't believe Dad's using the one thing I've got left against me like this. Would he *really* stop me going to art college? And if I can't study art then what's the point? What's the point of anything any more?

This art college I've applied to isn't just any art college. It's a *huge* deal. If I get in, it means I can forget about A levels altogether and focus on the one thing I love most: art. Every day! And I would get away from everything here and have my own life. I still can't believe Dad actually let me apply. Maybe that's it though – he's changed his mind and now he's just looking for an excuse to stop me going.

My thoughts spin and spin. The same thoughts, again and again and again. Painting is what I love. It's all I know. It's the only thing I want to do any more.

I paint a girl wearing a cap.

If Dad tries to stop me now, could I go anyway?

I paint a boy next to her, wearing the same cap.

How would I pay for it?

The cap is yellow and purple. It's Akash's cap. It's my cap now, but it's still Akash's, always will be. My chest goes tight. Dad can't take my art away from me. He just can't.

I should do breathing exercises to calm myself down. Count to ten. Or picture a nice, peaceful place or something. But instead, as I look down at the red paint, wisps of panic catch in my throat, making it difficult to breathe. What if that guy *was* wearing Akash's cap? Could he have taken it and attached the red lion logo himself?

I rush over to my dressing table. I have to check. I have to make sure it's in my drawer. I breathe a little more freely. The cap is still there. I laugh. Of course it's here! What is wrong with me? Why would I think that guy had stolen it? Why would he anyway? It doesn't make sense. Nothing I'm thinking right now makes sense.

I press my face into Akash's cap. I breathe him in, my brother. It stinks of cigarette smoke, even now, almost a year later. It's the most disgusting, beautiful smell, and it makes my throat hurt.

Akash wanted to go to art college too, but Dad never let him. And now Dad wants to stop me. But I have to go. For me – and Akash.

I put on the cap. *Be happy*. That's what Akash said to me. I need to find a way to keep Dad happy, and make myself happy too.

6

'To be, or not to be, THAT is the question . . .' Miss Taylor's head of frizzy brown hair appears from behind her copy of *Hamlet*. She peers around at the class dramatically. We're silent. Still. The way she demands her lessons are. But then her eyes meet mine and I see that flicker of pity I'm so used to getting from the teachers. I fidget in my seat and she quickly lowers her eyes, carries on reading. 'Whether 'tis nobler in the mind to suffer the slings and arrows of outrageous fortune . . .' She glances up at me again and this time she gives me this pathetic little sympathy smile.

Urgh. I wish she'd stop.

I don't want to think about *being* or *not being*, or how much I've got in common with Hamlet, and she's not exactly helping. I sneak my phone out of my bag to check if I've got any messages from Josh. I have! It was sent ten minutes ago and it says:

Thinking of you ☺ x

My heart beats far too fast. He's thinking of me in lessons. Then my stomach does a nervous dip as I think about Dad and his threat. But how would Dad find out about this? I have to reply.

What exactly are you thinking? ☺

I imagine kissing him again and the thought quickly escalates: we are in my bedroom, on my bed, lying down and kissing and . . .

What's wrong with me?

I force myself to look back up at Miss Taylor. Push the image out of my head. As if Josh would ever be in my bedroom anyway! That would be far too risky.

Talking about risks . . . I push my phone back into my bag before Miss Taylor catches me. She once caught Sophia messaging her mum in the middle of a lesson and took her phone from her to read the messages out to the class. Sophia had been asking her mum to pick up sanitary towels and her mum had wanted to know if she needed 'normal' or 'heavy' flow. Miss Taylor looked so smug as Sophia groaned and hid behind her hands. Teachers, huh?

And now Miss Taylor is going on and on, explaining what Hamlet meant when he said this, and that, and . . . yawn.

I glance across the classroom at Raheela. Her mouth is slightly open with concentration as her hand glides across the page, making notes. Her hijab frames her round face neatly, and her cheeks glow, as if under her smooth brown skin there's another layer of sunshine yellow. She's so neat and perfect. Still, I *do* kind of wish she was sitting next to me right now. And I wish I could tell her about Dad threatening to take art college away from me. But then she'd probably be on his side, tell me that I shouldn't be drinking, or sneaking out, that I'm not acting like myself, which isn't exactly the point. She *would* write me a funny note about Miss Taylor's hair though, which has a life of its own, and we'd giggle silently behind our textbooks.

I guess we were pretty childish together really. I miss that.

Her hand stops moving and she looks at me. She gives me a cold, hard stare. I roll my eyes and look away. I feel kind of bad, for everything, for stopping hanging out with her and for all the horrible things I said. But then *she's* the one who stopped talking to me altogether. *She* moved seats. *She* stopped coming to the house with her mum. *She* stopped messaging me. So I guess it'll just take time to get used to. We've been – sorry, we *were* – friends for, like, ever. Our mums met when we started nursery and Raheela's mum began looking after me while Mum worked. We were like sisters really. Called each other's mums 'Aunty'. But whatever.

Miss Taylor claps her hands, snapping me out of my thoughts. 'Right,' she says, 'enough of me talking – we're going to do a timed essay question.' There are a couple of groans around the class, but she quickly silences them with a glare before turning to write on the whiteboard.

I'm copying down the essay question when Miss Taylor comes and sits next to me. She leans in close enough that I can smell the vanilla perfume on her cream silk blouse and see the tiny lines around her eyes. She has a small brown mole on her right cheek, which has a couple of hairs coming out of it.

'Ms Jones would like to see you this morning, Neena,' she says. 'Now's a good time; you can finish this at home.' She smiles, but it's a tight smile, and my stomach goes hard. I want to ask her what it's about, but she stands and walks away before I get a chance. You only have to see Ms Jones if you're in trouble. The last time I was in her office, I was in Year Seven and we all got called in for doing the Mexican wave every time our maths supply teacher turned his back.

I force myself to get up. A feeling of dread swishes around in my stomach. As I walk past Raheela's desk, she glances up at me. I ignore her. The last thing I need is another disapproving stare from her. Why is everyone always so judgemental?

Ms Jones's office is down a narrow corridor with a rough red carpet. I have a worrying thought as I walk towards her room: *Has Dad told her about me drinking alcohol? Am I now in trouble for being underage?* I feel a bit sick as I stare at the gold plaque that says: MS E. L. JONES, ASSISTANT HEAD TEACHER. But then I push the thought away. *No, no, he wouldn't do that.* I'm being paranoid. Aren't I?

Either way, standing here worrying about it isn't exactly helping. I breathe in deeply and knock on the door. It's quiet and for a moment I think I've managed to escape, for now at least, but then there's an irritated: 'Yes? Come in.'

The tiny office smells of strong coffee and toast and there are books absolutely everywhere, not just packed on the bookshelves, but towering up from the floor and piled on the desk that Ms Jones is sitting at by the window. She's deep in concentration, staring at a textbook. She looks like she forgot to brush her hair this morning and her thick eyebrows are furrowed so that they join in the centre like a long, furry caterpillar.

'Just a minute,' she says without looking up.

'Yes, miss,' I say quietly.

I seem to be standing there forever. To distract myself from worrying, I imagine plucking her eyebrows. One, two, three – who am I kidding? – one hundred plucks, until we can see more of her eyes and forehead. It's a satisfying thought, her wincing the way she makes kids wince if they're even slightly disruptive in assembly. But also the idea that afterwards she might actually look human, instead of like an angry owl.

She finally raises her head and stares at me blankly.

'You wanted to see me?' I say, and I try a smile that I hope is totally charming and doesn't look like I'm sucking up.

'Oh! Neena.' She slams her book shut. 'Yes, yes, please sit.'

I perch on the edge of the cracked leather chair opposite her. She leans back and takes off her glasses. Her eyes are grey, matching her shirt, and she looks kinder without glasses, even with her humongous monobrow.

Pluck, pluck, pluck.

'How have you been, Neena?' she asks. 'I just wanted to . . . check in.'

Oh! I relax a bit. It's one of *those* talks. They seem to come every couple of months, though usually my art teacher, Mr Butler, does them. He sort of took me under his wing when everything happened and he really seems to care. Fi's super cynical about him though and says it's just so they can tick off some criteria to continue being considered a good school.

'Oh yes, I'm . . .' I pause. I never really know what to say when people ask me how I am. Some days I'd like to say: *Pretty shit. I mean, my brother disappeared – how do you think I am?* But I'm sure that would get me into all sorts of trouble. Or, worse, they'll look at me like Miss Taylor did earlier: *Poor girl.* But I also need to be careful not to go overboard and say I'm 'great' or 'good': they won't believe that.

'I'm . . . well, you know, I'm OK,' I say. 'Thank you for asking.'

I expect her to go on, asking how everything is at home, and if there's anything I want to talk about (there never is) and if they can do anything to help me (they never can). But instead she says: 'Your dad called me this morning.'

I hold my breath. *Oh God. She knows about the drinking. Are they going to tell the police? Can I get into serious trouble?* Surely not. I mean, practically every teenager I know has drunk alcohol by now. Maybe not Raheela, but most other people, I reckon. I focus on Ms Jones's eyebrows as a lump swells in my throat.

'He wants to know how you're doing in your lessons,' she continues. 'I told him I'd check – and that's why I wanted to speak to you.'

'Oh!' I breathe again. 'I see.' Of course. This is typical of Dad. He's checked up on me in the past, in the days before I started taking my antidepressants and wasn't keeping on top of schoolwork. I really should have guessed.

She nods. 'Yes. Hmm. So I followed up and spoke to some of your teachers this morning . . .' She looks down at her desk and frowns, searching for something. Her face relaxes as she reaches for a piece of paper and her eyes glide over it before she looks back up at me. 'Are you having difficulty concentrating in lessons, Neena?'

I fidget in my seat. 'Yes,' I admit. 'Sometimes.' Then I shrug. It's hardly surprising, given everything, is it?

The furry caterpillar on her forehead wiggles up and down. 'It's been a hard year,' she says.

'Ten months,' I say.

'Hmm?'

'It's been ten months.' Not that I'm counting or anything.

'Yes. Right. Well . . .' She pushes the piece of paper towards me across the desk, dodging a pile of books that look like they'll tumble down if they're touched. There's a column listing the subjects I'm studying for GCSE on the left, and then loads of marks and months beside them with arrows pointing up and down. There are so many numbers that it's hard to focus and I zone out. I look back up at her face.

'So,' she says, 'what I've noticed is that after the initial dip in your marks when you came back to school last June – *absolutely* understandable – you improved in September and kept more or less steady until January. But over the past few months your marks have dipped again. Is there anything we should know about?'

I stare at her and try not to roll my eyes. OK, so I might not be the most focused person in the world right now, but I try. I definitely try. It's just that everything feels a bit pointless most of the time. But that's got to be normal, right?

'Mr Butler is especially concerned too . . .' she continues. 'About your art projects?'

I frown. Mr Butler knows how hard I've worked in art to improve my marks. It's OK to have an off day, isn't it? Mostly, I'm doing so much better in art.

'So is there anything you'd like to share, Neena?'

'No,' I say. 'Everything's fine. I'll . . . I'll try harder.'

She seems deep in thought. 'Hmm. OK. So what I've decided is that we're going to watch you from now until the exams. Nothing formal, but with the exams so close we don't want . . . I mean, we want to support you the best we can.'

Great. More watching. It's like Neighbourhood Watch but Neena-Watch instead. The whole world might as well join in. 'Yes, miss.'

She smiles at me. 'It's nothing to worry about, Neena. You're a top-grade student! And so I'm sure – certain – you'll do brilliantly in the exams. But, if you can report back to me at the end of every week, that'd be great. And I'll call your dad and fill him in on the . . . the hiccup . . . that we're going to fix.' She smiles again. A fake smile. All lips and no eyes.

'Wait. What? No.' I'm shaking my head like crazy. She can't tell Dad about the marks. Especially not after everything that happened over the weekend. He'll go ballistic. There's no way he'll let me go to art college – it's like he's just looking for one more reason.

Ms Jones's head tilts so that she's practically resting her head on her own shoulder. Like a proper owl. 'I beg your pardon?' she says.

'About the . . . the *dips* in my marks. Do you *have* to tell my dad?'

She straightens her head. 'I can't lie to him, Neena.'

'No, no, of course not. I'm just . . .' I know I need to say something that will convince her and I desperately search for the right phrase. 'I'm not asking you to lie,' I tell her. 'It's just . . . it's Dad . . . He's not doing so great himself lately.'

I've definitely got her attention now. She's looking at me really closely. I used to think that teachers had this built-in bullshit detector until I saw the amount of stuff Fi gets away with. I keep my eyes fixed on Ms Jones's. I don't blink and I definitely don't look away – a sure sign of a liar. Fi taught me that.

'Please, just give me a week or two,' I say. 'Let me prove myself. I'm . . . not sure he can . . . you know . . . take much more.' The tears come gushing out now. I'm not exactly sure where they come from, if they're real or fake or what. I'm not usually much of a crier. But they're genius, even if I do say so myself.

The crying puts her into quite a frenzy. She pushes tissues into my hand and pats my arm across the table. 'There, there,' she says. 'I didn't mean to upset you. Let me see what I can do.'

The tears continue rolling down my cheeks.

Ms Jones looks a bit nervous. She bites the corner of her lip. 'I'll tell you what,' she says, 'let's give it a week and see how it goes. But then I *will* need to call your dad with an update – and hopefully it will be a positive one. How does that sound?'

I take a deep breath and nod. 'Thank you.' I actually want to hug her, but that would be a step too far, I reckon.

'You can do this, Neena,' she says. And that makes me cry a bit more.

'I won't let you down,' I say, and I mean it.

I'm going to work hard. And not just to get Dad off my back, but to get away from home. That's *always* been the plan – studying art is all I've dreamed of for years. It's weird, but it's like a wake-up call, as cheesy as that sounds: I suddenly can't understand why I haven't been working harder already. It's like I've been sleeping. Or sleepwalking. Or something.

I wipe my eyes and stand up. 'Thank you,' I say again. And then I get out of there, fast, before she changes her mind.

7

'Holy shit!' Fi says, when I fill her in on Dad catching me on Saturday night. 'Does he know about Josh?'

It's lunchtime and we're at the top of the field behind the school, leaning against the bike shed. It's much hotter than it was this morning and the air smells of freshly mown grass and smoke from Fi's cigarette. Although I've only been up here a few minutes, I'm getting twitchy about being caught. For months, it hasn't bothered me. Now it's all I can think about. And the smell of the cigarette is bothering me too. I don't want to stink of it and get into even more trouble.

'God, no, can you imagine!' I reply. I keep my eyes focused on the bottom of the field, in case any teachers come checking. No one ever does until the second half of lunchtime, I guess because they're busy having their lunch and gossiping in the staffroom. By that time, me, Fi and any others up here are usually at the chippy. But today I can't take any risks. There's no way I'm going to the chip shop; I'm not even sure what I'm doing up here, but it was either that or face Josh. And, with everything that happened with Ms Jones this morning, I'm really not sure what to do about Josh . . . I can't risk being seen with him and Dad finding out, but I'm also not ready to tell Josh that yet.

'But he knows I was drinking,' I explain. 'And now he's checking up on me and I'm on some sort of informal report with Ms Jones. Apparently, my marks aren't good enough. I have to check in with her at the end of every week.'

'Shit,' Fi says. 'That sucks.'

'Yep.' I glance back at her. I don't tell her about begging Ms Jones not to tell Dad. I definitely don't tell her about the crying.

She pushes her designer sunglasses up on to her head. 'God, Neens. You . . . want a cigarette?' She lights another for herself and offers me one. 'You seem totally stressed.'

I glare at her. 'This is serious, Fi.'

'I know, I know . . . I'm sorry. And seriously, if you ever need a place to stay, to just get away from everything . . .'

'Thanks, Fi.'

'Anyway, I say stick two fingers up at them all.' She waves two fingers in the air in the direction of the school.

I pull down her arm. 'Please don't do that. What if they see you?'

She stares at me, shocked. 'Are you *really* going to let them stop you living your life?'

'I . . . I don't know what to do! If I don't get good marks, Ms Jones will tell my dad and he's going to stop me going to art college.' I take a sharp breath in as the reality of everything hits me. 'No more parties for me,' I say, deciding this is it: I need to make some changes. 'And I'll have to end things with Josh too. It's just too risky.'

'What!' Fi grabs hold of my arm. 'No! I saw you two on Saturday night. You were *soooo* happy! I don't think I've ever seen you that happy, Neens.'

I look at Fi and I hear Akash's voice: *Be happy.* 'I know,' I say. 'But I've got no other choice.'

'You always have a choice,' Fi says. 'Isn't that what Akash would say?'

I stare at her, and I don't know what to say. Because she's right. It's exactly what he'd say. But I'm just not feeling too brave right now.

'Maybe I can help . . .' Fi continues, and she taps her chin with one of her perfectly manicured nails, thinking up a plan. Her red hair glistens in the sun.

I'm suddenly too hot. Too worried. Too full of all the things Akash said and the things I want to do and the things I can't. My eyes are frantically scanning the bottom of the field again. There's only one thing I know with absolute certainty: I want to study art. I *need* to. Akash would want that for me too.

'I've got to go,' I tell Fi, standing up. 'I'll . . . text you later?'

Fi stares up at me. She looks taken aback.

'I'm sorry,' I say, turning away. 'I just . . . I've got to go.'

'Wait.'

I turn back round.

'I . . . I *might* have a lead,' Fi says.

'What?' I sink down beside her. At the party on Saturday, she told me she had nothing. So is this a new development since the weekend? Or was she hiding it from me? 'Tell me everything,' I say.

'It's a real long shot. Nothing concrete yet. But . . . I just thought you should know . . .'

'Right. Long shot. I get it.' My stomach's bubbling. I know I shouldn't get my hopes up, but it happens every time, no matter how much I try to stop the excitement, or nerves, or whatever it is. 'Can you tell me anything?' I ask, my voice now small.

Fi shakes her head. 'I don't want to jinx it. But the moment I know anything, you'll know . . . I promise.'

I nod. 'Right. Yes. Don't jinx it. That makes sense.'

Fi looks away. 'Anyway, you better go before you get caught, right?' she says, an edge to her voice. 'The teachers will be out on the prowl soon. Go on. Fuck off. Abandon me, why don't you!'

'I'm not abandoning you!' I say, looking towards the school. The dread is taking over again.

She pulls down her glasses. Shrugs. 'Whatever.'

I hesitate. The last thing I want to do is upset Fi. She's practically the only friend I've got now. But Ms Jones is watching me – that's what she said this morning – so I can't risk being caught up here. I give Fi a quick hug and, although my stomach tenses when she doesn't respond, I make my way back towards the school.

That afternoon, in lessons, I block out all thoughts about clues and possibilities and I stop myself replaying the night it all happened in my head. I also ban daydreams about Josh. *Art college, art college, art college*: that is my mantra to help me focus. I make so many notes that my fingers ache from gripping the pen so tightly. I stick my hand up to answer question after question. I'm extra polite to the teachers. It actually feels good. 'You can do this, Neena,' Ms Jones said to me earlier. And, for the first time since everything happened, I actually believe it. I'll work hard and get good marks and Dad will let me study art. I'll have my own life away from Mum and Dad. Away from everything. A fresh start.

Towards the end of last lesson, Josh messages to ask when he can see me. I tell him I'll see him when the bell goes and we plan to meet round the corner from school, where there's a small park set away from the houses and the street. I need to get it over and done with. I have to tell him nothing more can happen between us. I feel a surge of anger towards Dad and Mum as I send the message, for all that has happened, and for all the things they won't let me do. But I block the feelings before they swamp my plan. *Art college*, I remind myself. *Art college.*

But, when I see Josh, art college slips out of my head. The plan is not so easy to stick to.

We stand huddled in the shade of an oak tree, far away from the street so that no one can see us together. We are in our own world. Nothing else matters.

'How was your day?' he asks. And I can't remember the last time anyone ever asked me that. But Akash used to. Every day, when we walked home from school.

I don't know what to say to Josh – there are too many things that I want to tell him. So instead I just nod. 'And you?' I ask.

He shrugs. 'Could've been better,' he says, and then a cheeky smile spreads across his face. His neck and ears go red.

He touches my hand, curls his fingers round mine, and I let him. I can't help it. And all I want is to kiss him.

Art college, I say to myself.

But I can't pull away. As much as I want to study art, I want Josh too. When we kissed on Saturday night, something inside me shifted. Everything else, all the crappy stuff that's happened over the past ten months, went away for a while. We were all that mattered. And I feel that again now.

But no – I can't sneak out of my window and kiss boys and drink wine any more. Not if I want to study art. Not if I'm ever going to get away from Mum and Dad. Not if I want to have my own life.

Josh leans forward and kisses me, and my body tingles all over. I kiss him back.

Could I maybe, somehow, do this? Could I carry on climbing out of my bedroom window when I'm sure Mum and Dad are asleep? We could meet up here at lunchtimes. I could say I'm studying at the library after school and see Josh instead. Maybe, just maybe, we can make it work.

I lean into Josh, and we kiss again, and I want to stay like this forever.

But then I remember Dad sitting on my bed, and staring up at Akash's cap. His clenched jaw. That horrible silence.

You're a mess.

I pull away, breathless from the kiss. Every bit of me wanting to kiss Josh again.

'My parents . . .' I say. 'I'm sorry but . . .'

Josh's face falls. He brushes his hand through his hair and steps back. 'I thought you said . . .'

'I know, I know. I . . .' How can I explain how different things were on Saturday? Where do I begin? He crosses his arms. Looks at the ground. Panic swirls in my throat. I'm losing him already.

I can't. I can't lose him.

'Wait,' I say. 'I don't know . . . I can't think straight.' I step towards him again. Close enough to smell his breath – coffee and apple and minty gum. I feel a bit calmer, but my mind is whirring, trying to figure out what to do.

I don't want to lose Josh.

Maybe, once Dad trusts me again, I can be with him.

Maybe we just need some time.

'I really like you,' I tell him. 'I've just got some things to sort out. Can we maybe . . . sort of press pause? Can you . . . wait for me?' I hold my breath.

'Wait?' he says. 'For . . . for how long?'

I swallow. 'I don't know. A few weeks?' I say, hopefully. I can't believe how nervous I am.

His shoulders loosen. He smiles. He takes my hand again. 'I'll wait,' he says. 'For sure.'

Relief washes over me and we grin at each other. We have one more kiss. OK, more like five. Then I *do* actually leave. I make my way home, smiling, and with a plan. I'm going to work hard. And I'm going to do some major sucking up to Dad when he gets home from work.

8

I like the brand-new me. She has more energy than I've had in a long time. She's organized. Crisp. Lighter somehow. I once saw a sticker on the back of a car that said WARRIOR NOT WORRIER, and that is how I feel.

I shut old me out of my bedroom and I sit at my desk. I don't move until I've done all my homework. Then I draw up a revision timetable, highlighting each subject in a different colour until the piece of paper is a luminous rainbow of times and topics. There are just eight weeks until the exams. Eight weeks! Why haven't I started revising? I bet Raheela's been revising for months. I reckon everyone in the year except me has started their revision. I don't quite understand it. I knew I needed to, but it's like I, well, forgot. Flutters of nerves burst in my chest. But no, I won't let them overwhelm me. I must focus now.

I stick the timetable to the wall above my desk, take deep breaths and open up my history book. Yes. Look at me! I am a warrior.

I'll prove myself to everyone: I'll get good grades; I'll get on to my art course; and I'll be able to see Josh again.

The front door opens and closes, and I hear the *click-clack* of Dad's work shoes against the wooden floorboards in the hallway. It's only five o'clock: he's home early, which hardly ever happens. I have the urge to see him straight away. I want to show him I'm taking his threat seriously. But no. I keep my bum on my seat and read through my history book, highlighting as I go. One whole hour of the Treaty of Versailles and Hitler's rise to power.

When I finally finish, I stretch my arms and then relax them into a warrior pose. I laugh. I'm pleased with myself. But, even better than that, I feel neater inside.

I scoop up my books to show Dad. I find him in the garden, dressed like he's at the beach: long beige shorts, T-shirt, flip-flops and one of Mum's straw sunhats. Hilarious. And the barbeque is out, which is totally typical. The slightest hint of sun and out it comes. Mum's wearing a similar hat, which is also pretty funny on top of her usual tent-like salwar kameez. She's standing in front of the patio table, staring at all the food: she must have been cooking all day because there's enough to feed ten families. I guess the whole gang's coming over today. Or she's hungrier than usual, but even Mum couldn't eat all that, I don't think.

She waddles towards the table, snatches a samosa from a plate and bites into it. She chews fast, as if someone might steal it from her if she breathes, making appreciative noises as if it's the best thing she's eaten. Ever. Honestly, Mum and her food. She used to be so fussy, super slim, always eating healthily, but now I reckon she'd eat anything anyone offered her. I can't help rolling my eyes.

Clutching my books to my chest, I step out into the garden. The air smells of barbeque smoke and flowers, and it's actually really hot out here. Mum glances at me, smiling, as she reaches for another samosa.

'Hi, Mum,' I say, heading over to Dad. I hover next to the barbeque, waiting for him to look at me, but he keeps poking at the coal with the skewer he usually cooks kebabs on. He's probably still angry with me, but that's OK because I'm going to prove myself to him.

I give a little cough to let him know I'm there. 'I've done all my homework already,' I tell him. 'Started this evening's revision too.' I offer him my books. 'Want to see?'

I feel a bit weird. Sure, I'm proud of myself for doing all that work, but I also feel like I'm ten years old again, waiting for Dad to tell me I'm a 'good girl'. I've spent the last ten months not worrying about pleasing Mum or Dad, and that was actually much easier. There's a knot in my stomach that's getting tighter and tighter as I wait for Dad to acknowledge me.

He finally looks up from the barbeque. His forehead creases into thick folds. Still angry.

'Not right now,' he says, showing me his hands, which are black from the coal.

I press the books against my chest again. 'Maybe later?' I say hopefully.

He looks at me hard. 'How was school?'

Oh God. Did Ms Jones call him after all? Did she tell him about my grades dropping? And that I asked her not to tell him? 'It was good,' I say, watching Dad's face carefully. 'Lots of revision for the exams, but it's going . . . well.'

I hold my breath.

Dad nods. 'Good, good,' he says.

I breathe again.

'Leave your books on the dining table. I'll check them later.'

OK. This is better. This is good. He'll see how hard I'm working, and he'll think I'm sorry and trust me again.

'Do you . . . need any help?' I ask.

'You can help Mum.'

I glance over at Mum, who's munching on yet another samosa, and I smile at Dad. Should I help her EAT all the samosas?

Dad frowns again. 'We need plates. Glasses. A couple of jugs of water. Ice.'

As I turn back towards the kitchen, Mum keels over. She grabs on to the edge of the patio table to steady herself and for a second I think she's going to pull the whole thing down.

We rush over to her. 'Mum!'

She pushes me out of the way and heads towards the patio door as fast as she can. But it's not quick enough; she grabs a plant pot from near the door, crouches down and pukes into it. I put my arm round her, even though I absolutely hate sick. I get a waft of it and heave too. I look up at Dad for help.

'She's OK,' he says, bending down to hold her hair back as she's sick again. 'She must have eaten too fast.'

I glance at the patio table of food. 'How many of those samosas did you actually have?' I ask Mum, laughing.

But, as I look at her, my stomach does this horrible dip thing, a bit like when you're going down on a roller coaster, but with this sick feeling that I've come to know as dread. Mum's pale. Puffy. Much puffier than usual. It's in her face, her hands, her feet. And this isn't the first time this has happened.

'You were sick last week too, weren't you?' I say. 'How long have you been feeling like this?'

Mum tries to smile. Her hat's fallen off and I notice how grey her hair is, silver streaking through the black. She must have stopped dyeing it. 'Just tired,' she says. And she really does look tired. But I also know that this is more than that. They're keeping something from me.

Bad thoughts, scary thoughts, tumble into my head. I try to bat them away. I do not want them. WARRIOR NOT WORRIER. That's the new me. But, like a boomerang, they keep coming back. *Mum's sick. Very sick. Is that why she's so overweight? Has she got a massive tumour or something? Oh God. Is she dying?*

'You need to go to the doctor's. I'll come with you. Or, if it's really too much to leave the house, the doctor will come here, won't she?' I'm breathless now.

Mum and Dad share a look that I can't quite figure out.

'We should tell her,' Mum says and her voice is shaky. My chest hurts.

'Tell me what?' I ask, though a part of me doesn't want to know whatever terrible thing they're going to say. I want to run away. Hide.

'Let's go inside,' Dad says, helping Mum up. 'I'll put the kettle on.'

*

We sit round the dining table and no one says anything for what feels like ages, but it's really probably only about sixty seconds. My palms are sweaty. My heart is racing. The kettle boils too loudly, taking up all the spare space in my head.

Dad puts his arm round Mum's shoulders. She starts crying and that's it, I can't take it any more. I look down at my lap. My ears ring.

'Just tell me,' I say in a small voice.

Then, weirdly, Mum starts laughing. 'I really shouldn't have eaten all those samosas,' she says.

I look up. Dad smiles. *Hang on. Laughing. Smiling. Maybe nobody's dying after all.*

'We've got some news,' Mum says. She sighs heavily. 'We've been trying to figure out how to tell you.'

'Good news?' I ask, because it still doesn't make sense, doesn't explain why Mum's been so sick. Has she just been overdoing the fried stuff every week?

'Yes,' she says. And I breathe, and breathe, and breathe. But then Mum starts crying again. It's all very confusing. 'You tell her,' she says to Dad.

Dad strokes Mum's hair. 'Neena,' he says, 'you're going to have a brother again!'

I feel dizzy. My brother. I'm going to have my brother again?

How? Is he back?

My breath is stuck in my throat, but I force the words out. 'Akash is here?'

I've dreamed of this moment. In my dreams, Akash would be standing in front of the fridge, stuffing his face with a cream cake. Or I'd hear the strumming of his guitar while I was painting in my room. Once, I heard him laughing in the garden in a dream, and when I woke up I quickly pulled back my curtains. But he wasn't there.

I'd have to remind myself that he wasn't here, and it would be fresh all over again: that sharp ache in my stomach, the huge, gaping emptiness that I fell into again, and again, and again. But now . . .

'Is this really happening?' I ask, breathless now. 'Where? Where is he?'

But Mum and Dad aren't smiling any more. They're staring at me, wide-eyed.

'No, no,' Dad says, shaking his head. 'That's not what I meant.'

And then it hits me: the sickness; a brother. I look down at Mum's stomach.

'Yes, I'm pregnant,' Mum says, nodding.

And now I'm the one feeling sick.

Mum reaches across the table and grips my hand. 'A baby brother!'

My head spins. But what about Akash? My big brother. I want him.

Mum's still speaking. 'I'm hoping the sickness will calm soon. It should have stopped by now – I'm just over twenty weeks.'

I feel like I'm floating outside my body. Like everything is very distant.

'We didn't want to tell you . . . until we'd had the scan to check things. With my age and everything . . . But everything looks good.'

I try to focus on Mum's words. 'So Akash isn't here?' I ask, just to be sure. I have to be very, very sure. Nothing is making much sense and I need to check if my brother is back.

Dad glances at Mum and she reaches into the drawer behind her, pulls something out of there and pushes a small black-and-white photo towards me. It's a blurry photo of a baby. I can make out a small head, a round body, tiny hands and feet.

'No Akash,' Mum says. 'But this is good news, Neena.'

'I want Akash,' I say, and that makes her cry again. Dad rubs his head like he's got a bad headache.

The front doorbell rings. But none of us move.

'No one knows yet,' Mum says, taking the photo back from me. 'We . . . we'll tell them soon. Just not yet . . .' She tucks it back into the drawer.

Then the door opens and Aunty Jasmine's voice calls up the hallway. '*Helloooo*. Anyone home? Ready or not, we're coming!' She laughs, like she's cracked a hilarious joke.

'We've got gajar ka halwa,' Aunty Sunita adds, which makes Mum dry her tears.

And then there's a commotion in the hallway, shoes being taken off, laughter, chatter, and I need to get out of there. 'I'm going for a walk,' I say, standing up. I feel unsteady on my feet, but I try to focus. I can't stay here any longer.

'Of course,' Mum says.

'Don't be too late,' Dad adds.

But I don't really care what either of them says any more. I stumble out into the hallway and squeeze my way through

Mum and Dad's friends, ignoring all the hellos, dodging the hugs. I feel like I'm in a weird dream. It's hard to breathe.

Finally, I escape out of the front door. I'm hoping that I'll feel better the further I get from the house. But no, it doesn't work like that. My ears are roaring and my heart is pounding and the pool of emptiness I try so hard to keep shut has been ripped open and is swallowing me whole.

All I can do is walk.

I don't know where I'm going, but at the same time I do. I've only been there once since everything happened with Akash. I think it was a few days after, but it's a blur, so I don't remember it properly. Now, I have no choice.

My feet: they're leading the way.

9

The Ridgeway was our place. Akash's and mine. It's the local beauty spot, which means anyone can come here, but it was *ours*.

I stand at the top of the long bank, looking out at the lush green rolling hills in the distance, at the curves and the slopes and the dips, and all the tiny houses in between. The sky is clear and bright. You can see across the Severn Estuary from up here; we thought it was the top of the world when we were kids. 'Little Switzerland,' Mum called it. 'Witzerland,' I would say, which made everyone laugh, especially Akash. But it was later that it *really* became our place. When we were teenagers.

My ears ring.

My heart races.

Behind me is the bench we always sat on. We came here when Akash wanted to smoke. And when he passed his driving theory test. When I got a crappy mark for one of my first pieces of GCSE art, I sat beside him on that bench and cried, and he told me how talented I was, that I just had to practise. Here we figured out who we were, away from Mum and Dad and all the noise of the world.

And then he left.

Dad's words replay in my head: *You'll have a brother again.*

I feel full. So full of everything. 'Akash!' I call out. Perhaps Mum and Dad are wrong. Maybe he really is coming back. He could . . . he could be here already. 'Akash?'

I shut my eyes and pretend I'm a child again.

I remember. I remember so clearly.

He'd make me race him down this hill. My stomach would bubble with excitement and nerves as we stood at the top. I can see his wide grin. Eyes dancing. 'One,' he says. 'Two . . .'

'Don't go too fast,' I say. 'Give me a chance!'

'But it's a race!' he says, laughing. 'Ready? Go!'

I run down the bank and it's like a long green slide. *We* run. I feel like I'm flying as my feet leave the ground. And then we're falling, rolling, rolling, down, down, down.

I stop abruptly in a heap at the bottom. Covered in grass. Mud. Aches. Akash's laughter pierces the air. Makes me laugh too. I look round, expecting to see him, forgetting, *almost* forgetting, he's not here.

I sit up, pulling my knees to my chest. As I catch my breath, I grab fistfuls of grass. I want to talk to him. Tell him Mum's having a . . . a . . . a baby. A fucking *baby*. It's ridiculous. A joke. She must be near the menopause. Forty-four, for God's sake.

I wrap my arms round my knees and close my eyes. I imagine a baby taking over Akash's room. Filling it with his things. His noise. His *smell*.

My throat burns.

I don't want some other new younger brother.

I want my old one, my big brother – I want Akash.

My thoughts spin and spin and spin. Mum and Dad's voices replay in my head. *Pregnant. No Akash. A baby brother.* And I think I knew, didn't I? Out in the garden, when she was being sick. It was like a part of me realized. But I didn't want to believe it. I still don't! A new brother. How can that be? I bury my face in my hands and try not to scream. If I could just trace Akash's steps . . . If I could find out what happened that night . . . If only I'd gone to the party with him . . .

And then I smell him. My brother.

I can smell Akash!

Cigarettes. Whisky. Deodorant. Mint. And something else that's just him – sweet, like the biscuit tin. I stand up. Look around. I can't see him, but I can definitely smell him. Is it a sign? Is he trying to tell me something? Sending me a message to let me know he's near, whatever Mum and Dad think?

I rush up the hill – but no, he's not on our bench either. My heart is going crazy; it's forgotten how to beat. 'Akash?' I call out. There's still no reply, but the air is full of his smell.

And then I get it. It's like hide-and-seek, isn't it? That was our favourite game when we were kids. We played it wherever we went. Is that it? Has he been playing it since the night he left?

I'm buzzing now.

I have to figure out where he's hiding.

I need to go home.

I need to check if Akash is there.

I'm in my bedroom, standing in front of my easel. I have a paintbrush in my hand. Mum and Dad's friends must have left because the house is very quiet. There was singing when

I got back from the Ridgeway, singing and music. I went into Akash's room to check if he was there; I was so sure that *he* was the one playing the guitar. But he wasn't there. I searched the whole house, but there was no sign of him. And then I couldn't smell him any more. I began to think that maybe I'd imagined it all, that there was no smell, and no clue, and that he really was gone forever.

But I smelled him, didn't I? At the Ridgeway.

I grab my phone to message Fi.

> I know you said it's a long shot, but do
> you have any more info on your lead?
> I'm desperate to know . . . N x

She hates me hassling her about this stuff – says I need to 'manage my expectations' or whatever, that these things take time and she'd always tell me if she knew more. But I can't help it.

I've just turned back to my painting when there's a knock on my bedroom door. My heart sinks. I really don't want to see Mum right now. She comes in anyway.

'I brought you food,' she says, her voice soft and sickly, like nothing has happened. 'You haven't eaten anything this evening . . .'

I keep my eyes on the painting. 'I'm not hungry.'

The picture in front of me is almost complete. Usually, it takes me days, weeks even, to finish. But not today. It's a bit of a blur to be honest – I don't remember painting it. I remember putting on some music to block out all the singing from the garden. I was shaking because I couldn't find Akash. I picked up my paintbrush, and then . . . *this*.

I inspect the way the dove-grey sky turns almost black in places. How it blurs into the dark green hills and tiny pink and white houses. My heart lifts and sinks, lifts and sinks. There's a bit of light, white, shining through the sky.

Mum sighs. 'At least eat the halva, huh? It has almonds, good for the brain. With all this study . . .'

I roll my eyes, my back still turned to Mum. She really is like a broken record. You know what else is good for the brain, Mum? Not having weirdo parents who think having a baby is the answer to everything. And also having some *space*.

I hear her getting comfortable on my bed, the mattress creaking. *Great. Make yourself at home, why don't you?* I ignore her, hoping she'll take the hint and go away. I focus on the painting, the bit of light in the sky. Something's missing, though I don't know what. I wait for it to come to me. For that tingle in my belly that reaches the tips of my fingers in those seconds before an idea arrives.

But nothing comes. I guess I'm too distracted now.

'Are you . . . OK?' Mum asks.

'Never been better,' I snap. I stare at my painting. *What is it? What's missing?*

'Oh, Neena. I thought you'd want this,' Mum says.

I swing round to face her. 'There are a million things I *want*, Mum. *Baby* is not on my list, strangely enough.' I laugh now. She looks so surprised. One of Fi's friends got pregnant recently and started acting really stupid. Weird stuff, like she couldn't remember the date, or the name of simple things

70

like cheesecake. Baby brain, or something, I think it's called. Mum must have that.

She peers at my face really seriously, like she's trying to figure something out. It's a bit intense. What's her problem? What doesn't she understand? I thought Akash was coming back. But he isn't here. And no one can take his place. Simple. If she doesn't get that, she *definitely* has the baby-brain thing. Is there something she can take for it?

'It wasn't easy, you know,' she says finally.

I screw up my face. *Oh. My. God.* Do I really need the details?

She looks horrified too. 'Leaving the house,' she says. 'I mean, it wasn't easy to leave the house for the scan. If that's why . . . why you're angry . . . I know you've asked me to go out . . . lots of times . . . And I haven't been able to . . .'

My breath catches in my throat.

Oh. Wow.

In all the confusion about Akash returning, I hadn't even thought about the fact that Mum must have actually left the house for the scan. Over six months of being housebound, and she actually went out? My faithful throat lump returns. I gulp and gulp but it stays put.

I'm remembering all the times I really wanted Mum to leave the house. I can't help it. The art exhibition that displayed my painting, chosen as one of three from the whole class; I was so happy but I missed Akash so much. Dad's birthday when I went out for a meal with him by myself, which wasn't awkward at all (spoiler: it was – we have *nothing* to talk about other than school). Parents' evening, when Dad was SO embarrassing, trying to tell the teachers how to teach. I wanted to die and wished Mum was there to stop him.

But for this baby – she went out.

'So are you suddenly cured?' I snap.

'Cured?' she echoes back, frowning.

'Yeah,' I say. 'Like, can you leave the house and stuff now? You're better?'

She stares at me. 'It's not like I'm ill, Neena. I just . . . I prefer staying at home . . . I . . . I can go out any time. If I want.'

'But you just said – you just told me – how hard it is for you! And all those times when you said no, you mean you could have?'

'No, no. It's not like that. But . . . I'm not *ill*. You're just exaggerating now.'

We stare at each other.

'Right, Mum. Sure.' I give a sarcastic little laugh and blow it out through my nose. I'm being a bit mean now. But does Mum seriously think she's OK? I guess she could be in total denial that something's wrong with her. We've never really talked about it – it hasn't come up properly, other than when I used to ask her to do things and she said she wasn't ready. That was a long time ago now, but even then we sort of accepted it as something temporary that she'd get over once she was ready. I wonder now whether she talks to any of her friends about it. They come *here* all the time, which is obviously because Mum can't – I mean, couldn't – leave. Doesn't she realize that it's a big deal?

She's staring at me again now. 'You're taking your medication?' she asks.

I blink at her. She's *never* asked about my meds. Not since the first evening. After that, she gave me the tablets every night like they were paracetamol, smiling, breezy, a glass of cool water in her hands. It was like that visit to the doctor's never happened. Now it feels like a dig. And as if she's using it to change the subject.

'Yes, I'm taking my meds,' I say firmly. 'But, more importantly, have *you* thought about taking any?'

Her lips tighten and she glares at me. But I know I'm not saying anything wrong. 'It's not normal, Mum, staying in the house all day. You know that really, don't you?'

Mum's fingers nervously pluck at the dupatta round her neck. 'I just . . . I've been worried about you . . . All this exam pressure . . . And what happened before with the Year Nine SAT exams . . .'

I cross my arms. Fine, so she's not going to talk about herself. She's going to make this all about me. I breathe in deeply through my nose. 'That was a long time ago, Mum,' I say. And I'm trying to convince myself of that fact too.

Mum sniffs. *Oh God. She's going to cry.* No. I can't handle her crying right now. Nothing's making any sense and I want to be alone. I need to get her out of my room.

I crouch down by her side. 'Mum,' I say carefully. 'I've been taking my medication. And everything is fine. I just . . . I have A LOT of revision for exams. Plus all this art. But it's OK. Really. I just need to get on with it . . .'

I give her hand a little squeeze. It makes me feel a bit sick, the way I'm so good at pretending. Mostly, though, I'm honestly thrilled at myself because Mum manages a smile. I smile back. Both of us pretending nothing is wrong. Not with her. Not with me.

'Yes,' she says, her voice a bit brighter now. She stands up. 'Yes, I'll leave you to it.'

I nod. 'Everything's fine,' I say again. *Nothing is fine. Nothing will ever be fine again.* 'Everything is completely fine.'

Once Mum leaves, I get one of my brown paper bags out of my bedside drawer and breathe into it: in for five, out for five. Slow, steady. My head's spinning. I can't believe Mum left the house. I should be happy for her, but it's hard to right now. The dark thoughts that have been creeping around on the edges of my mind sink in. Mum left the house for the baby, but not for me. Maybe I'm just not enough. Is that why they're having another baby?

My eyes fill with tears. Despite the brown bag, my breathing worsens.

I sink down on to the edge of my bed. After a few minutes, I hear Mum and Dad chatting happily as they use the bathroom, getting ready for bed. They flick off their bedroom light and the house is suddenly completely silent. It was never this quiet when Akash was here. I have the urge to blast out Bollywood music, like he used to. But then that would wake Mum and Dad and they'd hassle me. I don't want that either.

What I need is a distraction.

I keep breathing into the paper bag as I check my phone to see if Fi has messaged me back. I really need to know if she's got any more information on Akash. She's replied. My heart races as I read her message.

> Nothing, I'm afraid. Not getting anywhere.
> Sorry, Neens. I didn't mean to get your
> hopes up . . .

I screw up the paper bag. Chuck it across the room so hard it hurts my shoulder. It hits the wall and bounces back at me, landing beside my feet. A small yelp escapes me, rising up from my belly. I bury my face in my hands as my breathing worsens.

Fumbling for my bedside drawer, the tears coming fast now, I look down at the tiny tablets. I should take one; it will help to calm the thoughts, my brain, me. But, instead of reaching for one, I remember the day I got the pills. It was two months after Akash disappeared. Everything was extremely hard: my thoughts were racing so fast I could barely keep up with them; I'd stopped eating or sleeping; I cried all the time. I'd had a cold, a bit of a temperature, and Mum took me to the doctor. The doctor had been worried and chatted to Mum quite intensely; I was in a sort of daze. I don't remember what they were saying.

But I remember Mum had laughed nervously. 'She just needs some sleep.' And the doctor had frowned and scribbled something down.

Mum and I had picked up the crisp white bag from the pharmacy together. It wasn't until I was home, back in my bedroom, that I looked at the name of the medicine. It was such a long, strange name, not one I'd come across before, so I'd opened the package to get a proper look. Antidepressants.

I was shocked. It hadn't even occurred to me until that moment that I might be depressed. That the way I felt might be something 'curable', that I could take medication for it. I thought it was just the way I was. The way I'd always be now that Akash had disappeared.

Mum had perched on my bed, holding a glass of water. She took the tablets from me and handed me just one. I had to take one every night before bed, she said. And I felt ready for it, ready to try anything really. But then she added: 'No one needs to know about these, Neena. It can be our secret.'

God, the shame.

I already felt like a failure. I couldn't *function* like a normal human being. Sleeping, eating, these were such basic things. And Mum's words just made me feel that even more. But there was also this strange sense of relief and so I tried to hold on to that. I took the pill, gulping it down with my shame.

That night I slept. And so I continued taking the pills. I felt just a bit more together. I got out of bed in the mornings. I went to school. I didn't stop feeling sad, exactly, but they did help.

I never stopped being embarrassed though. The only person I told about the tablets was Raheela, one evening when she came to sleep over. I thought maybe she'd get it. That perhaps Mum was wrong and it was actually OK. Not normal but also nothing to be ashamed of. But Raheela had looked awkwardly at her lap. She didn't know what to say.

Was that the start of it? Us drifting apart. She blames Fi, I know, but maybe she actually thinks I'm too . . . broken? Messed up? Unmendable?

I slam the drawer shut. I don't want the tablets any more.

Sinking down to the floor, I reach under my bed and pull out the bottle of whisky I took from Akash's room. I unscrew the lid and drink. It burns my throat and I hate it. But I also want more. And more.

My muscles relax a bit. So does my brain. And so does my breathing.

But then I picture Mum and Dad all cosy in bed. Three of them now. Happy.

And I wonder, who do *I* have?

I know that there's only one person, really, who helps me forget everything. I want to see Josh. I want to kiss him. In our little world, nothing else matters. I give in and message him.

> Sorry about earlier. Things are so complicated . . .
> Can we start over? Please?

And then I finally do the deep breathing my brother showed me. I stand up and breathe deep into my belly. I do that until I feel calm again. Then I lie down on my bed and imagine Akash here. He'd drink this whisky with me. Make me laugh. Why, why didn't I go to the party with him?

My phone buzzes. It's Josh.

> Hey! What you thinking?

I'm thinking that I really like
you. So can we figure out the
rest? And forget whatever I said
this afternoon?

> So un-pause?

Yeah?

> OK!

I smile. Huh. *OK*. Simple. I like that. I wish I had his brain. I message him back.

Cool. What you up to?

> Confession: I was thinking
> about you when you
> messaged. Been revising.
> Now out for a walk.
> Stargazing . . .

My heart races. *Thinking about me.* It's probably the whisky, but everything's suddenly warm and fuzzy. I push the bottle back under my bed and curl up under the covers with a stupid grin on my face.

You and your stars, Josh! Lol!

Oh God, I wish I hadn't
mentioned stars now . . .

Ha ha. No, don't worry.
Stargazing actually sounds
perfect right now.

There's nothing for a few seconds and then:

Want to join me? No
pressure though. I know
it's complicated . . .

I swallow hard. I want to go. I really, really want to go. But I can't. If Dad catches me, I won't be able to go to art college. And I need my art more than ever now. I need to get away from Mum and Dad. Away from this . . . this baby.

And yet . . . Mum and Dad are asleep, aren't they?

I don't know if it's the alcohol or what, but I'm imagining sneaking out. I just need to be really careful that no one catches me. Josh sends another text.

> I'm actually heading to my
> dad's grave. Could do with
> the company.

Aha. That changes things, doesn't it? He needs me. Anyone would go, wouldn't they? I can't just leave him at his dad's grave alone. I sit up.

> Let me see what I can do.

I tiptoe down the corridor and press my ear against Mum and Dad's bedroom door. I hear A LOT of snoring. Dad's, like a minor hurricane, shaky and phlegmy. Gross. And Mum's, more like a distant whistle.

Definitely asleep.

I take a deep breath in. OK. Maybe I *can* do this. I'll be extra quiet going out and coming in. And I'll see Josh and no one will be able to stop us, not Dad's threats, not even a baby.

It dawns on me how happy I'm suddenly feeling. Maybe I don't need my meds after all.

I tiptoe back to my room. Stuff it. Mum and Dad are doing what they want. I'm going to live my life too. After all, you only have one, right?

What am I waiting for?

As I'm leaving, I take one last look at the picture I did earlier. I'm astounded. How did I paint it so fast? And why don't I remember doing it? It's still not finished. There's something missing, which I can't quite figure out, but it really doesn't look like something I would paint. It actually looks . . .

A shiver runs through me . . . It looks more like something Akash would do!

A thrilling thought dives into my head: *Was Akash here after all?*

Did he . . . help me?

I peer around my room for any signs of him. I don't even know what I'm looking for. Then I shake my head at myself. What is going on with me lately? I'd remember something like that, wouldn't I? And anyway I looked everywhere earlier: Akash isn't here.

But then I look at the painting again.

And I feel that shiver again. *Is he?*

10

It's totally dark outside the graveyard. Spooky. There are no street lamps, and branches from overgrown trees spill over the wall surrounding the cemetery, blocking any light from the moon. The air is cool. It smells of pine trees, moss and mud. I'm still warm from the whisky and the walk here and everything's fuzzy, but I hover next to the huge metal gates, having second thoughts. Is Josh already inside? Should I go in or is this actually a bit weird? Maybe we could go to the park or something instead. Somewhere a bit more . . . normal?

My phone rings. I jump and for a terrible moment I think it might be Mum or Dad. My heart hammers against my chest. But no, it's Josh.

'Hey. Whereabouts are you?' he asks. He sounds out of breath.

'Outside. Main road entrance. I can't see you . . .' I'm breathless too, still startled by the ringing. I need to get a grip.

'Stay there,' he says. 'I'll come and get you.'

A few seconds later, Josh appears, shining the torch on his phone to light up the worn, muddy path in front of him as he approaches the gates from the inside. He's wearing trainers, jeans, and a rucksack over his sweatshirt. His hair's messy. Cute. It's a relief to see him.

He comes right up to me, close, and I can feel the heat from his body.

'Permission to kiss you?' he says, instead of hello. His breath is warm. Smells of beer. I see that he's clutching a can in his other hand.

I chewed gum on the way over, so I'm hoping I smell of mint by now and not of whisky. 'Permission granted.'

'You're sure now? Not going to change your mind again?'

I shake my head. Smile at him. 'Nope.'

He smiles too, and we do this funny smile-kiss, which is a bit like trying to eat each other's teeth, and we end up laughing before it turns into a proper kiss. His body is right up against mine now. My skin tingles all over. My stomach buzzes. I put my arms round his waist. We kiss and kiss. I can't believe how fast everything's moving between us, but at the same time it feels totally natural.

A car drives past and it's suddenly bright, its headlights lighting up the road around us like a spotlight. I pull away from Josh. Oh God. Oh shit. What if it's someone who knows Mum or Dad? I turn my face away from the street to hide, peer up at the trees lining the graveyard. My heart's beating so fast I can feel it thudding against my chest.

'Let's go in,' I say, suddenly realizing the graveyard is possibly the best place in the world for us to meet. The chances of me seeing someone I know in there are zero. Right? And if that did happen, especially at this time of night, it would be so unexpected and weird that it would be like a sign from the universe, telling us we're not meant to be together.

And then I have another thought: *Or a sign from Akash maybe, wherever he is.*

'Sure!' Josh says, not noticing I'm being a bit weird. He grabs my hand, leads the way.

We're silent as we make our way through the woodland leading to the graves. My heartbeat steadies; my breathing calms. We're in our own little universe now, hidden from the rest of the world. Only the sound of our footsteps can be heard, twigs snapping beneath our trainers as we walk. Finally, we reach the graves. I try not to look at them until we stop because I find graves disturbing, especially all the names and dates on them. Once, when I was younger, I read them as I walked through here with Akash, a short cut to the park. It was overwhelming, imagining all those families who have gaps where people should be: empty dining chairs and beds and shoes and bedrooms.

Empty bedrooms that might one day be filled.

No, no, I don't want to think about that right now. I focus on Josh.

His dad's gravestone is big and black and shiny. It has gold lettering, which shimmers in the moonlight. It's smart, spotless, like someone has recently polished it. Josh crouches down on the grass next to it and slips his backpack off his shoulders. He pulls out a couple of cans of beer.

'Want one?' he asks.

'Sure.'

I sit down next to him and take the can. We sip beer while looking at the gravestone. It reads:

IN MEMORY OF

DANIEL STONE

(1968–2013)

FATHER, HUSBAND, SON.

LOVED DEARLY BY ALL.

I glance at Josh, waiting for him to say something. But he doesn't. And, although I'm glad that no one can see us in here, I can't help but feel it *is* a bit strange. Then, I don't know why, I have this sudden, terrible, uncontrollable urge to laugh. What the hell is wrong with me? It bubbles in my stomach, gurgles in my throat. I shake a bit from trying to keep it all in and I'm sure it's going to spill out any second and ruin absolutely everything between Josh and me.

I gulp down practically the whole can of beer to try to calm the giggles. It works, thank God. Bit like putting out a fire. I focus on how creepy this place is so that I don't laugh again. It's just so weird, all these dead bodies in one place, all those bones under the mud. I peer into the darkness. There could be hundreds of ghosts around us right now. A shudder goes through me. Great, now I've managed to freak myself out.

I shift a bit closer to Josh. 'So . . . do you . . . come here often?' I say, trying to lighten the mood. I watch his face for a reaction. I hope I'm not being *too* insensitive, but I need to do something.

Luckily, he laughs. 'This isn't the most romantic, is it?'

The beer fizzes in my belly. 'No, no . . . it's fine. Totally fine . . . Graves and ghosts and whatever else is lurking in those shadows is actually my idea of a perfect date.' I do a pretend shiver to cover up a real one.

He laughs again. 'It seemed a good idea at the time . . . I . . . I don't know why . . .'

Josh finishes his beer and gets himself another. He passes me another can too. I'm tipsy. I shouldn't drink it. But I take it. Who decides what we should and shouldn't do anyway? Why are there all these rules all the time? Would you like a drink? Yes, please. It should be that simple. Shouldn't it?

'I usually talk to him,' Josh says. 'You know, like if I'm upset, or worried about anything. It helps. It never seemed strange on my own, but now . . .' He looks at me sheepishly.

'It's OK,' I say, wrapping my fingers round Josh's. 'I get it.' And I get why he might want me here with him too.

'I wish you'd met him,' he says.

'Yeah. Me too.'

We look at the shiny gold words for a bit longer. FATHER, HUSBAND, SON. Funny how you can mean so much to so many people, and then suddenly be gone.

'Where do you think he is now?' I ask.

Josh squeezes my hand tight. 'Dunno, to be honest.' He sniffs. 'Mum believes in the afterlife. She never used to, but she completely changed after Dad died. Yoga and running was just the beginning. Then it was meditation, gratitude lists, incense sticks – like a whole different Mum. But . . . I guess that's what happens . . . Things happen . . . and we change.'

I swallow. *Things happen. We change.* 'Yes, yes, that's true.'

He drinks some more beer. This time, he downs loads in one go. 'What about you? What do you think happens . . . *afterwards?*'

I shrug.

'Do you ever wonder about Akash?' he goes on. 'What happened? How do you . . . How do you deal with that . . . that *loss?*'

I shrug again. The real question is, what have I *not* wondered about Akash? 'I find all that stuff . . . confusing,' I say. 'But, you know, weirdo parents, *that* is my forte too.'

Josh laughs. 'Trust me, your mum can't be weirder than mine. She's vegan now and completely obsessed with all things green. She even goes to these classes where they dance naked and stuff.' He groans. 'Oh God, I can't believe I just told you that. When you meet her, that's all you're going to be thinking about now. Naked dancing.'

I laugh too. But all I'm actually thinking is: *He wants me to meet his mum!* I try to play it cool. Totally cool. 'Honestly, nothing about parents can shock me any more. They reckon teenagers are hard to understand, but whatever. I can't keep up with old people . . .'

Josh looks at me, waiting for me to continue. 'Your parents are strict, right? That's why you were unsure of things earlier . . .'

'Yeah. I mean, they're so . . . I don't even know what the word is. Traditional. Old-fashioned. Weird. All of the above. It was always there, just much worse now. Proper weirdos.'

I laugh but Josh doesn't.

'So . . . if we're going to do this, it's not going to be . . . easy . . .' I try to explain. 'No one can know about us. It can't get back to my parents . . .'

Josh nods but he's frowning. 'Yeah, yeah, I get that. But how old do you have to be? You know, until you can have a . . . boyfriend?'

My heart sinks. 'Well, I . . . I'm not sure.' Then my heart flutters. Does that mean he wants to officially be my boyfriend? 'Oh.'

'But it doesn't mean . . .' I swallow. 'It doesn't mean I *can't* have a boyfriend.'

Josh nods slowly. He looks confused. I cringe. God, I wish we'd stuck to talking about graves and the afterlife. That was definitely less awkward. I'm actually feeling quite sick now. That combination of whisky and beer probably wasn't the best idea. 'My mum's having a baby,' I say suddenly. I don't know why I add that to the mix right then. But there it is. Maybe I need to prove just how bizarre my parents are. Because then perhaps we can laugh about it. Or maybe I just need to talk to someone about it, share the weight of it all.

Josh tilts his head. 'Wow.'

'Yep! She should've tried yoga and running, or even meditation first, right?' I force a small laugh. 'It's just so *weird*. And they're so *old*.'

We both screw up our faces.

'God, yeah,' Josh says. 'The thought of parents having sex. Gross.'

We stare at each other. Sex. All I hear is *sex*. And, from the way he's looking at me, I know he's thinking about it now too.

He turns to face me, kisses me, which I guess means he's OK with the secrecy thing. And, the next thing I know, we're lying on the grass, next to Josh's dad's grave, and we're kissing and kissing and Josh's hands are everywhere. In my hair, on my waist, my thighs. And I feel like I did at Fi's party the other day: as if the world and everything that has happened in my life before this moment is a distant and inconsequential thing.

A totally embarrassing sound escapes my lips. Like I'm enjoying myself a bit too much. Oh God, I want to die. But then Josh makes a similar sound back and it makes it OK. Sort of special even. A secret between us. We carry on kissing and it all feels so good – until I accidently hit Josh's dad's headstone with my elbow.

We both freeze. I clutch my elbow. Wince. Josh is above me and he looks at the headstone and then back at me. We smile at each other awkwardly.

'You OK?' he asks.

I nod as I rub my elbow. Talk about killing the mood.

'Do you . . . want to get out of here?' he asks. 'Maybe . . . come back to mine for a bit?' He coughs. A bit nervous maybe. 'My mum's cool about that sort of thing.'

I'm still doing the awkward smile. A part of me really wants to go back to his. The other part of me wouldn't know what to do, where to start, and it all feels a bit like it's too much too soon. Also I can't because I should probably get home. 'Oh, I uhhhh . . . well, my parents aren't.'

'Oh God, of course, yeah!' Josh shakes his head. 'Sorry!' He rolls down on to the grass by my side. We're squashed in between two graves, Josh's dad's and someone else's. Josh clutches my hand and presses his palm against mine. I press mine against his too. We are hot. Sweaty. My heart is racing again.

'We can still kiss though, right?' I whisper.

He smiles. I smile back. And we do that cute smile-kiss thing again that turns into a laugh-kiss, our teeth clashing together. Then Josh kisses my neck, and it feels good. Any awkwardness around the headstone or invite home slips away.

But now I'm thinking about home. *Have my parents maybe woken up?* No, no, I push the thought out of my head. I want to stay a bit longer and they've ruined enough already. I'm not going to let them spoil this too.

I kiss Josh back.

And eventually my parents and the bad thoughts drift away.

11

I wake up abruptly, as if someone has pushed me. My head's spinning and pounding all at once. At first I think I'm still at the graveyard: I'm cold, damp with sweat, a horrible sour taste in my mouth. But then panic fills me as I realize I'm in a bed that's not mine. Josh's bed? I sit up. Look around. My heart steadies. No. I'm in Akash's room: grey walls and lemon-yellow curtains and bookshelves full of thick art books. His guitar is balanced against the wall in the corner. Beneath me is his grey-and-white striped duvet.

I'm struck again by a horrible, sickening thought: *Soon this won't be Akash's room any more.*

But I push the thought away. I need to focus. Why am I in Akash's bed? How did I get here?

I'm in my pyjamas. I have my phone. But I don't remember coming into Akash's room, getting into his bed, or falling asleep. It must be very early; the sky is deep orange and the air is cool. I check the time on my phone: 5.30 a.m.

Images from last night flash through my mind as I try to piece everything together. I remember a feeling of dread coming over me as Josh and I said goodbye outside the graveyard. It was the thought of Dad catching me again. I practically had to drag myself home. The closer I got, the heavier my legs felt, and the more my chest tightened. And then, as I walked down the drive, I started shaking uncontrollably. I was still shaking once I'd climbed back through my bedroom window. Dad wasn't there. But, even though I should have been relieved, I kept shaking and shaking.

It was a full-blown panic attack. I hadn't had one like that since the Year Nine SATs. After that, I remember nothing.

Another buzz of panic flashes through my chest now. *Did I shut my bedroom window?*

Silently – and I'm seriously impressed by how silent I can be, especially considering how dizzy and tired I feel – I climb out of Akash's bed, straighten the covers, tiptoe across the hallway and slip into my room.

I look around. OK. Good. The bedroom window is shut. Everything looks normal other than the pile of clothes on the floor. Muddy, grass-stained jeans and the light blue top I wore last night. I grab them to put in the wash basket before Mum or Dad see them, but as I gather them together I discover the whisky bottle I drank from before I went out, hidden under the clothes. I freeze. *Weird*. I remember putting it back under the bed when I was messaging Josh. *Before* I went anywhere. I pick it up – it's practically empty. Whoa! Did I drink all that when I got back from seeing Josh last night?

No, I couldn't have. Why would I? There must be some other explanation.

But then my mouth *is* really dry. And I have a pounding headache. Urgh. I quickly shove the bottle back under the bed and chuck my clothes into the laundry basket. That's when I see it: my painting.

It's the one of the Ridgeway that I was working on before I went out yesterday. But it's . . . well, finished. And so *alive*. There's this painter called Jackson Pollock who my art teacher and I totally love. His paintings look like they're just splashes of colour. Like a kid could do them really. But people pay a ton of money for this 'messy' kind of art. And what you notice after looking at them for a while is that they're actually splashes of feeling. Well, that's what I think anyway. And it looks like I've used that style in this painting; there are flecks of white, red and gold paint all over it. It looks great!

It's not the kind of thing I would ever usually do. And I don't remember doing it. Did I get home, drink a ton of whisky, finish the painting and then sleep in Akash's bed? Is the whisky why I don't remember? Memory loss?

I stare at the painting. It *really* doesn't look like my work. My skin prickles all over. I feel cold and shivery. I know I brushed the thought off last night, but *was* Akash here? Did he do this?

No, no. It can't be. I haven't been sleeping much. I'm not thinking straight. Nothing's been making any sense since Mum announced she was having a baby.

And yet . . . Could that be why I don't remember the drinking or the painting? Because it *wasn't* me? Did Akash drink that whisky? Did he finish my painting? Did he . . . maybe pick me up off my bed and put me on his to sleep? As a sort of sign?

Is he sending me a message? Telling me he's still around?

I know, I really do know, that I could be imagining it. But I have to check if he's still here. I look under my bed, and peer into my wardrobe. My head's spinning. He's not here. I look around for more clues. I don't know what, exactly, I'm looking for. His shoes maybe? Or a footprint. But there's nothing.

I sit down on the edge of my bed. Take deep breaths.

Am I being *totally* unreasonable? Do I just need some sleep?

But everything's pointing towards him. Is he trying to *help* me? I was stuck with my painting, and he wants to help, like he always did. And didn't I smell him at the Ridgeway yesterday? Maybe that was him playing the guitar later; maybe he was just hiding. Hide-and-seek.

Where *is* he?

This is all too confusing. I need sleep. I need my thoughts to stop spinning. But I don't want to take any pills. Those days, they're over. I get into bed. Close my eyes. I keep thinking I'm falling asleep, but then my alarm goes off.

I sit up, confused all over again. It's 7 a.m. already? It doesn't make sense. I just got into bed! But I force myself up and start getting dressed. I need to work hard and get good grades. I can do this, especially if . . . if Akash *is* helping me. And I can't wait to get to school, where I'll see Josh again.

Maybe Akash will be there.

The weeks pass in a daze of schoolwork and revision. Dad makes me change my shift at the art centre cafe to Sunday afternoons, because I have to go to church with him in the mornings. And every week, on the way there, it's the same talk: *Stay on the right path, Neena; pray your worries and mistakes away, Neena; really think about your behaviour, Neena.*

I make a pact with myself, but for my own reasons: no more sneaking out, no more drinking, no more climbing over the school fence and going to the chippy at lunchtime. I don't want any more panic attacks, or any more memory loss; I need to focus on getting good marks to keep Dad happy, so that I can go to art college and get away from this baby.

I meet up with Ms Jones and she's thrilled with my progress. That's what she says, her grey eyes shining: 'I'm *thrilled* with you!' She calls Dad in front of me to tell him how well I'm doing.

I stay up later and later every evening, work harder and harder. The harder I work, the less I think about reaching for that bottle of whisky under the bed. Anyway, I want to leave what's left for Akash. In case he comes back again.

And then, like a reward for my good behaviour, the things I'm hoping for actually happen. Mum doesn't mention the baby again. It's like it never happened. And twice Akash finishes my paintings while I'm sleeping. Each time, I wake up in his bed. He drinks the rest of my whisky and starts a new bottle from Dad's cabinet. Hides the new bottle under *his* bed this time.

I see Josh at lunchtimes. We meet under the willow tree at the top of the front field. We lie on the grass and look up at the blue sky and hold hands. We talk about exams and revision and Josh's dad. But mostly we kiss. I find myself thinking about him in lessons. And at home, once Mum and Dad's friends come over for dinner in the evenings, I escape to my room to revise and message him.

Only once do I break my pact and sneak out to meet him at the graveyard again. This time, I don't stay out too late, and I don't panic as much when I climb back through the window. Everything seems to be going smoothly. Josh *does* keep asking to see me more, but, when I tell him I can't, he understands. I'm even feeling . . . *happy* . . . As if all the heaviness of the past ten and a half months is slipping away, and I'm being . . . *lifted*. No antidepressants, just real joy. But I don't think about happiness too much. I don't want to jinx it.

The only person who doesn't like me working hard is Fi. She keeps messaging to invite me to parties at hers, complaining she doesn't know what's up with me. I need to let my hair down, she says. At first, she's moody. Then she stops messaging altogether. She doesn't reply to my messages or answer my calls. I almost give in and go to her house, but stop myself.

Then it's Friday again. Unexpectedly, Fi calls as I'm walking up the field to meet Josh for lunch. I freeze, my heart pounding. My eyes fill up and I realize how much I've missed her. I answer straight away.

'I need to speak to you,' she says. 'Can you meet me at the usual place?'

'I can't,' I tell her. 'I don't want to get caught.'

'Please, Neens,' she says. 'It's *really* important.' She sounds upset. Her voice is heavy. I wave to Josh, calling him over to tell him. 'OK,' I say. 'I'm coming now.'

Fi is at the end of the field, loitering near the bike shed, as I approach. Her red hair shimmers in the sunlight as she runs her fingers through the long strands; she looks sparkly and fresh and I've missed her so much, the way I feel a bit more together when I'm around her.

'Everything OK?' I ask. I hug her tight. 'I haven't heard from you in ages. Are *you* all right?'

She lights a cigarette and I take a step back. I don't want to smell of smoke.

'Yeah, all good,' she says, puffing away. 'But we're going for a drive. I want to take you somewhere.'

I frown at her and then peer back at the school building. Whatever she wants, I can't do it. I've only just got Ms Jones and my parents back onside. And she doesn't seem upset, like I thought, after all. I look back at her. 'No, I'm not leaving school. I can't.'

Fi rolls her eyes. 'Do you realize what a *bore* you've become, Neens?' She does a fake, exaggerated yawn. 'Come on, we won't get caught. You know how easy it is!'

She starts walking but I stay put. A part of me wants to follow her. I want to make her happy. And I want to fill her in on everything that's happening with Josh. But I can't go with her. I can't risk it.

Fi turns back round and raises an eyebrow.

'I'm sorry,' I say, shrugging.

She stares at me. 'You can't be scared of *everything* all your life,' she says. 'What would he think? What would Akash think?'

I go cold. What would he think?

My brother wasn't scared of stuff. He was brave. Adventurous. Bold. I recall the night when it all happened. Remember how he'd begged me to go to the party at Fi's with him. But I didn't because I was too scared of getting caught by Mum and Dad. And look how that turned out.

I should have been braver. I should be brave now. More like him. But what about art college?

I keep my feet firmly on the ground, even though my mind feels like it's already left with Fi.

Fi sighs. I glance towards the school building again. I'm getting twitchy about getting back – and I mean *literally*. The skin on my face is twitching all over. It must be nerves or something. I'm about to walk away from Fi when I notice that she actually looks a bit nervous too. Is her lip also twitching, or is it my imagination?

She steps towards me and her face softens. She licks her lips and takes a deep breath. 'So, I might have a lead,' she says, and it comes out as a whisper. 'A proper one.'

Now my skin gets really prickly. Up and down my arms, my legs, my neck. I stare at the freckles on Fi's face, suddenly nervous as hell. 'What do you mean?' I say, and I'm also whispering.

Fi clears her throat. Her face hardens again, her eyes suddenly watching everything – the field, her watch, my face. 'Remember I said I might have something?'

'But . . . but then you said it was nothing.'

'I know, I know. But actually . . .' Fi rubs her forehead. Is she sweating? 'I didn't want you to get your hopes up, but this guy . . . He's a good friend of Akash's. He might know something . . .'

I take long, deep breaths. Slow and steady. The way my brother taught me.

'I've been chatting to him for months,' Fi goes on. 'I can't get anything out of him other than that he saw Akash that night.'

'What? That night? This is huge!'

She nods. 'But if *you* speak to him . . . If *you* try . . .' She pauses, catches her breath, swallows. 'He refused to speak to you for ages, but I've begged and begged, and he . . . he said yes, Neens.' Her voice breaks and her eyes fill. 'So . . . if you want to speak to him, you need to come now. He's expecting us.'

My heart races as my brain tries to process it all.

Fi puts her arm round me. 'You still want to get to the bottom of what happened, don't you?'

I nod. I put my arm round her too. And then we're walking towards the far end of the field, and my chest and toes are on fire. My skin is prickling all over now, even the soles of my feet, my palms, the inside of my ears.

'I just don't want us to get our hopes up,' Fi says as we climb over the gate to get to her car.

'Yeah,' I manage to say. But it's too late. My mind's racing ahead with the possibility of tracing Akash's steps that night. The possibility of finding *everything* out . . .

12

Fi drives fast as we head away from school. Too fast. But it doesn't bother me like it would have this morning. She glances at me apologetically as she runs a red light.

'I want to make sure we get you back in time for lessons,' she says.

I nod. But, right now, I don't care about that. All I care about is Akash.

As Fi drives, she fills me in on some basic details. Akash's friend's name is Jay. He's twenty. He's known Akash for five years, although she's not sure how they met. At first, Jay said he didn't see Akash the night he disappeared. But Fi kept hearing rumours that Akash was at his house that night. Finally, last week, when Jay was really drunk, he admitted Akash had been there – but he wouldn't give Fi any details like what time or for how long . . .

I do my deep breathing as Fi talks. Try to take it all in.

And then we're parking outside a grey-blue house with a faded yellow door. Overgrown bushes spill out on to the pavement. The rusty gate whines as we open it. Cracked tiles line the path to the front door. Fi rings the doorbell and it plays a happy tune. We look at each other and Fi rolls her eyes. I relax a bit, but my head is spinning. Although Fi and I have been trying to uncover clues for months, this is the first time we have something solid. A real person, who Fi has spoken to, and who I am going to talk to as well.

A guy opens the door. He's pale with round glasses and long, straight brown hair tied back in a ponytail. My skin twitches all over. Is this Jay?

'All right, Fi?' he says. He lifts a chin towards Fi as she steps into the hallway; she nudges her chin back at him. I follow her in and he shuts the door. My stomach is tight.

'Who's your friend?' he asks, as we stand in the dark hallway.

'Oh, she's cool. Neens, this is Gareth. Gareth, Neens. She's a friend of Jay's,' she says. I give a small nervous laugh.

'Cool,' he says. 'Come on in then. I'll get some drinks.' He turns towards the staircase. 'Jay!' he shouts up the stairs.

'What?' a gruff voice bellows back.

'Someone to see you.'

There's no answer; Gareth shrugs. 'I'm sure he'll be down soon,' he says. 'You know what he's like. Doesn't like to be rushed!'

I glance at Fi. 'Give him a minute,' she says.

I hesitantly follow Fi into the living room. There are plants everywhere and branches from a massive one brush my face as we go into a room with peeling wallpaper and rough, worn carpet. The curtains are drawn, and a round lamp in the corner is giving off a dull bluish light. Three guys are lounging on faded brown sofas, two playing a video game and the other one rolling something between his fingers. Looks like a spliff. Yes. I recognize the smell from Fi's parties.

'All right?' one of the guys says.

'Yeah, we're cool,' replies Fi.

My mouth is so dry, I don't even attempt to answer. I try to smile but I'm suddenly feeling awkward in my school uniform; we must look really young. Although Fi somehow manages to look cool in hers, the sleeves of her sweatshirt rolled back and her short skirt showing off her tanned legs. We sit down and the guys all carry on with what they're doing. I glance at Fi, hoping for a clue as to what's going on, but she's peering at the TV. I lick my lips to get rid of the dryness as I look around.

There are some weird-looking contraptions on the coffee table. But, even though they're unfamiliar, I'm pretty sure they're something to do with drugs. And there are also small, see-through packets of little white tablets. From here, they look like they could be painkillers. But of course I know they're not.

My throat and chest are getting tight. What exactly did Akash do here? Should we even be here? And where's Jay? I look at Fi again, suddenly scared. I desperately want to be with Josh, in the sun, under the willow tree. Fi doesn't see that I'm scared. She just smiles.

I concentrate on breathing. *We're here to find out about Akash*, I remind myself.

Gareth returns with pint glasses of blackcurrant squash. He hands one to Fi, one to me and keeps one himself. As he squeezes on to the sofa next to me, I get a waft of greasy hair and stale cigarette smoke.

'Will he be long?' Fi asks. 'We're in a bit of a rush.'

'I'll call him again,' says Gareth, downing some of his drink and bouncing up.

My stomach is flipping over with nerves. I want to know everything. But I'm also scared. Scared Jay won't know anything and scared that he will – that I'll find out the reason Akash disappeared. Find out that it really *is* my fault. That I could've stopped him if I'd gone to the party with him.

'All right, all right, I'm coming,' a voice calls.

Then a set of footsteps comes tumbling down the stairs. A six-foot guy with black hair and shiny, tanned skin comes into the room. He's gorgeous, his face almost pretty, he's that cute. He has high cheekbones, big brown eyes and long lashes, and a squishy nose like a baby's. He's wearing black joggers and a white vest that shows off his toned arms. I'm not sure what I was expecting, but it wasn't this. He grins when he sees Fi, and his teeth are so white and straight, his smile wide and reassuring.

Fi gets up and hugs him. He picks her up, swings her round. They laugh. Then he puts her down and looks at me. 'And this must be Akash's little sis.'

I nod, suddenly feeling more shy than nervous. Butterflies burst in my stomach.

'You look like him,' he says, and my throat tightens. 'It's your eyes.' He smiles. 'Come on. We'll chat upstairs.'

I look at Fi. 'It's cool,' she says. 'I'll wait here.'

'Cool,' I hear myself echoing back. And I follow Jay upstairs, like it's no big deal. Me and this total stranger. Perfectly normal. *What does he know that he doesn't want to tell me in front of everyone?*

We step into his bedroom. My heart pounds hard against my chest.

Jay's bedroom has hardly anything in it. There's a thin white wardrobe and a matching bedside table next to a single mattress on the floor that's pushed up against the wall. Like downstairs, the curtains are drawn, but up here the main light is on and it's all weirdly yellow. He seems even better-looking against the grimness of the room.

'Sorry about the smell,' Jay says, pointing to patches of damp on the cream-coloured walls. 'Landlord refuses to do anything about it. Dick.'

I nod. 'Dick,' I say too, because I don't know what else to say.

Jay makes himself comfortable on the mattress on the floor and pats the patch next to him. There are no other seats in the room so either I stay standing or I sit on the mattress. I don't want to seem rude so I give him what I hope is *not* an awkward smile and sit down. I almost spill my blackcurrant drink as I sink into the mattress.

'Steady there,' Jay says, and I do the hopefully-not-awkward smile again. I add a laugh for good measure. Why the hell am I laughing? There is absolutely nothing to laugh about.

And then there's this long silence. We're two strangers sitting on a mattress on the floor in a damp room in a house where I reckon the curtains are closed throughout and every room smells of either weed or damp. Jay's looking at me like he's waiting for me to say something. Which I probably should. I just don't know where to start, now that I'm actually here.

'You gonna drink that?' he asks, nodding at my glass.

Realizing how thirsty I am, I down half the blackcurrant juice. It's different but nice. Sort of fizzy, refreshing. I burp suddenly, a long, fat belch, which is totally devastating, but Jay finds it the funniest thing in the world. He pats my back while chuckling, like we're old friends.

'So,' he says, when he finally stops laughing. He rubs his hands together. 'Fi said you wanted to meet me?'

I look at him. Why does he have to be so damn cute? It's not exactly helping me concentrate. My mouth is dry again so I drink some more of the blackcurrant juice. But not too much this time because I don't want to burp again.

'You . . . you knew my brother,' I say, taking in this information myself properly for the first time.

I try to think now. Did he ever mention Jay? I can't remember. I don't think so. He had this whole life I didn't know about. Parties and friends I'd never met. Did he hang out here often? Did he maybe even kick off his shoes and sit on this mattress next to Jay?

My stomach is burning now.

I need to know everything.

'Yeah, man,' Jay says, nodding. 'Knew him for years. Good guy, he was. One of my best mates.'

'Years? Best mates?' I stare at Jay. Had Akash mentioned him? I try harder to remember. Maybe he did and I've forgotten, but how could I forget something like that?

And what if I forget more things? What if I forget *him*?

'Yeah, yeah.' Jay says. 'We were like that.' He crosses his fingers.

I stare at Jay's perfect face. I try to focus on what I need to ask him. 'So you . . . saw him that day? The day he disappeared?'

I hold my breath. My mind's racing ahead. Did Akash sit downstairs with Jay that evening? Did he smoke whatever was on that table before he went to a party at Fi's? Maybe swallow some of those pills? Could that explain his disappearance? Was it more than just drinking he was into? I can't imagine him getting together with Jay and painting.

Maybe all that would explain things.

If only I'd been there with him. If only I'd agreed to go to Fi's party . . .

Jay reaches for a lighter from his bedside table. I think he's going to light a cigarette, but then I see that it's actually a spliff, the smoke strong and sweet. Shit. My uniform is going to stink. I try not to breathe in. You can get stoned from breathing in secondary smoke. I know that from Fi. I finish the rest of my drink and put the glass down on the carpet next to me. I try to ignore absolutely everything, and just focus on this: he might know something about Akash and this is my chance to find out.

Jay's eyes are focused on the blank wall in front of him. After smoking some of his spliff, he finally looks at me.

'Yeah,' he says. 'Yeah, he was here.'

My chest tightens. I wait for him to tell me more. I smile at him, trying to encourage him to give me the details.

But Jay must misread my smile: he puts the spliff down in the ashtray on the bedside table and leans towards me. His lips press against mine.

I should pull away. Josh. I'm with Josh. But it actually feels nice, like he *really* knows what he's doing, and he smells of expensive aftershave, and he's Akash's friend, and older, and he seems to really like me, and –

No! I pull away. What am I doing? I'm with Josh.

Jay's face changes. He scowls. I think that this is it – he's going to chuck me out. He's not going to tell me anything at all. But instead he kisses me again.

This time, I stay perfectly still.

I'm sorry, Josh.

After months and months of nothing, finally I have a chance of getting some information about what happened that night. I can't mess it up. A part of me wants to run out of this room and go to Josh right now. But a part of me is flattered. Jay must think I'm attractive. And he's seriously gorgeous!

Most importantly, I'm the only one who can do this. I'm the only one who can find out what happened to my brother.

When Jay stops kissing me, I take a deep breath. Guilt swirls in my stomach. Jay, on the other hand, looks really pleased with himself. He does this weird nod, bouncing his chin from side to side, as if he's moving his head to the beat of music.

I try to focus. 'So, my brother . . . he was here . . .' I cough to clear my throat. Get rid of the lump that's growing and growing. *I just cheated on Josh. Did I?* 'Can you . . . can you remember the details of that night?'

Jay stretches. The muscles in his arms flex. 'I don't know. We'd had a lot to drink . . . Just a normal night, that's all.'

I glance at Jay's spliff. 'Did you . . . Did he take drugs too?'

Jay shrugs. 'Sure. We often smoked together. But not that night. He was trying to be good.'

My chest tightens. Akash smoked spliffs. I didn't know that. But it doesn't surprise me too much. What else though? What time did he come and go? What exactly did he drink? What did he talk to Jay about? Did he maybe talk about *me*?

'So he had drunk a lot? More than usual, would you say?' This is important. If he was really wasted, he might have made some bad decisions that night. It doesn't mean . . . It doesn't mean he *planned* any of it.

Jay holds his hands up in the air. 'Nothing to do with me if he did.' His face is suddenly closed, lips tight.

Shit. This is no good. I need him to tell me everything. He reaches for his spliff again, but I grab his hand to stop him. He turns to look at me, surprised, his brown eyes wide and questioning. I'm shocked at myself. But I'm desperate. I realize I'd do anything to find out what happened to Akash.

'I . . . I just miss him,' I tell Jay honestly. 'And I keep thinking that if I can just retrace his steps . . . back to when he was last seen . . . If I can just figure out what was on his mind that night . . .' The desperation is taking over now – it's all I'm feeling. 'He was here one minute, gone the next, and it's all so goddamn unfair and it sucks, everything sucks.'

Jay's face softens a bit. But not enough. He licks his lips. My body tenses, looking at those lips. They're not going to tell me anything.

'Yeah,' he says. 'I get that. But I don't have anything else to tell you.' He nods at my empty glass. 'You want another drink?'

'No. No, I'm fine. Thanks though.' My head is spinning. I need to get my thoughts straight before I have to go.

Our eyes lock, and he flinches. He knows something. I can tell. Suddenly I'm not feeling nervous at all. Desperation is making my whole body burn.

My hand is still on his. I squeeze it tight. 'You were good friends,' I say, changing the tone, really willing to try anything now. 'I know it must be hard for you to talk about . . .'

I lean towards him. It's not ideal, but it's better than him closing off. I kiss him. This, I realize, is the only way I'll get him to tell me what I need to know.

'Do you remember what time he left here?' I ask when we stop kissing. 'It would really help me to know.'

Jay is still staring at my lips. 'It was around two in the morning,' he says.

So he left Fi's party – maybe even to go home – and then came here and got more wasted.

'And did you . . . did you speak to him after that at all?' I ask. 'Because one thing still isn't making sense. He was last seen in town, but why would he have gone there *after* coming here? Unless he was meeting friends there too? But who?'

Jay ignores my questions.

'Did he talk to you about me?' I ask, to distract him, and because it's the main thing I want to know now. Was he thinking about me at all that night? Did he think twice about leaving me?

Jay ignores me. He kisses me again. Soft and light. My heart's racing. He's my brother's friend. I feel like putty in his hands. Relaxed. It feels cosy here with him. His kisses are making me tingle all over. He smells so good. I feel . . . alive. I'm so confused by everything I'm feeling. I know I should leave. I . . . I want Josh. Not Jay. I think . . .

'Jay, I . . . I'd better get back . . .'

But he ignores me again. He pushes me gently so that we're lying on the mattress side by side. I laugh nervously, suddenly not so confident. He presses up against me and slips his hand under my school sweatshirt, and unhooks my bra. I freeze. Shit. What's he doing? What the hell am *I* doing?

I should be in school. With Josh. *Shit. Josh.*

Then I hear Fi's voice calling me from downstairs. 'Time to go, Neens!' she shouts.

Jay freezes. I breathe.

'Neens?' Fi calls again.

I jump up, stumbling as I try to get my bra back on.

'It was nice to meet you, Neena,' Jay says, smiling.

'Er . . . Yeah,' I say, not knowing what else to say. I grab my schoolbag, flee down the stairs and follow Fi as she marches towards the car.

'We've got five minutes to get back to school,' she tells me.

I nod. I don't want to be late now. But why am I still tingling all over from Jay's touch? How can I feel so good and so bad at the same time?

It hits me as I sit down in the car. Any good feelings slip away. Instead, I feel really sick. I just cheated on Josh.

And – what would've happened if Fi hadn't called me just then? Oh God, what the hell was I *doing*?

Fi starts driving. 'So?' she says. 'Did you find anything out?'

The blackcurrant juice swishes around in my stomach. It's going to come back up any second. My stomach's burning like crazy. 'What was in that drink?' I say. My words come out slurred. 'I feel *really* weird.'

'Shit, Neens, you *drank* that?' She looks at me like I'm really stupid. Which I am. I really am. 'We've got lessons, you know?'

'I . . . I thought it was blackcurrant juice . . .' Everything around me is spinning now. 'Wasn't it?'

We stop at the traffic lights, and Fi leans across me and rolls down the window. 'It's called a snakebite and black. It's lager and cider. And probably vodka or some other spirit too, knowing that lot.'

I look at her, confused. 'And blackcurrant juice?'

'*And blackcurrant*,' she says, rolling her eyes. 'Shit-loads of alcohol and blackcurrant.'

Oh. I really am stupid.

'If you're going to be sick, tell me, OK? Don't do it in the car.'

I glare at her. I'm drunk in the middle of a school day and I cheated on Josh, and she's worried about her crappy car?

She glowers back at me. 'You've only got yourself to blame, Neens.'

I shrink into myself. She's right. What the hell was I doing in there? It makes no sense now.

I'm silent the rest of the way, but I notice my cheeks are wet. Sick rises in my throat; I swallow it down.

When the car stops outside school, I open the door and puke on to the pavement. It's all purple liquid. No lumps. I guess I forgot to eat anything this morning.

Fi rubs my back. 'You'll feel better now,' she says.

I look at her and burst into tears. 'He knows something,' I say. 'But he wouldn't tell me.'

'Shh,' Fi says, pulling me close. 'Come on now. Don't cry.' She hugs me tight. 'We'll find out. We'll get to the bottom of it.'

I cry into her shoulder until she stops hugging me. 'We need to get back to lessons now, OK? Can you do that? Or I can . . . maybe drop you home? Pretend you're ill?'

'I'm OK,' I tell her, sniffing. Home is the last place I want to go.

'If he knows something, it's going to come out,' Fi says. 'I promise you.' And she says it with such certainty that I believe her.

We slip back into school just in time for lessons; everyone's going in from the field and so we just join them. It's so weird. Like it almost never happened. But I'm not going to forget so quickly, however much I want to. My head is still spinning. I can feel Jay's lips on mine. Taste him. Smell him. *I'm an idiot and I hate myself.* I keep my head low, hoping I don't see Josh. I don't want him to see me like this. I need to figure out what to do next. Do I tell him about the kiss? *Kisses.*

I feel sick again.

I'm not sure how I make it through lessons that afternoon – it's a bit of a blur. But on the way home from school, my head is clearer. I firmly decide on one thing: no one will ever know about what happened with Jay. Not Josh. Not Fi. Nobody.

Even I won't think about it.

I'm an idiot. This morning, I was happy. But I jinxed it. I jinx everything.

I can't ruin things with Josh by telling him about Jay. Instead, I'll make it up to him. I'll go home and brush my teeth. I'll take a shower. I'll chat to Josh this evening as usual. We'll carry on like nothing's happened. I'm not such an expert at that, but I need to learn how.

13

But it's not so easy to forget things, is it?

It's the day after the incident with Jay, a Saturday. I'm doing an extra shift at the art centre cafe, trying not to think about what happened, but failing epically. *Why did I let him kiss me? Why did I kiss him? How did I let things go so far? Am I really a person who cheats on her boyfriend and then pretends nothing happened?*

I don't know the answer to any of these questions.

Everything's changed. Maybe I have too.

The cafe is buzzing with the lunchtime rush and I'm crouched on the floor, cleaning up a combination of squashed blueberries and carrot chunks that a family with a baby left behind. The white tiled floor is almost gleaming when a voice interrupts my thoughts.

'Can we talk?' Raheela's voice is firm.

I glance up at her. She's got one hand on her hip, pressing against her bright blue skinny jeans. Her fuchsia-pink vest top matches her lipstick. She looks bright and neat. My white work T-shirt on the other hand is covered in tomato juice and a dusting of hot chocolate powder. Not exactly my most glamorous moment.

'I'm *working* . . .' I say, standing up to face her. 'No time for chats.' I barely slept last night, thinking about Josh and how I can maybe make everything up to him; the last thing I need right now is Little Miss Perfect making me feel even crappier.

She glances at my hair and frowns. This is exactly the sort of thing I mean. I run my fingers through the strands at the front. OK, so maybe I forgot to brush my hair this morning. But who cares? I try to step past her, but she blocks my way.

'I won't be long,' she says, glancing around the crowded cafe. 'Is there somewhere I can speak to you . . . in private?'

I cross my arms. 'Not really.' Which isn't a lie: I'm on my own while Dominic takes his break so I can't exactly leave.

'Fine,' she says. 'We'll talk here. *You're* the one who keeps messaging me at weird times, Neena! So don't you think we should . . . you know, *actually* talk about it?'

I cross my arms, a bit embarrassed. 'Fine,' I say. And I stand there. Waiting. Aware of all the tables that need cleaning. *Spit it out then*, I think. And then she does.

'I know I haven't been replying to you properly – I've felt so hurt. But I just wanted to say that . . . I'm sorry . . . about everything that's happened between us.' She dips her chin, suddenly looking very upset. 'I came over to see you every single day after Akash . . . Every day!' Her voice is shaky and I feel like she wants to shout at me. I sort of want her to lose it too. She's always so contained; it's annoying. 'I made notes for you in *every* lesson. Called you *every* evening after I left yours, to make sure you were OK –'

'I didn't ask you to,' I interrupt.

'I *know* that,' she says. 'But that's my point – I *wanted* to . . . But I also wanted you to . . . to talk to me. To trust me.'

'Should've thought about that before you cut me off,' I say. I turn to walk away, but she grabs my arm.

'You're the one who shut me out!' she says. '*You* cut *me* off! Don't you get it? We used to talk about everything. And instead you went and talked to . . . to . . . *Fiona.*'

I cross my arms. So she's jealous. That's what this is all about. 'Yeah, and?' I say, quite enjoying this now. But I don't add that Fi gets me. That she knew Akash like I did. Or that she doesn't mind if I get wasted or if I don't talk about stuff. She doesn't judge me.

Raheela frowns. 'I just want to know – did I . . . did I do something wrong? You *can* talk to me about stuff, you know.'

I keep my mouth shut. Look down at my feet. *It's me, not you*, I could say. *I've changed.* And we could maybe even laugh at that, reel off a whole list of relationship clichés and take the piss out of them. But I just shrug instead.

'I don't know,' I mumble. 'Everything's just weird. Not how it used to be . . .' I want to tell her about what happened with Jay. I want to explain that I didn't mean for it to happen, but it did, and I feel awful about it.

She nods. 'Yeah. I know. I do still care though. You know that, right?'

I look back up at her. Her eyes are soft and kind. I wonder if I can tell her about Josh. I *have* known her forever, so I know

I can trust her. And maybe she'll help me out, cover for me so that I can see him more often, make up for everything with Jay.

'I've got a boyfriend,' I tell her, before I lose my nerve. And then quickly, before she can react, 'I'm finding it hard to keep it a secret and see him. It makes me anxious . . . But he makes me . . .' *Dare I say it?* 'Happy.'

She stares at me. 'Your parents will kill you if they find out,' she says, like I don't know that already.

'It's Josh,' I tell her.

She raises her eyebrows. 'Josh, Josh?' She looks almost amused, but like maybe she gets it.

I smile. 'Yeah. Josh, Josh. And I'm careful. Really careful.'

'I don't know, Neens . . . Is this a good idea?'

Someone taps me on the shoulder, and I jump, remembering I'm at work. I feel bad. But I also need to quickly finish what I'm saying to Raheela. So I ignore them for a minute.

'I don't know!' I'm suddenly feeling very emotional. 'But I just want to be *normal*. I don't want to be the girl whose brother's gone any more! I want to do something for me. Can you help me out? Cover for me while I see him? Tomorrow maybe?'

Raheela shakes her head. 'I'm sorry.'

'Please?' I beg. 'It's the only way . . .'

'We could both get into so much trouble!' Raheela goes on. 'You know what my mum's like – worse than yours.'

Something inside me snaps. Why has she come here to tell me she cares when she clearly doesn't? 'Fine!' I shout. 'FUCK OFF.'

'I'm sorry!' Raheela says, her voice raised too. She's peering over my shoulder now; she looks really uncomfortable. 'But I can't get involved in all this!'

There's another tap on my shoulder. I swing round. 'WHAT?' I shout in the woman's face. Can't she queue up by the till like normal people?

My boss, Rosie, glowers back at me, her blue eyes wide. She's sucking her lip, like she does when she's angry. I cover my mouth. My breath stalls somewhere in my throat as I stare at her pale, freckly face.

'A word,' she says, through gritted teeth.

I tune back into the cafe. People are staring at me. There's a massive queue at the counter. A woman is helping herself to one of the pastries that only I'm supposed to give out. Oh God. It's chaos. I glance back at Raheela, hoping she might share some of my embarrassment, make it a bit easier, but she's gone. Typical.

'I'm sorry, Rosie,' I say, calming down. I don't know what just happened. I totally freaked out. I breathe in deeply. 'I'll get back to serving. I've got all this under control. You don't need to worry, I promise.'

I seem to be always making promises I can't keep lately. But at least I intend to try with this one.

She shakes her head and her blonde curls bounce round her shoulders. 'Dominic can sort this out,' she says, waving him over as he comes back in from his break. She sucks her lip again. 'You come with me. We need to talk.'

*

Rosie ushers me into a room I've never been in before. It looks like an unused office, all clean and white: empty white desk; a few white chairs; bright white walls. Something about all the white makes me feel uneasy. Like there's nowhere to hide. I cross my arms over all the stains on my T-shirt as I sink sulkily on to one of the chairs. 'She started it,' I say. 'It really wasn't my fault.'

Rosie sits down opposite me. She crosses her legs. 'Neena,' she says, her voice soft but firm, in that way she has. 'I gave you this job as a favour to your brother. You know that. And you know how much we all loved him and his work.'

I look down at my lap. Pick some hot chocolate powder off my black trousers. 'I know,' I say. 'I'm sorry. I'll try harder.'

She clears her throat. 'Why don't you . . . take some time off. Have a rest. It might help you feel . . . better.'

I look back up at her. She has that horrible pitying look on her face. Oh God, no, not her. Those *eyes*.

'I'm fine,' I tell her. 'It was just . . . That stuff, it . . . it goes back years . . .' I lie. 'It's nothing to do with anything.'

She nods but her lips stay stiff. Then she breathes in deeply and runs her fingers through her curls. 'Think of it as us letting you have a break. You'll be sixteen soon. You can reapply for your position then.'

I stare at her unsmiling face. Oh. I get it. She's just like everyone else. All this bullshit about loving Akash and wanting to help me – but actually she's ready to move on.

'You're sacking me?' I ask, just to be sure.

'Like I said, you can reapply officially. And listen . . .' She leans forward and touches my arm. 'I know how much you love the galleries, Neena. You can come in any time. Don't feel –'

'You're sacking me!' I say again, as it sinks in. I came here with Akash when I was a kid. It was our special thing. Dad would drop us by the door and Akash would take me round the exhibitions: 'Look at the colours in this one, Neens!' We'd make up stories to go with the paintings. Afterwards, we'd always sip hot chocolate with cream at the cafe.

This place brought out the best version of him.

I don't want to leave.

Everything about Akash seems to be slipping away.

But Rosie squeezes my arm, and I realize she wants me to leave right now. 'I'm sorry, Neena . . .' She stands up.

I stand too. My legs are wobbly. Rosie opens the door and I walk out with her. She smiles a proper smile now, like the Rosie I know, the Rosie Akash knew. 'Come back and see us, OK?' she says.

Suddenly I'm angry. With absolutely everything. With Rosie, and Raheela, with Mum and Dad, and with Jay. With the whole goddamn world.

'Forget it,' I say, giving her a hard, cold look. 'Just forget it.'

I storm through the rush of people coming out from an exhibition, past the busy cafe and out of the double doors. Then I'm outside, and I'm on my own. Again. I try not to think about how much I'll miss this place. Or how much I miss Akash. I concentrate on breathing.

Everyone pretends they care, but they all push me away.

Ever since everything happened, everyone just pushes and pushes.

14

As I walk through the centre of town, heading towards the bus stop, I realize how much trouble I'm going to be in with Dad. I can just hear him now. *Sacked?* His face incredulous. *And what have you done now, Neena?* What will I say? What can I tell him? No, I can't tell him I got sacked. But I have to tell Mum and Dad something: they aren't expecting me home for hours. Maybe I could tell them I've quit to focus on exam revision? Yes, that's a brilliant idea. It'll keep me in Dad's good books.

But then, as I hover in the middle of a busy street in town, I have an even better idea. What if I *don't* go home? Instead, I could go to see Josh. Mum and Dad will never know. I could see him *every* Sunday afternoon when they think I'm working. I will be a brilliant girlfriend – he keeps saying he wants to see me more often out of school. And I can make up for the kiss with Jay.

I message Josh to see if he's home. He replies immediately, telling me to come over.

A small fire starts to burn in my belly as I get on the bus. I squeeze on to a seat next to an old lady and take a deep breath. Maybe I'm not jinxed after all. Maybe I was supposed to lose my job.

Could this . . . could Akash be helping me? This is *exactly* the sort of thing he would do. I message Fi to tell her – she'll be proud too.

She replies straight away.

Good girl! Come see me too!

I will! I'm freeeee!

I do worry as I get off the bus and walk down the road to Josh's: I can't help it. My throat and chest go tight. I mean, I'm walking to Josh's house in broad daylight when I should be at the art centre. But I concentrate on inhaling and exhaling and I keep an eye out for signs of anyone I know, and it calms me. The street is completely deserted and the better thought that I'm holding on to takes over again: I'm going to make everything up to Josh.

Then I'm standing on his doorstep. I reach up and press the bell and watch the sky-blue door until it opens. Josh grins at me. He's wearing shorts and a T-shirt. I wrap my arms round his neck. He smells of soap and apples. All clean and crisp and fresh.

'I came straight from work,' I say, suddenly aware that I must look a mess.

He looks down at my clothes and laughs. 'Yeah, I see you've made an effort for me!'

I feel awkward, and he must see it in my face because he adds: 'I'm just teasing you!'

I force myself to laugh too.

'Come on in,' he says. 'My mum's out.' And he holds my eyes with his until my stomach feels tickly inside. My heart beats fast. He takes my hand, pressing my fingers against his warm palm.

Inside, the house smells of cinnamon and vanilla. Instead of curtains, frilly lace covers the windows. Coloured wooden beads sway in the doorways rather than actual doors. Josh leaves to get us some drinks and my hands shake as I look around the living room: I'm suddenly very nervous. Above the fireplace there's a beautiful painting of a single boat at sea by moonlight. My heart skips a beat. I want to look at it properly, take it in, but I can't focus.

Josh returns with two hot chocolates. 'Shall we go up to my room?' he asks.

I nod. I don't trust myself to talk. Klaxons and alarm bells are going off in my head left, right and centre – this is literally the exact opposite of everything my parents have ever told me to do. I try to shut them out.

Josh glides ahead of me, like this is no big deal. As I follow him up the stairs, I spill hot chocolate on my white T-shirt and quickly rub it in. Not that it'll make a difference along with all the other stains.

But I need to pull myself together.

Fi would waltz on ahead, leading the way. She never seems to get nervous. Cool and calm, that's what I want to be. Like

Fi. Like Akash. My brother was the coolest and calmest. I count backwards from ten to calm myself, like Akash taught me to do as a kid.

We get to a doorway and Josh parts wooden beads to let me into his bedroom. Once we're in, they clatter behind us like musical notes. It feels weird not to have a proper door for privacy, but there's something reassuring about it too. Makes it feel less official, I guess. We are alone, but I could easily leave the room if I wanted. Not that I want to. I don't.

I look around the room. Light blue walls. Normal blue curtains in here. The smell of zesty aftershave. Schoolbooks on a shelf. Astronomy books on another shelf. A telescope by the window, pointing towards the sky. It's cosy. Very Josh.

He sits on his bed and messes around with his phone, flicking through different songs until he settles on one I don't recognize. Some old guy singing and playing a guitar. Mellow. I put my hot chocolate on the floor and sit on the edge of the bed next to him. All I can think is –

Oh. My. God. I'm in Josh's bedroom. Sitting on his bed.

I can't mess this up, but my mouth's so dry. I pick up the hot chocolate and drink a bit. No alcohol in this one. Suddenly I'm thinking about Jay. I feel sick.

'What's wrong?' Josh says.

I must have zoned out. I look at his bright, kind face. *I cheated on you*, I want to tell him; I want to spill it all out so that it stops taunting me. But that's selfish, and I can't hurt him like that. I can't ruin everything between us. Instead, I say: 'I can't stop thinking about Akash.' And I realize it's true. I am thinking about Jay, but I'm also thinking about

Akash, wondering if he sat on that mattress next to Jay, wondering what else Jay knows about him that I don't, and if he ever had one of those purple drinks and drank it too fast.

Did Mum and Dad know that he smoked weed? Is that why Dad was always so angry with him?

Josh fiddles with the string bracelets round his wrist. 'You want to . . . you know . . . talk?'

I shake my head. Once upon a time, I would've talked to Josh. But what I want right now is to kiss him and forget about everything else.

I slip off my shoes and lie down on the bed. Josh kicks off his shoes too. Lies next to me. His fingers comb through my hair and massage my scalp. My whole body relaxes. His lips touch mine. Lightly. Dry bits of skin brushing mine. My face tingles. Then he kisses me harder, and I kiss him back.

And then we're kissing like there's no tomorrow. Our hands all over each other. And this is what I want, this feeling of being *alive*. If this is what I'm going to be doing instead of serving coffees, then I think I know which the winner is! Rosie can go to hell.

Mum and Dad's faces drift into my head, but I push them out. I'm not going to let guilt ruin this; it feels too good.

I'm shocked to find myself climbing on top of Josh. His hands slide just under my T-shirt and lift it off. It's all happening really fast, but I feel better without my T-shirt and all its stains. Lighter. Sexier. I'm wearing a pretty purple bra that makes my boobs look bigger than they are. I feel a bit pleased with myself.

Josh pulls his T-shirt off too, and I admire the muscles in his neck as his hands trace along my hipbone and then up, up, until suddenly they're cupping my breasts. Then they move round to my back and I realize he's trying to take my bra off. It shouldn't *really* come as such a shock: what did I think was going to happen after he took off my top? But my chest tightens. My body freezes up.

Josh freezes too. I search for words, try to express what I'm feeling. I want this. *Don't I?*

'I'm sorry,' I mumble. 'I . . .'

Josh looks unbearably hurt, but worried too. 'What's wrong? Was I . . . too rough?'

'No, no! Not that!'

'Don't you want to?'

'I do. I think! I don't know . . .'

My heart's racing. I want him to like me. Want me. And I like him. Want him too. I thought I might be ready, but maybe I'm not. You can't just go from nought to sixty when it comes to boys, it seems.

I lie down next to Josh. 'I'm sorry,' I say again.

'Shhh.' Josh kisses my forehead. He's breathing fast. 'It's my fault. I just . . . you know, like you so much – I got carried away.' He grins at me sheepishly, this crooked smile that somehow makes everything better by cutting through the tension.

We lie there for a while, catching our breaths. The silence is soothing. Then Josh props himself up on his elbow and looks at me seriously.

'I've never really spoken to anyone about my dad,' he says. 'But it helped, taking you to the graveyard.' He takes my hand

and intertwines his fingers with mine. 'You can talk to me, Neens. I shared my . . . my pain – you can share yours too.'

A lump swells in my throat. I swallow it down. 'What is this, Pain Club?' I say, trying to sound jokey. But it comes out with an edge. I laugh to cover it up. But Josh doesn't laugh.

'It can be whatever we want,' he says seriously.

The memories of the weeks after Akash disappeared come rising up inside me. I want to tell Josh all about it, every single detail, but I'm scared too, worried that if I start talking I won't ever stop feeling all this pain. I tug my hand away from his. Feel a surge of anger towards him. For asking. For caring.

'There were weeks when I couldn't get out of bed,' I snap at him. 'Is that what you want to know?'

He looks hurt but I can't stop.

'I didn't want to continue living. My body didn't know how. I couldn't move. Could barely breathe. Is that what you want to hear?'

Josh touches my arm. 'No, no. I just meant if you . . . you know, wanted. I thought it would help . . .' And then he touches my face, and it's so tender that all my anger towards him fades. It's not him I'm angry with. Of course I know that. I close my eyes.

'It's all a blur . . .' I try to explain.

'It's OK, Neens. You don't have to –'

I open my eyes. 'No, I do want to.' The smell of those days comes back to me. The sharp stink of my unwashed bedsheets. But I don't tell him all that. 'I felt numb for ages. Blocked off from the rest of the world. And then one day I couldn't do it any more. I knew it wasn't what he'd want, you know? He wanted me to be happy. So I got up, got dressed and went to school. Promised myself I would live my life.'

There's so much kindness in Josh's face that I know he understands.

I smile. 'So the let's-talk-about-our-pain-and-then-forget-it club?' I say.

'Yeah. Only it's not so easy . . . Forgetting . . . Is it?'

'No.' Now that I'm talking, I don't want to stop. 'And, if I'm honest, I still don't believe my brother's actually gone.' It suddenly feels so easy to talk about all this. Or at least talk to Josh anyway. 'I keep waiting for him to come back. I even think I've seen him a few times.'

Josh nods enthusiastically. 'I know what you mean. For ages, I'd think I'd seen Dad crossing the road. Or I'd walk into the dining room, expecting him to be sitting at the table with a coffee in one hand and a newspaper in the other . . . It always felt so *real*. Like they could come back any minute.'

'Yes! Exactly!' I feel a huge surge of love towards Josh. He gets it. He's the only one who understands.

My stomach bubbles with the excitement of it all. Because Akash was in my room, wasn't he? He drank whisky. Hid the bottle under my bed. Finished my paintings. I smelled him at the Ridgeway. And I'm not the only one who believes he's coming back!

Josh puts his arm round me and pulls me close. 'Oh, Neens,' he says.

We sit in silence for a few minutes and I allow myself to think about Jay. He knows something and Fi promised me she's going to find out what it is. I'm feeling more optimistic than ever now. If anyone can do it, it's Fi.

Then Josh seems suddenly excited. 'We should do something nice,' he says, kissing my forehead. 'I'll take you out. Cinema and dinner. Cheer you up.'

I look at him and shake my head. I'm the worst girlfriend in the world again. 'I can't,' I say. 'You know I can't . . .'

He shakes his head too. 'Of course. No. But not even if we're *really* careful?'

'I'm sorry, Josh.'

'No, don't be sorry. I just want you to be happy.'

I smile at him. 'I am happy,' I say. 'I'm happy when I'm with you.'

He pulls me close again. Our skin sticks together from heat and sweat, but he doesn't let go. I look up at him, wanting to kiss him again. And he presses his lips against mine.

I'm running. I feel like I'm flying. I'm late. The heat is stifling and the worry is taking over: I've got ten minutes to get home from the end of 'work'. I'm kicking myself: how could I lose track of the time like that? But I need to calm down. Keep focused. There's a heatwave, that's why I'm sweating so much, I tell myself. Not because I'm late. Not because I got sacked. Not because I went to Josh's house. No, nothing to do with any of that.

I can *still* make it home in time. I just need to keep going.

I turn into the park, deciding to cut through it: it'll be faster and also I'll get some shade. But, as soon as I'm there,

I regret it. The park is all noise. It's children laughing and screaming and splashing in the pool. It's perfect trees and ice cream and happy families.

I'm intruding. I pause near the entrance, thinking that maybe I should stick to the road after all, but then I get caught up in a big group of mums and tiny kids and I'm being swept along with them towards the play area. There's no way out – children and smiley mums surround me.

When we reach the playground, they all spread out. And I'm left standing there, alone. I could carry on home. I should. But instead I'm staring at the big red slide at the centre of the play area. I walk towards it, wooden chips lumpy beneath my pumps. I go right up to the red slide. I touch it. It's smooth and warm and has tiny scratches.

'Watch out!' a little girl calls from the top. She has big eyes and is wearing glittery pink trainers. Her feet come rushing towards me and I move my hand out of the way just in time. The girl gets off the slide and comes up to me.

'Are you OK?' she asks.

I'm shocked to find that I'm crying.

'Oh! I . . .' I wipe my tears away as fast as I can, but they keep coming. I want to go down that slide with Akash waiting for me at the bottom. I want to be nine years old again.

I'm being ridiculous. Absolutely ridiculous.

'I'm OK,' I tell the girl.

She makes a sad face. 'You don't look OK,' she says, before running off.

I walk over to the grassy patch near the slide and sink down on to the grass. I feel heavy. My whole body – legs, arms, feet, hands – feels too heavy to move. I have no idea how long I sit there. It's hot and I'm sweating and there are kids everywhere. I need to get home. But, for some reason, I can't get up.

I just want to be nine years old again.

My phone is buzzing in my bag. It's Fi. I answer it.

'I thought you were popping over?' she says. 'Or were you too *busy*?' She laughs. 'Tell me *everything*!'

'I want to be nine again,' I tell her, sobbing into the phone.

'Oh! Bloody hell, Neens,' she says. 'Is it happening again?'

'Is what happening again?'

'Don't worry. Where are you?'

I explain where I am. I tell her about the red slide and how much Akash loved it.

'I'm coming,' she says. 'Don't move.'

When I hang up, I see that I have twenty-three missed calls from Mum and Dad. I have a feeling that I'm in deep, deep trouble. I look across the playground, at the black pirate ship. And I feel like I'm on it. I'm on a ship and it's sinking. Sinking fast.

Fi's arm is round me and we're walking down the drive to my house. When we reach the door, she rings the doorbell, which is a bit confusing. She has walked me home from the park. Her arm has been tight round me all the way. She smells of expensive perfume. It's nice. Comforting.

'I think I can just go in,' I say, giving her a little smile.

She smiles back, which I'm pleased about. She seemed angry on the way here. She said I'm working too hard and I need a break and why won't anyone give me a fucking break. I think she's angry with the world, not with me. But I somehow feel responsible.

She hugs me. 'Oh, thank God, Neens. I think you're OK now. Are you OK?'

'I'm fine.' I'm not sure why she's asking me that. Though I do feel a bit weird. Weak, tired. But then I haven't slept properly for weeks. There's something else too: my head feels stuffy and it's hard to think straight.

'Oh, good.' She hugs me again. 'I'd better go. I'll message you later.'

'Wait,' I say, remembering something important. 'Have you found anything out? From Jay?'

Fi shakes her head. 'I'm really sorry, Neens. Not yet. But I'm working on it. OK?'

I nod. She gives me another hug and then I watch her designer skinny jeans race up the driveway. Turning back to the house, I push down the door handle.

'Hello?' I call as I step into the hall. I'm nervous. I'm very late home. But Fi said I should say I went to the library after work and that everything will be fine if I say that.

'Oh, thank God, Neena,' Mum says, rushing out of the kitchen and towards me. Her face is swollen from crying. She grabs me, pulls me in for a hug.

'Oh, hey, Mum,' I reply, like it's no big deal. 'Sorry I'm late. I went to the library to study after work.'

She stares at my face. 'Why didn't you call? Why didn't you answer *my* calls?'

'I . . . I forgot to call. And I turned my phone on to silent at the library. I'm sorry, I should have messaged.'

She starts full-on crying now. 'I was so worried. When I couldn't get hold of you on your mobile and the minutes turned to hours . . .' She breathes in deeply through her nose. 'I started getting all these thoughts . . .' she continues. 'Bad thoughts . . . Terrible, terrible thoughts . . .' Mum presses her forehead into my shoulder and cries.

'Shhh. I'm here now,' I say, pulling her closer. I feel awful. I understand the bad thoughts. The bad thoughts are agony. I hate them so much. 'I'm so sorry, Mum.'

'It just made me think . . . you know . . .' Mum goes on. 'It was like it was happening all over again.'

Like picking at an old wound, I remember the day Akash didn't come home. I start crying too, and we just stand there, in the hallway, getting each other's shoulders wet.

Mum's broken.

Everything's broken.

But I'm also out enjoying myself, feeling all these new, crazy, wonderful things with Josh. How could I do this to her?

When we finally stop crying, I lead Mum into the living room. We sink on to the sofa, side by side. Mum looks at me. Her mascara has smudged so she looks like she's got two bruised eyes. She touches my cheek.

'I know you hate me calling you my jaan,' she says. 'But you really are, you know.'

'I know, Mum,' I say. 'I know that.'

Fresh tears drip down Mum's cheeks. I lean forward to get her a tissue from the box on the table and catch a glimpse of her swollen ankles. 'Mum! Your feet! What's happened?'

She takes the tissue, wipes her cheeks, and laughs. 'Can't tell where my ankles end and my calves start. Cankles! Another joy of pregnancy.'

'I don't know, Mum,' I say, looking more closely. Mum's right – everything's swollen together. 'It doesn't look right to me. You should see someone.'

She frowns and shakes her head.

'Mum! You need to.'

She shakes her head again. 'I'm not going anywhere.'

'Shall I . . . shall I call someone? I'm sure a doctor could come to the house?'

Mum sighs and waves a hand at me. 'Really, you're worrying about nothing. This is normal in pregnancy.'

'Oh! It is?'

'Sure. I just need to rest. It'll go down.'

'OK,' I say, feeling just a bit less guilty now that she's happier. 'Put your feet up,' I tell her. 'I'll make you some tea.'

Mum nods and closes her eyes. 'Help yourself to food,' she says. 'I already ate. They say you don't need to eat for two but this little one's definitely hungry!' She laughs again.

I manage a little laugh too, but I ignore the comment about the baby. I've been quite happily ignoring anything to do with the baby for weeks. It's amazing how much you can ignore when you want to.

I'm waiting for the kettle to boil when I get a message through from Raheela.

> Your dad's just been over looking for you.
> My mum told him you haven't been here.
> **BE CAREFUL.**

I take Mum's tea to her. 'Dad out?' I ask, as casually as I can.

'He was looking for you,' she says. 'But I've just messaged to let him know you're home.'

I nod. 'OK, I'm going to get on with some homework.'

Mum smiles. 'I'm glad you're home,' she says.

'Me too,' I lie.

I sit on my bed, waiting for the inevitable. But maybe it's not going to be as bad as I think, I tell myself. I'll just tell him the same thing I told Mum. I was at the library. Lost track of time. It'll be fine.

After a few minutes, the front door opens and then slams shut.

I was at the library. Lost track of time. No one knows otherwise.

My bedroom door swings open.

'Where have you been?' Dad asks, his face all screwed up. 'Have you seen the time?'

'I went to the library after work,' I say carefully. 'Lost track of time.'

He glares at me. 'You're lying. I went to the art centre. You were . . . *sacked*.'

Shit. 'Yes,' I say. 'They had to let me go. That's why I went to the library instead.' I'm surprised by how steady my voice is. How calm I am, considering.

Dad slams his fist against the door. 'You're a liar. LIAR!'

Mum is behind him now. 'Arré!' she says, trying to shoo him away from my room. 'She went to the library, forgot to call. She's home now. Let's forget it, huh? She's OK. That's the main thing!'

But Dad pushes past her and comes into the room. 'Get up,' he says to me.

'What's got into you?' Mum says, coming to stand next to me. She clutches my arm.

'She's a liar!' Dad says. 'I went to the library. Three times! Like a madman. In, out, in, out, in, out. I went to the school. I went to Raheela's. Neena says she was at the library, but she wasn't. WHERE WERE YOU?'

His face is so close to mine that flecks of spit land on my cheek, my nose, my lips. I don't dare move to wipe them. Dad's breath stinks of coffee and egg. I stare at him and imagine spraying him with air freshener. I find that hilarious. The idea of him smelling of flowers and pine instead.

'WHERE WERE YOU?' he repeats, but this time so loudly it makes me jump.

Mum starts crying. 'Please, stop shouting,' she is saying. 'I don't like the shouting.' She rubs her stomach. 'The *baby* doesn't like the shouting.'

I know I need to say something. Me being silent is making everything worse. But I don't know what to say.

'Are you taking drugs?' Dad says now. 'I caught her sneaking into the house at five in the morning!' he tells Mum. 'Drunk.'

Mum stares at me. I look down at the floor.

'She looks like she's taking something. Lost weight. Tired all the time.'

'I'm not on drugs,' I say, firmly.

'LIAR!' Dad raises his hand and it stops just next to my face. At first, I think that Mum's stopped him, but she hasn't. He's stopped himself. He pulls his hand back to his side, keeps it there in a fist.

I've never seen Dad like this; I should be scared. Instead, it sounds weird, but I don't care if he hits me. I almost want him to.

'That's it,' he says. 'You're grounded. School, home, nowhere else. You understand? And no art school. That's it, final. We won't support you.'

Mum starts crying harder. But honestly I just feel numb.

'I understand,' I say. I feel like I'm on that ship in the park again. Sinking further down. I don't deserve to go to art college anyway. Why should I go when Akash isn't? He's the one who really should've gone.

'Enough now,' Mum says to Dad. 'Stop. Bas. You've done enough.'

Dad shakes his head at her. 'You spoil them! You keep spoiling her and it's . . . it's going to happen . . . all over again.'

'Ignore him,' Mum says, pulling me closer to her.

But she needn't worry. I already am.

Dad leaves the room and the front door slams.

'Let him go,' Mum says. 'You, you listen to me.'

She sits me down on the bed and gives me a tablet from my drawer. There's some old water on the table and I swallow it down with that. 'You get some rest. It's been a long day. Unless there's anything you want to tell me? Are you . . . are you taking drugs, Neena?'

I shake my head. 'No.'

She nods. 'I believe you.' She turns off the main light and flicks on my lamp. 'OK. Sleep first. Then we will talk about anything else.'

Sleep. Such a good idea. I lie down on the bed and close my eyes. I think of the red slide. I wish I was nine years old again. 'I just miss Akash,' I tell Mum.

'Oh, Neena,' she says, stroking my head. She keeps stroking and stroking and stroking. 'So do I.'

Slowly, her voice gets more and more distant, and so does her touch. Just like it has been over the past eleven months.

Eleven months.

It's been eleven months.

15

Stillness spreads through the house on Sunday. Dad stays in bed, doesn't even drag me to church. No one mentions the day before. Mum cooks and cooks until the house smells of roasted garlic, chicken, crispy potatoes. But Dad doesn't join us for lunch. And, in the evening, none of their friends come over. It's a still day and a still evening. The air feels empty.

Then it's Monday again. I meet Josh as usual at lunchtime. Fi sends me messages all day to check how I am. She tells me she's trying her best with Jay, but nothing yet. And, in the evening, I paint and paint. The next morning, I wake up in Akash's room. There's a fresh bottle of whisky on the bedside table, which I hide for him under his bed. Back in my room, I see that he's finished another painting for me. *He's here. He's here again.* I feel better for a while.

But, as the week goes on and Dad continues ignoring me, the reality of art college hits me. Every time I think of not going, my chest hurts. Every day, the pain gets worse. It lasts for longer each time until it's there for hours.

Then, towards the end of the week, something really weird happens. Time speeds up. The world speeds up. I speed up. I can't sleep during the nights any more, but they're not long, restless nights. They whoosh past. The gap between night and day is close. Too close. Dark and then light. Like someone simply flicks a switch.

And the days rush past. I try to grasp hold of the hours. I attempt to study, the urgency of exams on everyone's lips around me, but it's hard to concentrate in lessons. I tell Fi and one breaktime she gives me her old GCSE books and hugs me tight. Tells me it'll be OK. I feel lifted for a few minutes. Like when I see Josh. But they're slippery feelings I can't hold on to.

At home, I sit at my desk and stare at Fi's books. She messages me to check if I'm still grounded and if I'm studying. I try. I try and try. But my eyes glide over words, numbers, equations, and nothing goes in.

Mum and Dad's friends don't come over in the evenings any more. Dad spends more and more time out. Mum tries to feed me, cooking plates of rice and lamb curry, spicy chicken legs, daal decorated with fresh coriander so green it hurts my eyes. She gives me roti after roti. And so many almonds, blanched white. *Good for the brain*, she keeps telling me, pushing them into my palm like a secret jewel. But I'm never hungry. I hide the food in tissues and carrier bags and drop it into the bin when she's not looking. 'Are you taking your meds?' she keeps asking. I nod. I always nod. And I make sure I bury a tablet in the kitchen bin every night in case she checks.

My thoughts swirl round and round in my mind like a whirlpool. There's no break from them. They seem to be living, breathing things. They demand my attention, pulling me away from whatever I'm doing. They don't stop until I give in to them.

They tell me, *PAINT, PAINT*, when I should be revising chemistry. And I walk over to my easel and splash paint at the canvas.

They tell me, *LOOK FOR AKASH*, when I'm walking home from school. And so my eyes peer into cars, stare at the faces of people walking past.

Because he's been in my room, finishing my paintings. So he could be anywhere. *Anywhere.*

I live for lunchtimes, when I meet Josh under the willow tree. There everything slows down for a while and the feeling that I'm racing against myself fades. He's the only thing that makes sense any more, in this seriously messed-up world of mine where my brother disappeared and took me with him.

But with Josh, for a while, I find myself again. His kisses are soft and his breath is warm and he listens as I tell him all about my memories of Akash.

'Here one day, gone the next,' he says sadly. 'You don't really know what happened.'

'Exactly,' I say. And I kiss him again.

It's Thursday, and we're three-quarters of the way through the last lesson of the day, which is maths. The class is quiet, copying equations from the board, when someone knocks on the door. A small girl with mousy brown hair to her waist creeps in and hands a note to Mr Baker. He looks across at me and scratches his white beard. 'Neena, pack up your things,' he says. 'You're wanted.'

I glance at Raheela and for some reason she smiles at me. She usually looks away whenever she sees me and she hasn't spoken to me since she messaged to say Dad was at her house. I ignore her, collect my things and make my way to the front of the classroom. Mr Baker passes me the scrap of paper. It says:

PLEASE SEND NEENA GILL TO ROOM 21A
IMMEDIATELY. SHE WILL BE REQUIRED
FOR THE WHOLE OF THE LESSON.

It doesn't say who it's from or why I'm 'required'. And, as I walk down the corridor towards the history building, I have a sinking feeling inside. I hover outside room 21A, staring at the chipped blue door.

I tell myself to stop being silly. It could be about anything – it doesn't have to be bad news. I gulp in some air and push open the door.

As I step inside, I see that there's some sort of meeting going on. The tables have been arranged into a square in the middle of the room. Mr Butler and his bright orange tie-dye jumper smile at me. But it's a sad and serious smile. Ms Jones is sat at the table next to him, but her grey eyes aren't shining at me like they usually do. And next to Ms Jones is Miss Taylor, her hair as frizzy as ever, but even she seems oddly still, her arms folded tight. And then I see Mum, her eyes full of worry, her hands resting on her stomach.

She's out of the house! What's she doing here? Oh God. This must be bad.

Dad's next to her, wearing his work suit, frowning. Which just confirms my suspicions.

'What's going on?' I ask. My voice quivers. I try to calm my thoughts: maybe it's not such a big deal. Maybe Mum really is OK, like she's been claiming. It seems the baby has cured her phobia. This could just be . . . a friendly visit?

Who am I kidding?

Mr Butler stands up. 'Hello, Neena,' he says, like I've come in for a job interview or something. 'Please sit. We want to talk to you.'

He rubs his hands together nervously and then indicates his chair. But I don't sit. My skin itches all over. I want to get out of here. Everyone's got a mug of tea in front of them and there's a plate of biscuits in the middle of the table. Maybe this should feel cosy. But it doesn't.

'What's going on?' I ask again.

Mum wipes her head with her dupatta. She looks really hot and bothered. Dad shoots me a look. 'Sit down, Neena,' he says, and his voice is so deep and strong that it forces me to move. I sit down on Mr Butler's chair and he sits next to me. The smell of strong coffee hits me. Miss Taylor stares into her mug.

'I've been concerned about Neena for a little while now,' Mr Butler says to Mum and Dad. 'And so have other teachers.' He glances at Miss Taylor, who nods, and then he points to a pile of notes in front of him. 'It's been a tough year, Neena. You've struggled to keep up at times, which is understandable and we all sympathize. But, over the past couple of months, we've noticed . . . Your work's been . . . erratic. Possibly due to exam pressure? It seemed you were improving, but there's been a sudden dip in your grades over the past couple of weeks or so.'

I look at Ms Jones for reassurance. I think Mr Butler has got it all wrong.

'My work's been brilliant, hasn't it?' I ask her.

Mr Butler coughs. 'You had a good few weeks – that was all. But, Neena, we're not here to tell you off. We'd like to know, are there any extenuating circumstances that are affecting your work and concentration right now? Anything that might potentially affect your exams?'

I cross my arms. So I've had a bad week. But that's only because everything's been happening so fast. I've been working hard. I've been trying.

Mr Butler clears his throat. 'OK . . . I've also noticed . . . *We've* noticed . . . that Neena has been acting out of character. Withdrawn. And . . .' He clears his throat again. 'We suspect she's been getting help on her artwork – there has been a vast improvement in some of her paintings while others have been . . . not so good.'

'"Getting help"? You mean cheating?' Dad says, and his voice sounds dangerous.

'Now wait a minute, I didn't say that,' replies Mr Butler.

I glare at Mr Butler. We all know what he means. How could he? Him, of all people. Mr Butler has been the one teacher who has helped me through everything. He let me spend lunchtimes in his classroom, drawing, when I first came back to school after Akash disappeared. He was the one who told me to use what I'd been through and put it into my art.

'I haven't cheated,' I tell him. But then I realize that I have. Because Akash's been helping me.

Mr Butler's still talking. This is beginning to feel like an ambush. 'We're very concerned, especially with the exams so near. We'll need to investigate further, but Neena is producing work that's either outstanding or very poor. Not just in art, but in English too.'

What! I stare at Miss Taylor. Now I know that they really are setting me up. Akash *definitely* hasn't been helping me with English. He was rubbish at English. Hated writing essays.

'Like I said, we're going to need to look at this closely,' Mr Butler continues. 'But, at the moment, we want to know how we can help. Is this . . . like what happened before?'

I don't dare look at Mum and Dad. But, from the corner of my eye, I can see Mum fanning herself with a piece of paper. The bell for the end of school rings and the corridor is suddenly filled with shouting and cheering as everyone rushes out of lessons. I want to get out of here and join them.

'There's been a lot going on,' Mum says. She's fanning herself like crazy now. She looks really uncomfortable. 'Lots of changes . . .'

'We do understand,' Mr Butler says, nodding, and I think I see him looking at Mum's bump. 'But what can *we* do for Neena? We spoke to Fiona – Neena's friend in Year Twelve. She's also worried. Could we arrange some counselling perhaps?'

I feel dizzy. 'Fi?' I say. I don't get it. Fi's involved in all this? Why would she do that? She's supposed to be someone I can trust.

My hands begin to tremble.

Everyone's turning against me.

What do they want from me?

What are they trying to DO to me?

I think of Raheela's smile as I left the classroom. I bet she knew about this too. Trying to trap me as well. My heart slams against my chest. Everyone's staring at me now. Turning on me. The whole world is turning on me.

'There is one other option,' Mr Butler continues, and I try to tune in again. 'Due to everything Neena's been through this last year, there might be the possibility of deferring a year.'

It feels like someone's stamping on my chest. 'No! I'm not stupid. Why are you picking on me?'

Mum stands up suddenly. She's shaking. She tugs Dad's arm. 'I . . . I need to go home,' she says.

Dad looks super concerned. 'Are you OK?'

'Please,' Mum says. She's beginning to cry now.

I push my chair back and the screech of the legs against the floor pierces the air. A sign that I need to get out of here. Quick. I see Mr Butler get up – he's saying something to me, which I don't catch – and then Dad stands up too. I leap for the door before anyone can stop me. Before Mum and Dad reach me. Before they trap me and keep me here forever.

'Get back here, Neena,' Dad calls after me, not quite allowing himself to shout in front of the teachers.

But I don't stop. I almost trip over a chair by the door, which they've probably put there on purpose, but I fling it aside and it crashes against the wall.

I need to find Josh. He's the only one I can trust now. If I find him, I'll be safe.

16

I glance over my shoulder to check if anyone's following me as I charge towards Josh's house. No one. Nothing. I keep checking until I reach his front door. I need to be careful. Very careful.

KNOCK. KNOCK. KNOCK.

I peer over my shoulder again. Swallow. Breathe. 'Hurry, hurry. Please,' I whisper at the door.

The air is hot but I'm shivering. I wrap my arms round myself. Have the teachers followed me? Mum, Dad? Are they watching? Waiting? What will they do if they catch me?

KNOCK. KNOCK. KNOCK. KNOCK. KNOCK. KNOCK. KNOCK.

The door swings open. A lady . . . Josh's mum . . . Short blonde curls . . . Lots of bracelets and necklaces . . . Warm air . . . Vanilla . . .

'Hello,' I say. 'I'm . . . I'm . . .' I can't remember my name.

'Neena,' she says, smiling. 'You must be Neena.'

'Yes! Yes, I'm Neena.'

The woman holds a hand out for me to shake. Her palm is soft and her skin is warm. My hand must feel so clammy to her.

'Come on in. I've heard so much about you. I'll call Josh – we just got in ourselves.'

I step inside. The door closes. I feel a wash of relief. 'I'll go up . . .' I tell her. 'I just need to see him. I . . . I just . . .' My hand is aching where I've been banging it against the door.

Josh's mum frowns, and I'm worried she won't let me see him. But then she smiles again. 'Of course, love. Go on up.'

I rush up the stairs and stand outside the beaded curtain to Josh's room, catching my breath. I don't go straight in. There might be another ambush inside. 'Josh?' I say. 'It's me. Is it safe to come in?'

The beads part and Josh appears. He grins. Perfect teeth. I step into the room, into his arms. The beads close and clatter behind us like they're clapping.

Josh gives me a quick kiss. 'I didn't know you were coming over today,' he says. 'Good surprise.'

My eyes dart around the room. My breath is shallow. I need to check I'm definitely safe here. 'Can you shut the curtains?' I say. 'I'm worried they're following me.'

Josh frowns. 'What do you mean? Who's following you?'

I rush on, the words spilling out. 'If they're not following me, they might be watching, spying – they're always watching me.'

'Slow down,' Josh says. He takes my arm and manoeuvres me to the bed. We sit on the edge of the mattress. 'Who's watching, Neena? I don't understand.'

'Mum. Dad. The teachers. Everyone.'

Josh squeezes my hand. 'Shhh. Hey, breathe. Just breathe. There's no one here but me. Well, me and my mum, I suppose. I promise.'

'Please,' I beg him. 'Shut the curtains.'

He gets up and pulls the curtains shut. Turns on the lamp.

'No!' I say. 'No light. They might see it.'

Josh is looking really unsure now. 'Neens, I –'

My chest is tight. I'm desperate. '*Please*, Josh.'

He does as I've asked and I expect to feel better, but I don't. They could still be out there. Josh kneels in front of me and wraps his arms round my waist, presses his face into my neck. 'You're shaking,' he says. 'Did someone follow you here? Why are you so scared?'

I'm not shaking; it's more like my skin's twitching and jumping all over. 'What's happening?' I ask, pressing my head against Josh's shoulder.

'I . . . I don't know. But you're safe here.'

I can't stop twitching. 'Do you ever feel like you're in hell, Josh? Are we both in hell? Why are they trying to get me?'

Josh strokes my hair. 'Shhhhh. No one's after you, Neens. You're safe.'

'No, no, I'm not.'

He strokes my hair some more. 'Everything's OK. I promise.'

I look him in the eyes. I know I can trust Josh. He's the only one I can trust.

'I promise,' he says again. 'You're OK.'

He's so sure that I begin to believe him. His words crowd out my other thoughts. The image of Mum and Dad and the teachers and Mr Butler's orange jumper slowly fades. No one is here. I'm with Josh. They can't get me here.

'So we're not in hell?' I ask, just to make sure.

Josh presses me closer to him. I feel his heart, beating, strong.

'Feel that?' he says. 'We're definitely alive.' I smell his wonderful, familiar scent – shower gel and apples. His fingers stroke the back of my neck and he kisses me.

His touch, his kiss, his breath – they all calm me, soothe me. I kiss him back. The world stills around me. My breathing steadies. The twitching eases.

After we stop kissing, Josh presses his forehead against mine. 'We wouldn't be able to do that in hell, now, would we?' he says, smiling.

'No,' I say, managing a smile too. 'No, we wouldn't.'

I'm calmer after seeing Josh, but I'm furious with Fi. I've had a message from her while I've been at Josh's house. She wants to know where I am. As if I'm going to tell her.

Liar. Traitor.

I dial her number while I hurry home, ready to demand some answers, when Dad's car pulls up beside me. It screeches as it stops. I freeze. Were they following me after all? I hang up the phone before Fi answers.

Dad winds the window down. 'Get in,' he says. 'Now.'

I don't know what to do. I want to go back to Josh, but how can I without Mum and Dad seeing me? 'I . . . I'm fine walking . . .' I tell him.

He glares at me. 'GET IN!' he shouts, which makes me jump.

I see Mum in the passenger seat beside him. Her face is swollen and blotchy, tears running down her cheeks. She looks genuinely worried. I try to hold on to what Josh said . . . They aren't trying to hurt me. No one is trying to hurt me. I believe Josh. I can trust Josh. I climb into the back seat. Wait for one of Dad's lectures. But he doesn't say anything; he just drives. I peer out of the window to see where he's taking me – but luckily it's in the direction of our house, not the school. So maybe Josh was right.

Mum peers back at me from the front passenger seat and sniffs. She wipes her cheeks with a tissue. 'We've been so worried, Neena. Driving around, looking everywhere for you. You can't just . . . *disappear* like that. After . . . after the other day as well. It's too much, Neena . . .'

Disappear.

I'm forced to think about Akash, as I know she's thinking about him too, but this isn't the same. She needs to realize that. They both do.

'I just needed some space,' I say. 'I needed to think.' *And you and the teachers were trying to trap me.* But I don't say anything about trapping or following. If they *are* planning it, they can't know that I know.

Mum's eyes fill with tears again. 'Space? No,' she says. 'Not space like that. Not between us.'

I cross my arms. No space for *me*. Mum's allowed to stay in the house and cut off the whole world. Dad spends all day out. But *I* can't want some space. I stare out of the window. Hypocrites. They're all hypocrites.

Dad's still scowling as he reverses the car down the driveway. I watch his reflection in the mirror. Why isn't he saying anything? What's he planning? He parks the car and turns off the engine. My body tenses.

'Your behaviour today was unacceptable,' he says. His voice is calm and controlled, but deeply furious.

I think about this. I'm beginning to see just how badly I behaved. I shouted at Mr Butler in front of Mum and Dad. I threw a *chair* across the classroom. I stormed out of the meeting. It sounds weird, but I don't even know how I ended up at Josh's house. I have a vague memory of meeting Josh's mum, of her hand being warm and soft, of her voice being soothing and calm. She has green eyes and long lashes like Josh. I remember that. What did I say to her? But I do remember Josh kissing me, feeling his breath against my ear, his arm round my waist, as secure as a seat belt. I remember his words as I left his house: 'Your parents and teachers aren't out to get you, Neens.' I'm still not *completely* sure I believe it, but I try to hold on to it.

'Yes, Dad. I'm sorry.'

'Your poor mother,' Dad continues. 'She had a panic attack in the middle of your school. Do you ever think about her, Neena? Do you ever think about anyone other than yourself?'

I feel so small, like I'm shrinking. I'm always thinking about everyone else, but I don't tell him that. And I'm surprised he even knows what a panic attack is. He's never used that term before.

I glance at Mum. It seems maybe the baby hasn't cured her after all. 'I'm sorry,' I say, even though I really don't think any of this is my fault.

She nods. 'It's OK, Neena. I'm OK.'

No, you're not, I want to say. *None of us are OK*. But I know that won't go down too well right now.

'Here's what's going to happen,' Dad goes on, loosening his tie. 'You're going to write a letter of apology to your teachers. I don't know what you've been up to, but absolutely no more getting help with your artwork or English –'

'But I –'

'And you're going to catch up on all your work.'

'They've got it in for me,' I tell Dad. 'I haven't been cheating! They're picking on me!'

Dad shakes his head. 'No! No more excuses! You'll work extra hard, understand?' He turns and glares directly at me. Mum looks at me too.

I know the answer to Dad's question, the right one to get this over with. 'Yes, Dad.'

'The teachers aren't out to get you,' Mum says. 'No one's against you.'

That's exactly what Josh said. I'm so confused. Everything's so confusing. Maybe *I'm* the one who's got it all wrong. 'I'm sorry,' I say.

Dad's face falls. 'I just . . . I don't know what to do any more,' he whispers.

We all sit in silence until Mum undoes Dad's seat belt and takes him into the house, her arm round him. I follow them in and go to my bedroom. It seems the right thing to do. No one tries to stop me, and again I realize I must have got it all wrong. No one's trying to trap me.

I sit down at my desk, ready to work, ready to try to make things right. I'm exhausted. Today has been very confusing. But I know I need to work hard to get back on track.

I hold on to Josh's words. I say them to myself quietly, under my breath. 'No one's after you, Neens. You're safe,' I whisper. I say it until I believe it. 'You're safe. You're safe. You're safe.'

17

Mum comes into my room later that evening, just as I'm finishing an English essay. I'm surprised by how well it's gone, considering what a shitty day it's been, and I'm feeling good, ready to prove to Miss Taylor that I'm not a cheat. Well, at least not when it comes to English. A bit of hope fills me. Once Miss Taylor tells Mum and Dad I haven't been cheating, Dad might even change his mind about art college.

Mum leans against my desk. She smells of fried onions and garlic. 'You'll eat with us today,' she says. 'I know you're studying, but you need a break.'

I look up at her puffy cheeks and messy hair. 'But I've got so much to do!' My throat tightens with worry as I glance back at the revision timetable above my desk: I still need to do maths and history.

Why is she trying to stop me? Does she want me to fail?

No – I push the bad thoughts away. No one's out to get me: that's what Josh said.

'I'm not hungry,' I say honestly and without thinking. 'I'll just work through.'

Mum's face drops.

'I mean, I *am* hungry,' I say quickly, correcting myself. 'But . . . can you maybe make me up a plate? I'll heat it up later. Please?'

Mum shakes her head. 'You've been sitting at this desk for three hours, Neena. You need a break. *And* you need food.'

Her eyes glide over my body and I feel uneasy, remembering what Dad said about me looking like I'm on drugs. I wrap my arms round myself. I know I've lost weight, but that was harsh. I hope Mum's not thinking the same.

'OK, Mum,' I say, to reassure her. The last thing I need is any more hassle about anything from my parents. I'll do whatever keeps them happy. 'I'll eat.'

Mum smiles and nods. 'I'll call you when it's ready.' She goes to move, but then she leans back against the desk again. Her fingers pick at a spot on her chin.

Then she crouches down next to me and looks me straight in the eyes. 'We want to talk to you about something over dinner,' she says. 'And I just want you to hear us out. That's all I ask . . . OK?'

I swallow. This is about the cheating. They're going to ask me about it again. Suddenly I can't take any more of everyone being so disappointed in me. I need Mum to know the truth. I need her to know everything.

'I haven't exactly been cheating,' I tell her. I'm light-headed as I speak. I can't believe I'm going to tell her, but I know I need to. 'It . . . it's Akash. He helps me.'

Mum covers her mouth. She hiccups. Her eyes fill and I have no idea what she's thinking. Is she angry that he's been helping me? Is it cheating, even though I didn't ask him for help? Or is she upset that he hasn't been to see her too? Maybe she's thinking something else altogether.

I need to explain properly. 'The thing is . . . he . . . he taught me everything I know about art. He's always helped me. That's why he's helping me now . . .'

Tears roll down Mum's cheeks. She nods. 'I know,' she says. 'Oh, my darling, I know.'

'You do?' I'm breathless now. Am I hearing her right? She *knows*? How? Has she seen the alcohol? Has she seen the paintings? Has she seen *him*?

Mum sniffs and wipes her face. 'Of course I know. He's your brother. He'll *always* help you, Neena.'

My body feels so weak. 'And that's OK?' I ask, my voice tiny.

Mum tilts her head. Her eyes fill again. She reaches forward and gently places a hand on my cheek. Usually, I feel so awkward when she does this, but today all I feel is her warm, soft skin. She's looking at me with so much tenderness and, as I look into her eyes, I feel bad for doubting her earlier, for thinking that Mum and Dad were trying to harm me. How could I have thought that? They're my mum and dad. My family. Just like Akash.

'Of course it's OK,' she says. 'Of course.'

A weight lifts from my stomach. I feel feather-light, flimsy. I wish Mum would hug me tight, tell me everything's going to be OK. I don't know if it's true, if *any*thing will be OK, but I just really want to hear it right now. And it's been so long since she's given me a hug. I can't even remember the last time.

'I love you, Neena,' she says. 'You know that, don't you?'

'Yes,' I say, 'I do.' And the lump in my throat burns with all the love I have for her.

A fat tear rolls down Mum's cheek. She presses her hand against my face harder. 'We just want you to be well,' she says. 'You want to be well, don't you?'

'Yes,' I say, though I'm not sure what she's on about. I *am* well. Aren't I?

'Good,' she says, nodding. She peers at me a bit longer, and then pulls her hand away from my face before kissing me on the forehead. I get a waft of her sweet, lemony perfume before she stands up.

'Come through when you're ready, huh?' she says, glancing at my books. 'Take your time. I still need to make rotis.'

Once she's gone, I glance over my English essay. I feel a surge of happiness. So many words! Good words. And Mum loves me so much. I open my maths book to do some revision, but my stomach starts rumbling. I didn't realize how hungry I was. Maybe Mum's right – I do deserve a break. And food will help with my revision, as Mum always says – energy for the brain. Maybe she'll even peel me some almonds.

But, before I leave my room, I go on my phone. Now that I know I can't trust Fi, I need to somehow get information from Jay myself. I don't want to see him until I've got something solid to talk to him about, so I've started doing my own research online. I'm not on social media – I came off after everything happened with Akash – so I log into Mum's Facebook account and check Jay's timeline. He hasn't got very good security settings and I can see quite a lot of his photos.

I looked earlier, before I started my English essay, and couldn't find any of Akash. But I'm going to keep checking. I flick through, but most are of Jay's beautiful face, which just makes me feel more and more guilty again for kissing him. I log off, my heart sinking. Nothing yet.

As I'm about to leave the bedroom, I catch my reflection in the dressing-table mirror. I'm shocked by what I see. I don't look like me. My school trousers and sweatshirt are baggy. My face is gaunt. Hair messy. And my eyes, they're open too wide, like I've seen something shocking.

I don't look like Neena Gill.

My phone buzzes, and I'm glad for the distraction, so that I can stop looking at the person in the mirror. But then I see that it's Fi. She's been trying to get hold of me all afternoon, but I don't want to speak to her, not after she betrayed me with the teachers.

Leave me alone. We aren't speaking.

I send a quick message to Josh too, while I've got the chance, thanking him again for earlier. Then I make my way to the kitchen.

I pause in the hallway. Mum and Dad's voices are raised. Something's wrong.

'. . . but what else *can* we do?' Dad is saying.

'I know, but is it really the answer? Maybe we should be getting her help *here*? Maybe . . . we should get someone in, to pray for her?'

I freeze. I'm not exactly sure what they're on about, but I know they're talking about me. I push myself up against the wall and move a little closer to the kitchen door to hear them more clearly.

'I don't know,' Dad says. 'I've tried taking her to church. I pray for her every day. Everyone's praying for her.'

'But does *she* pray? Do we need some direct prayer – *on* her?'

A shiver runs through me. Prayer, on me? What exactly do they think is *wrong*?

'We can keep praying, and sure, let's get someone over, but we also need to *do* something,' Dad says. 'Saleem says it will help.'

I like Dad's friend, Uncle Saleem. I've always thought he'd make a great Father Christmas if only his skin was white instead of brown. He's got the perfect belly for it and the laugh too. But what's this got to do with him?

'His niece changed completely when they took her there,' Dad goes on. 'Neena's been cheating! Most of her grades are poor. And all the drinking. What choices are left? Are we going to wait until it's too late again? Tell me that.'

My face goes hot. So that's what this is about. They want to *change* me. 'Fix' me somehow. They're disgusted with me. Mum's quiet now and I hear pots and pans being moved around. Then she sighs. 'Maybe you're right,' she says. 'She's going to be on those tablets her whole life otherwise. Something needs to be done . . .'

A wave of shame rushes through me. Mum's changed her mind about loving me. Those tablets in my drawer, that I don't even take any more, have made her think about me differently. My ears ring, like an alarm going off. And then, after a few moments, it's quiet again.

'Neena!' Mum calls.

I try to think straight. I back away from the door and towards my room, in case Mum comes out to call me again. There, I take deep breaths. I still don't actually know what Mum and Dad were talking about. But I'm going to find out. I wonder if they want to take me on a pilgrimage or something. Dad went to Lourdes in France once to pray for his mum to be healed of heart disease and she lived for fifteen years after that. He told us that when we were younger and Akash said church was boring.

'Neena!' Mum calls again. 'Dinner's ready.'

I head towards the kitchen again, ready to find everything out. And to test Mum and Dad. Can I trust them or not? I'm so confused now. What else has Mum been saying behind my back?

I join them at the dining table. Mum's cooked chicken curry and rotis and she spoons the curry on to our plates.

'Done your homework?' Dad asks. I notice he's holding a glass with amber liquid in it. Is it whisky? He hasn't drunk alcohol since everything happened. This isn't looking good.

I swallow and realize that my mouth also tastes of whisky. That's strange; I definitely haven't been drinking. I nod at Dad. I don't trust myself to speak. I don't trust anything right now.

'Good,' Dad says. He looks away; sips his drink.

'Let's pray before food,' Mum says suddenly.

We used to pray before eating as kids. Me or Akash would say a prayer we learned at school. But I can't remember the last time. Still, we all bow our heads now and Mum says a few words about family and love and strength.

Then we eat in silence for a few moments. The curry is too hot and burns my mouth. I down some water. When I look back up, Mum and Dad are staring at me. It reminds me of earlier in school, the ambush. They both look annoyed and a bit angry. I peer at Mum, think of her hand against my cheek earlier; was it all an act?

'We've been talking,' Mum says. 'And we think you should take a long holiday when the exams are over.' She looks at Dad. He sips more of his drink.

'Holiday?' I ask. That can't be right. After everything that's happened today, I'm being rewarded?

Mum and Dad both nod.

I don't say anything. A holiday sounds great but Mum always says that, if something seems too good to be true, it probably is.

Mum fiddles with the dupatta round her neck. 'A holiday to Pakistan for the whole summer,' she says. 'How would you feel about that, Neena?'

I frown. I've never been to Pakistan. I've only heard stories from Mum and Dad, seen it in films. 'On my own?' I ask. The thought of getting away on my own *does* sound appealing. I almost don't care where I go. But what exactly is going on here? Am I being 'sent away' because they can't handle me any more?

Something needs to be done. That's what Mum said. So this isn't *just* a holiday.

And then my heart contracts as I realize what that would mean: I wouldn't see Josh for the whole summer.

'No, no,' Mum says. 'We'd come with you. All of us together. A last holiday before the baby . . .'

The baby. I haven't thought about the baby for so long. I'm getting so good at not thinking about the baby.

'You can meet the family,' Mum continues. 'And it will be good for you, to see our culture.' She glances at Dad again. 'But really it's just a holiday,' she adds quickly.

'I don't think so,' I say. 'Not for the whole summer.'

Dad downs the rest of his drink and leans back in his chair. 'This isn't up for debate,' he says. 'We will go. All of us. And you'll see exactly how easy you've had it here. You and your brother – you don't realize!'

Mum puts her hand on Dad's arm. 'Bas now,' she says. 'Stop.'

I glare at him. How can he bring Akash into this? When he's not here to defend himself.

Dad scowls at me. Then he shakes his head and gets up and walks out of the room, his dinner only half eaten. Mum doesn't stop him.

'I'm sorry,' I say to Mum. 'But I can't go for the whole summer.'

'Just eat your dinner,' she says. 'We'll be going to Pakistan, Neena.'

I look into my plate, but I can't eat now, my hunger's gone. Why do they want to take me to Pakistan so badly?

A weird feeling comes over me. My skin prickles, like it did when I was at Josh's earlier, and like it did when I was going to Jay's with Fi. I look back up at Mum, and the prickling spreads until it's all over my body.

I'm remembering this film I once saw, where a family took their daughter back 'home' when she was caught clubbing. They then surprised her with an arranged marriage. I can't remember the exact details – it was a long time ago – but I watched it at Raheela's when we were friends. We'd kept looking at each other in horror, while her mum had watched as if it was the most normal thing in the world.

Mum sighs. 'I knew you wouldn't want to leave your friends for the whole summer,' she says. 'But all this fuss! Really, Neena? It's just a holiday. You'll see them when you're back.'

Just a holiday.

I swallow and force myself to eat my food. 'I know,' I say, and I'm the one pretending now. 'I'm sorry.'

What I really know is that it's *not* just a holiday. But I can't let Mum know that I know. I was right, about everything. They're conspiring against me. I can't trust them. But I'll act like everything's normal until I come up with a plan. As I chew the spicy chicken and smile at Mum, I send out a little prayer to Akash for help.

Where is he? Where is he now?

18

Be happy. That's the last thing my brother ever said to me. The very last thing. That's important, isn't it?

It's eleven o'clock. Mum and Dad went to bed hours ago, though it only feels like five minutes, but I can't sleep. I've been lying in bed, tossing and turning, thinking about Josh and everything that happened today. I can't go to Pakistan in the summer. I can't let Mum and Dad force me into anything. But I'm not sure what to do.

And I keep thinking about what Josh said when I was at his earlier today. *No one's after you*, he said. Has he got it wrong? Or have I?

I wish someone could tell me it's all in my imagination. But I can't trust Fi – she might even tell my parents that I know what they're up to. And I could call Josh, but I'm not sure he'll get it. The only person who'll really understand about Pakistan is Raheela.

I wanted to speak to her earlier, to tell her about Mum and Dad and ask if she remembers the film we watched. I kept picking up my phone while I was revising and then bottling out: she's made it clear that she's not willing to help me. But now I'm thinking of those sleepless nights after Akash disappeared; she slept on the floor by my bedside for weeks. And I remember spending every lunchtime in the toilets at school after her dad left when we were younger, hugging her as she cried into my shoulder day after day.

You can't just forget that stuff, can you?

When you've shared times like that, you can't just stop being friends because things have changed.

At the art centre, she said she still cared about me. And I believe her now, because you don't just stop caring about someone, do you?

I grab my phone and dial her number. She doesn't answer. I call her again. And again.

'What!' she snaps, on the third call.

My heart lifts. 'Please, don't hang up. I . . . I need you.'

She sighs. 'What is it, Neena? I'm trying to sleep.'

I swallow. 'My parents want to send me to Pakistan for the summer,' I tell her. 'You think it means anything?'

'Really? The whole summer?' She sounds surprised. 'They wouldn't do that, would they?'

'That's what they said.'

'Oh God . . . Are you . . . are you thinking about that weird film we watched with my mum?'

My heart races. 'Yes!' I knew she'd understand, but I'm even more afraid now.

'Shit, Neens,' she whispers. 'What's happened? Tell me everything.'

I try to stay calm as I fill Raheela in, but her reaction is making me even more worried.

'Crap,' she says, when I finally stop talking. 'You reckon they know about Josh?'

I think about the ambush at school. The feeling that they were spying on me. If they have somehow found out, it would explain things. 'Maybe,' I say, my chest becoming tight.

'Shit, Neens. Maybe you should end things with Josh?'

My chest gets even tighter. I feel like I'm *in* that film me and Raheela watched. I think about never kissing Josh again, never sitting under the willow tree and talking about stars or the meaning of life, or about Akash, or Josh's dad. This makes me very, very sad. No. I won't let that happen.

'I need to live my life. I need to be happy,' I tell Raheela. My head's pounding.

'Neens, I really think –'

'No,' I say. I can't bear for one more person to tell me I'm doing something wrong. It feels like it's Josh and me against the world.

She sighs. 'OK, Neens. But don't say I didn't warn you.'

After we hang up, I stare into the darkness. I have this weird feeling that someone's in my room. My heart misses a beat. 'Akash,' I whisper. 'Are you here?' But there's no reply. I switch on my lamp and look around. He's not there. Maybe I imagined it.

I climb out of bed and walk over to my easel. A half-finished painting of a castle is sitting there, and it's absolutely awful. It looks like a child drew it. I did it after revising this evening and, although I tried my absolute best, I just couldn't get it to work. There's no way I can hand that in for my art homework.

'Akash,' I whisper again, looking around my room. 'Are you here? I *really* need your help again . . .'

No answer. I check under my bed and find some whisky. So he *has* been here. My chest buzzes. He'll be here again soon, I know he will. I take a few gulps of the whisky and stow it under the bed again. Maybe it will help me sleep . . . Then I walk over to my dressing-table drawer and put on my brother's cap. I look in the mirror, at the small, pale version of myself. The cap is like sunshine on my head. It lifts me. I smile.

Be happy, Neens. That's what Akash said. *You deserve that.*

'Yes,' I say to Akash because I know he's listening. 'I do deserve to be happy, don't I?' Sneaky thoughts slip into my head, and I know that Akash has put them there . . .

Mum and Dad are asleep. Go out to see Josh. He makes you happy.

I smile at the mirror. Yes, I could, couldn't I?

I look over at my bedroom window. No, I'm being stupid. Mum and Dad could catch me again. And, after what happened at school today, they'll really hit the roof. They've already taken art school away from me. What if they try to get me married off sooner?

But he makes you happy, Neena.

On the other hand, this might be one of the last times I see Josh. I should see him as much as I can before the summer. I could have one last happy night with him. Not think about all the crap in my life. And Josh will still be awake: he said he was going to revise until midnight, and it's only 11.20.

Already the sadness is fading away. I'm grinning now. We can go on an adventure together! A happy adventure. Another idea slips into my head . . .

My stomach's buzzing with excitement as I rummage through the cupboard next to the kitchen sink. I dig out an old grey wicker picnic basket. Mum used to pack it with treats, like spicy spring rolls, when we went on family day trips. But that was a long, long time ago. From the fridge, I grab samosas, pakoras, chicken curry and rice. My hands are shaking. I'll be in so much trouble if I get caught. But I think of Josh's deep kisses, how safe I feel with his arms round me, and it spurs me on. I find leftover rotis in the bread bin. I pile it all into the basket without heating it – that's too risky, making all that noise. Finally, I close the kitchen door and tiptoe back to my bedroom.

I sit on my bed, the picnic basket at my feet, and text Josh, telling him to meet me for a midnight picnic at the park.

Be happy. That's the last thing my brother *ever* said to me.

'I'm trying, Akash,' I whisper. 'I'm trying my best.'

Then I wait, searching the internet for any more information about Jay, any more clues about Akash's disappearance, as I wait for Josh to reply.

The moon is full and bursting with brightness. Akash speaks to me. *Keep going*, he says. *This way, this way.* I clutch my wicker basket and keep walking. The streets are quiet. Still. Houses are darkened. There's no noise other than the occasional passing car. The silent air carries the beat of my desperate heart.

Boom-boom. Boom-boom.

I pass a row of shops: an old post office, hairdresser's, charity shop. Traffic lights change for no one but me. Street lights illuminate the road ahead. And the moon, he holds my hand, holds it tight. *You can do this, Neena*, he says. *You deserve this.*

Josh is waiting for me next to the entrance of the park, his hands buried deep in his jeans pockets. His dark hair shimmers in the moonlight. I run to him. He lifts me up, kisses me. I press my face into his soft hoody; breathe in his soapy scent.

Together, we climb over the railings like fierce, wild rabbits. We run down the path hand in hand, laughing. The park is dark – trees and bushes hidden in shadows – but we find a spot on the bank leading down to the playground. Here moonlight shines over the neatly mown grass. We sink to the ground, breathless, and I pull out the picnic blanket from the basket.

'What's this?' Josh asks.

'A feast,' I tell him, taking out the containers of curry. 'My mum's food. You won't have tasted anything like it.'

We settle down on the blanket. Josh reaches for a samosa and bites into it. I take one too, bite into the crisp pastry, the spicy lamb.

'Oh my God! How have I not tried your mum's food until now?' Josh asks. 'You could have snuck me some before!'

I look out towards the city lights beyond the park. 'I guess I've always been a bit embarrassed,' I confess.

'Embarrassed? About what?'

I stare down at my samosa and think of all the times I've changed my clothes before going out because they've smelled of Mum's cooking, of curry. 'Well, about being different,' I confess.

Josh doesn't say anything. I force myself to look up at him again. 'All I *ever* wanted was to be different from everyone else,' he says. 'It makes you special, Neena Gill.'

I gaze into Josh's eyes. I'm so happy right now, with the whole world locked outside those gates. No one can reach us here. None of the day's events seem real. It's perfection. We grin at each other, eat in silence, dipping rotis into the daal, sharing chunks of buttery chicken. We watch the stars and the moon, our legs spread out in front of us. Josh names some of the stars as we eat and it makes me laugh.

'What *is* it with you and stars?' I ask him. 'Do you seriously want to be an astronaut?'

Josh shrugs. 'Anything that'll get me far away from here,' he says. 'I just think it would be . . . cool.'

Suddenly I remember us as kids, in primary school, reading out our accounts of what we did in the holidays. We'd all written about things like going to theme parks and getting pet guinea pigs. But Josh had described camping in the garden with his dad, stargazing. How had I forgotten that?

'I get it,' I tell him, nodding.

He smiles but then frowns. 'That was kind of freaky when you came over earlier, wasn't it?' He gives a nervous little laugh.

The moonlight seems to dim. I don't know what to say.

'But you're OK now?' he continues. 'Aren't you?'

I don't tell him I still think the teachers are plotting against me – does that seem *freaky* to him too? And anyway I don't want one of our last nights together to be weird or serious or sad. I just want it to be happy. 'Yes, I'm OK,' I tell him. 'I feel . . . normal.'

Josh smiles again and I cheer up a bit. 'Talking about normal . . . I know we've talked about this, and that it's tricky, but I'd love to take you on a proper date. I don't know – to the cinema, or dinner, or even just for a walk . . . Anything. Can we find a way?'

I rub the back of my neck. I feel hot. 'I don't know,' I tell him. What if Mum and Dad catch me? Send me to Pakistan immediately? 'But I . . . I'll have a think . . . I do want to . . . But . . .' My neck is getting hotter.

Josh leans into me; plants soft kisses on my neck. 'It's OK,' he whispers. 'I just thought I'd ask. But really it's OK.'

'It is?'

'Of course.'

He continues to kiss my neck. They feel so good, his kisses. No one's kisses will ever make me feel like this. I close my eyes. Josh kisses my ear. My cheek. My mouth. I kiss him back.

But then, for some reason, I think about Jay. 'I have to tell you something,' I say to Josh. 'Something I should've told you a long time ago.'

'Sure.' Josh raises his eyebrows. Waits.

'I . . . I . . .' But I can't tell him. It won't come out.

For a moment, I think I see Akash in the distance, standing under some branches. But, when I blink, there's nothing there. Just shadows. I wish he'd come and see me right now. I just want a hug from him. I look back at Josh.

'What is it?' he asks.

I want to cry, but I smile instead. 'I want to kiss you forever,' I say.

Josh smiles too. He leans forward and kisses me again. When he stops and looks me in the eyes, he laughs. 'I can't believe we're in the middle of a park, having a picnic at midnight!' he says, shaking his head. 'This is definitely the craziest thing I've ever done for love.'

'Love?' I say, and it comes out light and breathless. Am I hearing him right?

He laughs again. 'Isn't it obvious? I've loved you for years, Neens. Ever since you held my hand when I fell off that bike in primary school and the other kids laughed. Remember?'

I nod. I remember! I do!

Josh tilts his head towards the dark sky, the stars, the moon. 'I love you, Neena Gill!' he howls.

I laugh. I want to say it back but I can't speak. All I can do is kiss him, and hold on to his words. I let them wrap themselves round me like a blanket, soft and warm. Josh loves me. He loves me!

19

My alarm rings in my ears like a siren. I jump out of bed. Pull on trousers. Shirt. Sweatshirt. No time for a shower. I need to get to school: I can't wait to see Josh and I need to show Miss Taylor my essay to prove I'm not a cheat. I rub my sore eyes. Another sleepless night, but this time for the most amazing reason . . .

Josh loves me. He loves *me*!

I waltz down the hallway to the bathroom. Brush my teeth. Wash my face. But, when I go back to my bedroom, I'm shocked. It's a total mess. The carpet's covered in clothes and books and pages and pages of revision notes. The duvet's been flung to the floor. It's as if someone snuck in here while I was in the bathroom and messed everything up. I feel dizzy. Unsteady. I need to clean it up. If anything in my life is ever going to be OK, I must sort all this out, get organized.

My phone buzzes as I start cleaning. A message from Fi. Again.

Meet me at breaktime? Nd to talk!

I push my phone aside. 'I can't trust Fi. She's been spying on me for the teachers,' I remind myself. I focus on tidying up, whizz round the room, folding clothes, putting books on shelves, lining up my shoes against the wall and making my bed again and again until it's perfect. Getting everything in order. When I stop, I feel much better. I pick up my phone to check the time, but see that I'm late for school! It doesn't make sense – it seems I was cleaning for five or ten minutes tops, not over an hour. I've missed first lesson and now it's double English, which I absolutely can't miss. I need to see Miss Taylor. I need to hurry.

But, before I leave, there's one last thing I have to do. I step up on to my dressing table and take down my framed sky-sea poster. I know my brother gave it to me but that was before. Now I'm not someone who worries. I'm not someone who takes medicine for her anxiety. I don't need to look at the picture to feel better, or less alone. I tuck it behind my dressing table.

I shout goodbye as I dash out of the house. No one answers. The house is very, very quiet. I guess Dad's already left for work and Mum must still be sleeping. She did seem extra exhausted yesterday.

Miss Taylor is halfway through the lesson when I get there. She's standing at the front of the classroom, her curly hair wild as she waves her arms around like she's conducting an orchestra. I barge in and she stops talking. I go straight up to her, push my essay into her hands. 'To show you I can do it,' I tell her. 'I did a plan and everything.'

I grin and grin at her. I am so pleased with myself.

But she frowns back at me. 'Oh . . . uh . . . Thank you, Neena. Do join us.' She waves a hand at the desk in front of her and I sit down.

'But aren't you going to read it, miss?' I ask. I plead with my eyes. I can't wait.

She sighs. 'OK, class,' she announces. 'Enough of me talking. Let's do a timed essay!'

There are groans around the class, but she ignores them and writes a title on the board. Then she bends down next to me. 'OK, Neena,' she says. 'I'll read this now. And, if you can prove yourself in this timed essay too, it might be enough to get you off the hook. Can you focus?'

I nod enthusiastically. I know I can do it. Josh loves me. I can do anything.

'OK,' she says, smiling now. 'I'll be very happy to be proved wrong.' She pats my arm. 'Good luck.'

After the lesson, Miss Taylor keeps me back. She's smiling again, her eyes bright, so I know it's good news.

'This essay's very good, Neena,' she says. She straightens her perfectly ironed cream blouse and presses her hands against her hips. 'But are you sure you didn't have any help?'

I shake my head. 'My brother's been helping me with art,' I confess. 'But not English. I've done that all by myself.'

She looks a bit shocked. 'Right. I see. Well . . .' She waves my essay in the air. '*This* is very good. I always knew you had it in you, Neena. It's just been . . . confusing . . . to see your marks be so erratic.'

She squeezes my arm and it's like an electrical current passes between us, filling me with even more energy. I beam at her. I get it. She's on my side now. I can trust her again.

'Thank you,' I say, before rushing out. I can't wait to tell Josh the good news. Is this what love is, I wonder? Wanting to share all the good *and* the bad with someone?

Josh is sitting under the willow tree at the end of the field, leaning against the tree trunk, eating his usual cheese roll. I feel like I'm flying as I hurry towards him. I can't stop smiling. I can't remember the last time I smiled so much.

He loves me. He loves me!

'Guess what!' I say, sinking down beside him. 'You were right! Miss Taylor isn't against me! Maybe Mr Butler isn't either. I've got him next lesson so I'll –'

'Neena,' he interrupts. And I see that he's not smiling or happy. He's frowning. 'We need to talk.'

I freeze. I want to reach out and hold his hand, or kiss him, or hug him. But I don't move. I hold my breath because I know that whatever he's about to say isn't good. Maybe this is about me kissing Jay. Has he somehow found out? I stare at him.

His cheeks go red. 'It's just something . . . something Fiona said,' he says. 'I was going to mention it yesterday, but you were so upset, and then . . . Anyway, it's been playing on my mind.'

'Fi?' I'm furious. My feet are hot. She's been talking to Mr Butler, and now Josh too? 'What did she say?'

'She thinks things are moving too fast between us. That

I should back off. That you have a lot on your plate – and I know, I know you have, but . . .'

I can't believe what I'm hearing. 'What? Why would she say that?' First the teachers and now she's trying to sabotage my relationship too.

'I mean, she *had* been drinking,' Josh continues. 'And she sort of went off on this little rant about men just wanting one thing, and then said I should leave you alone. I'd been drinking too; can't remember her exact words. But she basically said . . . something about . . . about you not knowing what you want. Have you been talking to her . . . about us? Did you say something?'

'No! And I don't want you to back off. I thought that was obvious!' I don't understand where all this is coming from. None of this bothered him last night. Fi must have really got her claws into him. The cow.

'When did she say all this?' I ask, trying to understand.

'Last week. Fi had a party and then we ended up going into town. We were all pretty wasted.'

'Last week?' That doesn't make sense. 'Why didn't you tell me? What party? You went to Fi's without me?'

I suddenly have this cosy picture of Fi and Josh in a bar, doing shots and dancing. I try to push the image away but it sticks. I feel sick. Has she got her eye on Josh? Is that why she didn't mention them going out? What else has she been hiding from me?

'We weren't going to tell you about the party,' Josh says. 'You were having such difficulty getting out in the evenings –

we didn't want you to feel left out. That's why I didn't mention it before . . . But hang on, you're missing the point! *Do* you want me to back off, Neens? It's not exactly the message I've been getting from you, but . . . I need to make sure.'

I take Josh's hand. 'No! None of that's true. I don't know why she said all those awful things. I know exactly what I want. Especially after last night.'

Josh looks briefly puzzled but it passes, and he grins. 'So I shouldn't back off?'

'No!'

I stare into his eyes to make him believe me, as if our lives depend on it, and when he smiles again it feels like we're invincible. And I think: *Our lives do depend on it. Mine does anyway.*

Josh moves a strand of hair off my face. 'Then prove it to me,' he says.

I gaze into his eyes. 'OK,' I say. 'I think . . . I think I'm ready.'

Josh's face and neck go red. 'No! I didn't mean like that!' Then he smiles. 'But let's maybe talk about that later too?'

'So what are *you* talking about then?' I ask, confused again.

Josh takes my hand. 'Well, a bunch of us are going out in town tonight. Come with me?'

I squeeze Josh's hand. I want to but I can't risk it with Mum and Dad. Especially with all this talk about going to Pakistan. 'I don't think I can, Josh. I'm sorry.'

Josh's shoulders sink. He looks down at his lap, at the remainder of his lunch.

'I thought you understood?' I say. I'm beginning to feel like the world's worst girlfriend again and it sucks. Especially after the thrill of last night.

'I . . . I do . . . I try to anyway.' Josh screws up the last bit of his roll in the foil wrapper. 'It's just . . .' He hesitates.

'Tell me,' I say. 'I want to know everything. I don't want us to have any secrets.'

He nods. 'It's like, logically, I know that it's your parents' rules. And I know you'd be seen in public with me if you could. But . . .' He swallows. 'You hiding me away, it feels like . . . I don't know, like I'm not good enough, I guess.'

I touch Josh's face. 'Oh, Josh. I'm so sorry, but you know that's not true, right?'

'I know, I know, it's silly . . .' He perks up a bit. 'And I know I'm putting pressure on you. But I think I just got my hopes up for no reason. Fiona said you wouldn't be able to go.'

My whole body tenses. 'Fi?' *Her again. What's she got to do with this?* 'Is she going too?'

'Yeah, she's organizing it. But she said you wouldn't be able to get away. Though we both think you need to let your hair down.'

My stomach churns. Fi will be there. They'll be drinking in pubs, dancing in clubs. Fi is beautiful. She's a great dancer. I've never even been to a club. Something inside me snaps.

'You know what?' I say, moving closer to Josh. I look deep into his eyes. 'You want me to come? Then I'll come.' I'm not going to let Fi steal Josh away from me. I'm going to watch her every move. He loves *me*. Me.

Josh's eyes smile at me. 'Really? You think you can? We can be like a proper couple on a proper date.'

I'm shocked by how desperate he is for a 'proper date': he's been so cool about it until now, it's barely even mattered. Has it? This is Fi's work. It must be.

'Yes,' I say, like it's no big deal. I know how risky it is, and I have no idea what I'll wear. But I know that I have to be there to keep an eye on Fi.

I lean forward and give Josh a long, deep kiss. I press my whole body against him. *You're mine*, I tell him with my body. When I pull away, he's breathless and staring at me like he did last night. *He loves me. He loves me.*

'I can't wait,' he whispers in my ear. His voice is deep, his breath warm. The skin round my ear tingles.

We really are invincible, I think. *Nothing, and no one, can get in our way.*

'Neither can I,' I whisper back.

20

After my chat with Josh, I have a brilliant afternoon in lessons, and even come up with a plan for tonight. 'I need your help,' I tell Fi on the phone as I walk out of school. I smile down the speaker so that it comes out friendly. Fi can't know that I don't trust her. This, me asking her for help, is a test. But I'd also really like her help. Let's see.

'Ahhh,' she says. 'I knew it was only a matter of time. And what the hell is *up* with you anyway? I've been trying to get hold of you since yesterday! You've been ignoring my calls, haven't you?'

I keep smiling. It's not exactly hard: I'm buzzing. In art this afternoon, Mr Butler apologized for suggesting I'd been cheating. Said he shouldn't have jumped to conclusions. Apparently, a piece I did in class under timed conditions was brilliant. He'd be calling home to apologize to Mum and Dad too, he said, and explaining that, considering everything, it's OK if I have bad days. He also said that Miss Taylor had spoken to him AND that it's OK about Akash helping: he's my brother and he always will be. But maybe I should get some counselling?

I didn't really understand that last bit, but the rest left me on a high. I'm feeling pretty GREAT.

'You're right,' I joke. 'I can't live without you, Fi!' I hope it comes out friendly and not sarcastic. 'But I'm not ignoring you. Things have just been pretty . . . intense . . . at home.' It's not exactly a lie.

'But *that's* why I was calling, Neens! I saw your mum leaving school yesterday. She's *pregnant*? Why didn't you tell me? And what the hell is that all about? Are you OK about it?'

I stop walking. Fi knows! She thinks it's just as weird as I do. I could talk to her; she might make me laugh about it and I might even feel better. But no, I can't trust Fi. I need to remember that. And then I see what she's doing. She's trying to trick me. She *wants* me to think about the baby. She wants to snatch away the happiness I am feeling right now.

I laugh down the phone. 'You've got it wrong,' I say. 'Mum's just . . . She can't stop eating . . . you know . . . since everything.' The best part of this is that it's not an absolute lie. Mum's about twice the size she was a year ago. Even before the baby, she'd put on a ton of weight. Her stomach is so flabby that you can't even tell she's pregnant, to be honest.

'Oh!' Fi says. 'I thought I saw her rubbing her belly, like she was pregnant!'

'Well, she was probably just hungry . . .'

Fi goes silent. She doesn't know what to say. One point to Neena Gill.

'Anyway,' I add quickly, before I lose my nerve, 'my favour?'

She sighs. 'Tell me, Neens. What can I do? Your wish is my command.'

Is *she* being sarcastic now? I need to be extra sweet to get her onside.

'I'm going to come out with you all tonight,' I tell her. 'It's been *ages* since we've spent any time together.' And then I add: 'Josh asked me.' I can't help it. And here's the bit I genuinely need her help with: 'But I need a cover story. And a dress.'

She shrieks down the phone. 'Oh, I'm so glad, Neens!'
Fake, fake, fake.

'Dress I can totally sort. I've got this little black one that will look *stunning* on you. Cover – what you thinking?'

'Well . . .' I've been thinking about this all afternoon. 'Raheela's house is the only place my parents will let me stay the night. Do you think you could . . . maybe ask her to cover for me?'

'Me? Ask Raheela? I . . . I don't know. Wouldn't it be better coming from you?'

I knew it. She doesn't really want to help me. She doesn't want me there! But she's not getting off that lightly.

'It's just . . . she won't listen to me, Fi,' I explain. 'But it's the only way I can go out . . . *Please?*'

'I really want to help you!' Fi says. *The liar.* 'But I honestly think this would be better coming from you. I mean, I don't even really know her . . .'

I feel crushed. But Fi not helping is just making me more determined to go tonight. She's failed the test: I can't trust her around Josh. 'Fine,' I say, all sickly sweet. 'No worries. I'll let you know the details, but I'll *definitely* see you tonight!'

'Cool,' Fi says, all fake right back at me.

I'm about to hang up – I'm so annoyed with her – but I quickly add: 'Do you have any new leads, Fi? Something from Jay, perhaps?' My heart beats fast with desperation and I hold my breath. But she explains that she has nothing new, and that she's still working on Jay. These things take time, she tells me, like she always does.

'Yeah, sure,' I say, though I don't believe her any more.

When I hang up, I see that I have twenty missed calls from Dad. Twenty! Wow, they really are trying to track my every move! I quickly push my phone back into my bag. I can't even think about all that right now.

I'm shaking. I don't know what to do about tonight. I can't leave Fi alone with Josh. I *have* to go. But how? The ground sways. People whoosh past me. The traffic on the road seems super fast. Everything's suddenly in a major rush, even more than usual. A weird buzzing sound vibrates in my ears. I feel dizzy. What's going on?

I sit on the wall outside school and rest my head back on the rails. I'll just stay here until the buzzing and spinning stops. Until the world steadies itself again. But time ticks on and the world doesn't still. It gets faster. The sun is hot on my face. I breathe in the smell of the nearby bushes. And, as I watch everyone walk home from school, chatting and laughing, I miss Akash so much. We used to walk home together.

My chest hurts. I wish he was here with me right now. He'd know exactly what to do about tonight. I feel a sudden surge of anger towards him. He's been helping me with my paintings and I know he's nearby but why is he hiding?

I want to see him. I want to hug him. I want to talk to him.

'Akash,' I say, looking up at the sky. 'I need you. I need you to tell me what to do.'

My phone buzzes in my hand. A message from Fi flashes across the screen.

> Just be honest with Raheela. Tell her how
> much tonight means to you.

I can't trust Fi – I know that – but I actually think she might be having a moment of kindness and that she's right. Because what else can I do? I peer back up at the clouds and take a long, deep breath. And then there he is! Akash! I stare at him, his face, there in the clouds. I don't say all the things I really want to say –

I'm going to have a new brother.

What if I forget you?

I wish you were here.

I don't tell him how devastated I am that Mum and Dad are trying to replace him. I want to protect him from that. I don't want him to feel like I do. Alone.

'Is it really you?' I ask, my eyes filling.

'Yes,' he says, and his voice is so clear, so deep and warm, that I have no doubt it's him. The clouds move as he smiles.

'Why are you up there? Can you come down?' I ask him.

'I will,' he says. 'Be patient.'

And then we laugh because patience was never my strong point.

Another sharper sound of laughter pierces the air. I pull my eyes away from Akash's face in the sky to see what's going on. Some people are walking past. Two guys.

It's him! He's here! Just metres away. His pale brown skin and dark hair.

'Akash!' I call out. I jump to my feet and run towards him. The guys turn round – but he doesn't look like Akash.

'Oh, it's not you'. Akash has darker skin. His eyes are bigger and shinier. He has different teeth.

'Er . . . you OK?' the guy says, glancing at his friend.

I edge backwards, back towards the wall, and they carry on walking. I look up at the piercing sky again, back up at Akash. But he's not there any more and the sky is so bright that I have to look away.

He's gone. Akash has gone.

'Will Raheela help me?' I whisper, not expecting a reply.

And then, although I can't see his face in the clouds any more, Akash says: 'Yes, she will.'

And my heart lifts and lifts and I feel even more joy than I did this afternoon.

Although I can't see him in the sky now, my brother is near.

21

I'm grinning as I knock on the door to Raheela's house. She's going to help me. My brother said so. Raheela opens the door and stares at me. 'Neena!' Her eyes are wide. 'A baby? I can't believe it!'

I stop smiling. 'What?'

'Your mum?' she says. 'Having a baby! You didn't tell me. I know we haven't been speaking, but something like this . . .' She steps outside and puts her arms round me. Squeezes hard. She's surprisingly strong for such a small person. 'This is crazy!' she goes on. 'What do you think of it all?'

'I don't know,' I say, wondering how she knows about the baby. Maybe Mum and Dad have decided it's time to tell their friends. But none of that matters. What matters is that she helps me. So far, she's being the most friendly she's been in months, so I'm feeling even more hopeful.

She hugs me again. 'Well, are you OK? Is this why you've been acting so weird?'

'Weird?' *Have I been acting weird?*

'Forget all that though – I'm here for you,' she says. 'We literally just heard the news.'

'Is that her?' Aunty Ruby calls from inside. And then she's standing behind Raheela. 'Oh, Neena! I'm so glad you're here.' I look up at her. She's extremely tall and has big white teeth, but she has one of the gentlest voices ever. Her wavy hair falls right down to her waist like a waterfall. 'Are you all right? Come in, come in. There's nothing to worry about.' She tugs at my arm, pulls me into the hallway.

The house smells of coconut hair oil, like it always has. I've missed this smell; it reminds me of long summers playing in the paddling pool in the garden and chatting with Raheela far into the night. Aunty Ruby always let us go to bed late.

Now she sits me down on the red velvet sofa and pushes something cold into my hands. It looks like lemonade. I can't remember the last time I drank anything and I gulp it all down in one go. She sits on a chair opposite me, smiling nervously.

'More?' she asks, looking at me, but waving her hand at Raheela. 'Get some more lemonade, sweetie.'

I shake my head. 'No, I'm fine, thank you.'

'Something to eat?' she asks.

I shake my head again. 'Not hungry,' I tell her. I haven't been hungry for weeks and weeks. But then I guess that's what love does to you. Josh. Love. I try to focus. I'm here because I need to talk to Raheela about seeing Josh this evening.

'I was just explaining to Raheela that I have to work tonight,' Aunty Ruby says. 'I am *sooooo* sorry. Really. But it *is* an emergency – one of the other carers is in hospital.

I've cooked food so you can help yourselves. And, in case of any emergencies, the number for the nursing home is on the fridge.'

I must look really confused because Raheela says: 'Are you OK, Neens?'

'I have no idea what either of you are talking about,' I confess.

They look at each other. 'Oh,' Aunty Ruby says. 'Haven't you spoken to your dad? You know about your mum? Isn't that why you're here?'

I shake my head. *Is this why he's been trying to call me? About Mum? Oh God, something awful has happened, hasn't it?*

'I . . . I just came to see Raheela,' I explain weakly.

My breath is tight in my chest. I look around for Akash, hoping he might be here, to help me with whatever bad thing they're talking about. But he's not. He never did like Aunty Ruby much, said she was nosy, so I'm not exactly surprised.

Aunty Ruby comes to sit next to me. 'Oh, don't look so worried!' she says. 'Everything's going to be fine.' She pats my knee.

I take a small breath.

'Your mum's in hospital; they're checking the baby. These things happen sometimes.'

My heart thumps against my chest. As I'm trying to get my head round what she's saying, my phone buzzes. Dad. I look up at Aunty Ruby, who nods at me sympathetically. 'Speak to him,' she says, then she ushers me up the stairs, into Raheela's room.

My heart is beating crazy fast as I sit down on Raheela's pink bedspread. A thick lump is blocking my throat and I want to cry. But I force myself to answer the phone.

'Hi, Dad.' My voice is small.

'Neena!' Dad's breathless. 'I'm so sorry – I didn't call during the day because I didn't want to worry you at school. And then I couldn't get hold of you. Are you back from school now?'

My heart thumps in my chest. 'Yes,' I manage to say.

'Mum's waters have broken early, so we're at the hospital. It happened first thing this morning. She's in with the consultant now.'

I try to think back to this morning. That's why the house was so quiet. I can't believe I'm only finding out now.

'We were hoping it was a false alarm,' Dad continues. He sounds nervous.

Shivers run down my neck. This is my fault. The stress of yesterday has caused this. 'Is Mum OK?' I manage to ask.

'Yes,' Dad says, and I breathe. 'But it looks like the baby's coming early.' There's a hint of excitement in Dad's voice now. 'He's coming, Neena. Your baby brother's coming.'

'Will you call him Akash?' I blurt out, and it's like someone else is speaking, someone inside me who isn't me but has my voice.

'What? What did you say?'

I try to find myself again, through all that I'm feeling. 'Nothing.'

He's silent for a few seconds and then he continues. 'They're giving Mum steroid injections to try to develop the baby's lungs. Twenty-six weeks is very early. Will you pray, Neena? That everything goes smoothly? I'm going to stay with her, but I'll try to keep you updated –'

'Shall I . . . come to the hospital?'

'No, no,' Dad says. 'Try not to worry – and keep up with your schoolwork. I've arranged for you to stay with Aunty Ruby and Raheela. Just get your stuff together and call Ruby when you need picking up. She'll collect you. And please, just pray.'

I can't believe what I'm hearing. *He's* arranged for me to stay here tonight? So that's what Aunty Ruby was talking about! A sudden, sneaky, awful thought occurs to me. If Aunty Ruby is working, that means it'll be just Raheela and me. I couldn't have planned this any better myself.

'So you'll stay at the hospital tonight?' I ask, just to be sure. And then I add: 'I'll pray.'

'Yes. Will you be OK?' he says. 'Ruby will look after you.'

'Of course,' I say. 'I'll head to Aunty Ruby's now.' I feel horribly guilty about tricking them like this, but it quickly passes. I think about Akash, and how they're replacing him . . . No. Let them worry about this baby. I don't want to think about it.

Raheela is going to cover for me. That's what Akash said. And I'm optimistic that he's right. I can trust Raheela.

I'm going to meet Josh in town tonight.

I'm going to make sure Fi can't get to him.

And I have a brilliant, bright feeling that Akash will be there.

I wasn't there the night he disappeared, but I'll be there now. I'll make everything up to him.

22

Town's buzzing. I hover near the taxi stand as I wait for Josh, watching cars pull up to the kerb and groups of people spilling out of them. The air's warm. Electric. Music's blaring out of bars, and chatter and laughter bursts around me. I catch the smell of perfume. Strong aftershave. Chips soaked in vinegar. And I'm so glad to be here that I feel light and free. But I'm also nervous. There's no sign of Josh yet.

My skin's prickling all over and I fiddle with the golden bracelets on my arms to distract myself as I try not to check my phone again. He said 9 p.m. and it's now at least twenty past. I try not to worry. Akash never worried about the time. He was too cool for that.

Akash.

Is he here yet? I peer around but I can't see him. I feel a bit deflated. I'm so desperate to see him now, and I'm also hoping that, when Fi sees Akash, she'll forget about Josh. We all know that Akash is the person she really wants. Why isn't he here yet? But then I laugh to myself. Of course he isn't here: he was always late for everything!

A guy wearing ripped baggy jeans and a vest top walks past me. He smiles. He has tattoos all up his arms and his eyes are twinkly. I smile back at him. Do I know him? But then his eyes move down my body and stare at my legs a bit too long. And I think no, I don't know you. And I don't like the way you're looking at my legs.

Where is Josh?

I pull my dress down a bit, wondering if I should have worn it. It's black, strapless, short. I've never worn anything like it, but Fi brought it over once Raheela's mum had left for work and made me try it on. She said I looked amazing in it. I wasn't sure whether to trust Fi, but then I saw myself in the mirror. I looked like Fi. I looked like someone who might have a cute boyfriend. I looked like the other girls from school. I didn't look like Neena Gill, and I was happy about that.

Raheela wasn't sure about the dress; she didn't want me to go out clubbing. But, once I explained about Fi trying to get Josh, she softened a bit. 'I need this,' I told her, and when I pressed my head against her shoulder I cried into it. She hugged me back and her eyes filled too. 'Fine,' she said, 'but just this once.' Then she marched over to her wardrobe and pulled out the red heels she wears to family parties. 'Here, do it in style and *please* don't get caught.'

After that, everything was very easy. We rang Dad to tell him we'd eaten and were going to study. He said everything was going as well as it could at the hospital. When he asked to speak to Aunty Ruby, Raheela said she was in the bath. The hardest part was trying not to think about the hospital as I left the house, but it's easier now I'm out – so much else to focus on. Still, the thoughts keep coming and going . . .

The baby's coming.

I take a deep breath, stand straight and smile. I'm not going to think about the baby. I'm going to have a good time.

A taxi pulls up and I recognize a girl with very straight, long blonde hair from the year above. Another blonde-haired girl follows her out of the cab. They could be twins: both wearing short red dresses and huge gold hoop earrings. Then Josh emerges. He's wearing a white-and-green stripy shirt and smart navy jeans. I smile and wave as I catch my breath.

I can't believe I'm out in town on a Friday night – with Josh!

He jogs over and kisses me on the cheek. 'Wow!' he says. 'Look at you!' He scoops his arm round me, and I'm filled with that buzzing feeling I had this afternoon.

Josh introduces me to the girls. They smile at me and I feel like I'm part of a secret club as I smile back. Then we're on our way. They walk ahead of us; Josh and I follow. Look how totally normal we're being! I just wish my skin felt a bit less prickly.

'My mates have gone off to some sporty bar so we'll go in with Rhian and Tash; they know the bouncer at Club 22,' Josh says. 'So he definitely won't ask for ID.'

I nod. 'Cool,' I say, like this is the sort of thing I do all the time. 'And Fi's meeting us at the club a bit later,' I tell him, though I'm really not in any hurry to see her.

Josh squeezes my shoulder. 'Great.'

I sneak a look at his face, to see if he's pleased she'll be there. But he looks normal. Not too pleased. More interested in what's going on around us . . .

We walk past a row of bars. Outside one, a group of guys are singing – if you can call it that – at the top of their voices. Beer spills from their pint glasses as they raise them in the air. The stench of sweat hits me as we pass them. Josh tightens his grip round me.

I spot an Asian guy, and his eyes meet mine. *Is it someone who might know me? Does he know Dad?* I quickly look away and focus on the street in front of me. I pull my dress down a bit. I don't want to care – I know I can't be the perfect daughter my parents want any more. I want to be here with Josh. I want to go dancing with him. But, at the same time, I do care. If this guy knows Dad, he'll tell him he's seen me – in town on a Friday night, wearing a tiny dress, with a boy's arm round me. I'm literally dead.

I'm just wondering how I can slip out of Josh's arms without it being obvious when we turn down a side lane. It's practically deserted. I relax. I can't imagine anyone who knows Mum and Dad will spot me down here. But the cobbled stones make it hard to walk in high heels, though Rhian and Tash don't seem to be having any trouble. I hug Josh's waist tight for support. We pass run-down shops and a couple of small bars and it stinks of wee and cigarette smoke. I start to feel a bit uneasy.

'Is this where we're going?' I ask Josh quietly.

'Yeah, not far, just up there.'

I smile. Not at anyone in particular. To myself. At the air. And the cobbled path. If I just smile hard enough, everything will be OK.

We stop halfway down the lane. A blue neon sign flickers outside a huge red door: CLUB 22.

Rhian and Tash turn round to us. 'No queue!' Rhian grins. 'We can go straight in.' Tash pulls a small, round mirror out of her handbag and refreshes her lipstick.

I suddenly feel the need to do mine too. 'Can I borrow that?' I ask.

'Sure.' She pushes the mirror into my hand. 'It's broken,' she says, shrugging, 'but it still works.'

'Let's go!' Rhian says, tugging on Tash's arm. 'I need a drink!'

'Wait, what about Fi?' I say, suddenly unsure about going in. This is beginning to feel a bit much, and, although I don't want Fi flirting with Josh, I wish she was here to reassure me. The club looks like a complete dive. Maybe Fi knows somewhere better we can go. 'I . . . I said I'd meet her outside,' I lie.

The girls look at each other. 'We're going in now,' says Rhian. 'You coming or what? You won't get past the bouncer without us. Unless you want us to introduce you to Baldwin? He's Tash's brother's mate so he'll definitely get you in.'

Tash nods. 'Sure, I'll introduce you. Or just come in now? Fiona will find her own way in.'

I look at Josh. 'I'm waiting for Fi,' I tell him firmly.

He squeezes my arm. 'Don't worry,' he says. 'I'll pop in with Tash and quickly meet her friend.'

They all disappear through the red door, into the dimly lit club. I lean against the wall, feeling totally out of place. This lane is so creepy. I message Fi to tell her we're at Club 22 and ask how long she'll be. Then, seeing that I've still got Tash's mirror, I pull the red lipstick Raheela lent me out of my clutch.

But, when I look in the mirror, it's very confusing. I can't see my whole face. The mirror is cracked all over, so I can see my lips, eyes, cheeks, nose – all in different parts of the mirror. It's me, Neena Gill, but in a million pieces. The million pieces of Neena Gill.

And I think about how this is exactly how I feel inside. I'm still there, the old me, somewhere deep inside. But I'm all muddled, like everything's in the wrong order, and I can't put myself back together. My skin goes even pricklier as I stare at the pieces of myself.

I shove the mirror and lipstick into my bag. I concentrate on breathing. I try to remember what I used to look like – inside and out – but I can't remember.

My breathing gets tighter and my chest begins to hurt. A lump the size of an orange is in my throat, stopping me from breathing. I try not to cry as I realize I'm probably going to have a full-on panic attack outside a club I don't even want to go into.

I close my eyes and try to breathe. Deep breaths that reach my stomach. I breathe through the pain that's spreading throughout my body. And it works a bit.

Seconds later, someone calls me. I look up to see Fi hurtling towards me, her arms wide open. I'm both glad and annoyed to see her. She looks amazing. Her red hair is straight and sleek. She's wearing a silver, metallic body-con dress. Her cheeks are shimmering. I feel a fizz of jealousy and wish I'd gone in without her after all. Or that Josh and I had gone somewhere else altogether, just the two of us. I wish we were in his bedroom right now, cosy beneath his duvet.

Then I see there's a guy coming up behind Fi. She hugs me hard and then looks me in the eye. 'Neens,' she says. 'I have a new boyfriend. I didn't want to tell you like this, but he insisted on coming. And I figure you need to know at some point. But are you . . . OK with this?'

I stare at Fi. *A new boyfriend?* My prickly skin burns all over. Akash. Josh. And now a new guy too. She really wants to get her claws into everyone!

Fi smiles as the guy reaches us. 'This is Chris,' she says. 'Chris, this is my Neens.'

Chris is tall, dark and handsome. He's wearing a plain grey T-shirt and jeans, but he somehow looks smart. He could be a male model.

'I've heard so much about you,' he says, kissing my cheek.

I shoot Fi a look. *What exactly has she said about me?* And then Josh walks out of the club and another horrible thought hits me. My skin burns and burns. Is this all a front? An act? To make me less suspicious about Fi trying to get to Josh?

I glance up and down the lane. Where is Akash? If Akash was here, it would make everything better – I'm sure Fi would forget about any other guys.

'All sorted,' Josh says, reaching us. He hugs Fi and I feel a sting of jealousy as her perfectly manicured hand curls round his waist. I push the jealousy away.

No. Josh loves me.

Fi must notice me staring because she quickly wraps her arms round me again. 'How you doing, Neens?' she asks, while Josh shakes hands with Chris and they introduce themselves. 'You feeling . . . OK?'

'Why wouldn't I be?' I snap.

Chris puts one hand on my shoulder and one on Josh's. Squeezes, slightly too tightly. 'It's good to finally meet you both.' He grins. 'And you guys are going to love me. Look what I've got for us.' He carefully pulls a joint out of his wallet. 'You want?'

Fi squeals and kisses him on the cheek. Josh looks behind him, to where the bouncer was standing, but he's no longer there – he's half inside, arguing with some kid who looks about twelve trying to get into the club. He pats Chris on the shoulder. 'Nice one!' he says. 'Let's go round the corner.'

I frown at Josh. Since when has *he* been into smoking weed? Is this Fi's influence too? Did they maybe even smoke together that last time they went drinking without me? But I don't want to look like the only uncool one so I quickly smile instead and try to look enthusiastic. But drugs are really not something I want to do – not after . . . everything.

Tonight's already feeling overwhelming and we're not even in the club yet.

'Isn't there somewhere nicer than Club 22?' I whisper to Fi as we make our way round the corner.

'*Whaaaat?* No! Don't worry, you're going to love it,' Fi says, her arm round my shoulders. 'It's the best! SO much fun! And, by the way, you look *ah-may-zing*!'

I feel briefly reassured, lifted even, but the alleyway we're now in is even seedier than the one before. Bits of rubbish – empty crisp packets and beer cans, cigarette butts, a dirty nappy – are strewn on the ground. It's starting to get really dark. I get away from Fi and hold on to Josh's arm. We all huddle in close, against the wall, as Chris lights the spliff. He takes a couple of drags and passes it to Josh. 'Mind out, it's good stuff,' he says.

'Yes, mate,' Josh says, grinning.

Whether I like it or not, I'm going to stink of this stuff, and I'm going to breathe some in. There's nothing I can do about it. Although I guess I don't need to worry about that with Mum and Dad at the hospital. Raheela probably doesn't even know what weed smells like.

I wonder how Mum's doing, and quite a big part of me wishes I'd gone to the hospital after school. I want to see for myself that she's OK. I'd rather be there than in this alleyway.

But Mum's having a baby. The baby is coming.

Josh takes a few drags and then passes it to me. I don't know what to do. I don't want to look stupid – I just want to fit in. I don't want Fi to be the cool one and me to be uncool.

I feel like I'm thirteen again, and the only one who isn't allowed to go on the school trip to France. Only I'm not thirteen and there's nothing stopping me from fitting in now . . . I think of my brother. I know he'd have some.

'Have a bit,' Chris says. 'It'll relax you.'

Fi frowns at him and for a moment I think she's going to stop me. She doesn't want me to relax! She doesn't want me to have a good time.

I take it. I watch my fingers carefully pinch the end, and I'm so pleased my hands aren't shaking because everything's vibrating like crazy inside me. It looks so small and harmless. Neat. Just a home-made cigarette.

Akash smoked cigarettes. Jay said he smoked spliffs too. He probably still does. *Where is he?* Is he inside the club already?

They're all looking at me. I swallow.

Just take a drag, Neena. Just one drag. It will relax you.

I definitely need to relax. I take a drag. Inhale. It's strong and stings my throat. I try not to cough. Instead, I blow out the smoke as slowly as I can. It comes out smoothly. I can't believe how easy it is. I smile at Josh and wait to feel something. Nothing happens. Fi looks annoyed but doesn't say anything. Her look urges me to have some more before I pass it to her.

It's weird, us all sharing it. Like we're taking Holy Communion in church or something. All of us united. I think I like it.

Josh puts his arms round my shoulders. He looks up at the sky and sighs. I lean into him and follow his gaze.

'They really are beautiful, aren't they?' I whisper, pressing my head against his chest as we peer at the bright stars. I can hear his heart beating and, for a moment, everything is just perfect. His arms are warm round me. It's like we're alone.

'Yeah,' he says. 'They are. I wish I had my telescope.'

I close my eyes. Breathe in Josh's soapy smell. But the moment doesn't last.

'We should get going soon,' Fi says, her voice too loud, too demanding.

I glare at her. She obviously didn't like me and Josh getting close.

Josh doesn't notice. 'Sure,' he says. 'My friend had a word with one of the bouncers so we should be fine getting in.'

Fi clutches Chris's arm as he hands Josh the spliff again. 'Oh, don't worry about that. *Chris* will get us in. He's *nineteen*.' She's such a show-off. Look at how she's poking out her boobs. *Urgh*. I can't believe Akash ever liked her. I can't believe I ever trusted her.

'Just be cool, guys,' Chris says, stretching. His muscly arms flex and relax. He yawns. 'It's no biggie.'

Suddenly my focus is no longer on Fi. I'm thinking about the club. My stomach flips. It's easy for Chris to be cool about it all: he's legal. I glance at Josh. *What happens if we get caught underage drinking? What if someone catches us right now, smoking DRUGS!*

'Of course, yeah, no biggie,' Josh says, passing me the spliff again. I take some more quickly, before someone sees. I really do need to relax! Everyone is relaxed apart from me. Still nothing happens. I must be immune to it. I take one more drag, inhaling extra deep this time. I feel a bit sick but that's about it.

'Hey, leave some for me!' Fi says, stealing it from my hand. She shows off again as she blows the smoke out in perfect rings.

'Like a piece of art,' I think I hear my brother whisper. My eyes dart from side to side, peering through the darkness. But I still can't see him. Did I imagine it?

'How do you do that?' Josh asks, gazing at Fi.

I put my arm round him tightly. She shrugs and passes the joint back to Chris. 'Don't know really. Just sort of do it.'

She doesn't mention that Akash taught her. Instead, she flicks her hair. She's flirting now, not just showing off. I need to be extra careful.

'Let's go to the club,' I say, wanting to get out of this stinky alleyway and away from Fi.

Chris chucks the end bit of the spliff on to the ground. Stubs it out, grinding it down with his beige suede shoe.

'Yeah, let's get out of here before someone sees us,' Josh says, looking down the alleyway.

Before Mum and Dad catch me, I think, suddenly worried that they're somehow watching me. They're always watching!

A familiar, strong, metallic taste fills my mouth. My skin prickles all over.

'Yeah,' Chris says, clapping his hands together. 'Club 22, here we come!'

23

All I can taste is metal.

Blood. It tastes like blood. I swallow and swallow but can't get rid of the taste.

My skin is prickling all over and I wonder if anyone else can see it twitching. But no one says anything.

Josh grabs my hand. Holds it tight. This makes me feel better as we follow Chris and Fi through the arched doorway of the club into a dimly lit passage. 'Don't look so worried,' Josh whispers, squeezing my hand.

I smile at him nervously. We walk past the bouncer and Josh buries his face in my hair; he kisses my neck. As I turn into him, I realize his hair smells of sharp lemons. It's a new smell. A brand-new shower gel? I laugh as his lips tickle my neck.

But, as soon as he stops, the cool air inside the club makes me shiver. I wish I had a coat. I glance at Fi, wondering how she isn't cold in her tiny silver dress.

Has she done something to mine? Something to make me extra cold? To make me look stupid or even want to go home? I'm not going home. I'm staying with Josh.

Mum's having a baby. I will have a brother.

Where's Akash?

At the desk, a woman with long black hair and a tattoo of a purple flower on her arm is flicking through a magazine. She peers up at us. Fi props her elbows on the desk. So relaxed. Showing off again. Chris does the same. They deserve each other. Josh and I stand behind them and their perfume and aftershave are so strong together that it makes me cough and cough.

'You OK?' Josh asks, rubbing my back.

'Yeah,' I say. 'It's just all the smells.'

Josh frowns, sort of shakes his head and looks at the woman again.

'All right?' Chris says to her. 'Busy tonight? There are four of us, please.'

The woman looks Fi up and down and then peers round her, at Josh and me. I shiver even more. I just want to get in now, before someone sees us.

'Which way are the toilets?' Fi asks, twirling a strand of hair round her finger. 'Can I use them?' She exaggeratedly crosses her legs. 'I'm dying here.'

'That way,' the woman says, pointing down a passage decorated with fairy lights. 'OK,' she says, looking back at Chris. 'You're in.'

I rummage in my bag for some money. 'I'll get this,' Josh says, pulling out his wallet.

But Chris waves it away. 'I've got this, guys,' he says, handing over a few notes. 'Buy me a drink later.'

'Cheers,' the woman says, taking the money. She turns back to her magazine and that's it. We're in!

It's suddenly warm. I stop shivering. There must be weird air conditioning in here. Music vibrates through the soles of my feet as we make our way down the steps to the basement. The club is dark and loud. It smells of stale smoke and sweat, mingled with perfume, aftershave and beer. There's a bar to the left-hand side and a huge dance floor in the middle.

Fi squeals and lifts my hands in the air. 'Drinks! Dance!' she shouts. 'How amazing is this? I can't believe you're out with us! IN A CLUB!'

'Yeah!' I shout back, pretending. 'Great!' This is *not* the glamour I expected a club to have. I think Fi has been lying to me about a lot of things.

'Told you we'd get in,' she says. 'We look at least twenty.'

'Sure!' I say. But I know that's not true either.

My stomach suddenly rumbles and I smell Mum's food. Fresh, grassy coriander. Fried onions. Sweet garlic. I look back towards the stairs we just came down. *Is she here?*

There's no one there. I shake my head. Of course she's not here! I'm being ridiculous. Mum's in hospital, having a baby.

My brother.

No. I already have a brother. *Akash.* Where is he?

Josh and Chris barge their way to the bar and buy shots of sambuca for us all, a bottle of wine for Fi and me to share and pints of cider for themselves. We down the sambucas. I pour myself a glass of wine and down that too. It tastes off, like it's been open too long, almost salty. But it's better than the taste of blood in my mouth, which is still lingering.

'You OK?' Fi asks, grabbing the bottle from me. 'Slow down a bit! You're swaying!'

My head is spinning but it's just the music. I frown at her. 'Why's everyone *always* telling me what to do?' I shout above the music.

Fi looks hurt. Chris puts his arm round her. That should be Akash's arm. Fi is a traitor. She's betraying both Akash and me at once.

'I'm sorry,' I say, not wanting to cause a scene. I have to be careful. Fi can't know that I'm on to her now. 'Look, I'll be fine. I've just got this bad taste in my mouth. Pour me a bit more.'

'Just take it easy, Neens,' Fi mumbles as she pours.

'Hey!' Josh says. 'Lighten up, girls. We're here to have fun.' He clinks his glass with mine and I try very hard to relax. He smiles. 'Come on, Neens. Let's dance!' And he drags me away from Fi, like he knows she's up to no good.

Josh. I can trust Josh. He loves me.

The dance floor is packed. My eyes lock with Josh's as we move to the *boom-boom boom-boom* of drum and bass. Our drinks spill from our glasses. We move closer to each other. Our bodies touch. I'm breathless.

He puts our half-drunk glasses on the side, and then his hands are on my waist, up my sides, in my hair. He kisses my neck, my mouth. I kiss him back.

The metallic taste in my mouth disappears. I taste Josh. Cider. Lemon. That sweet taste of apples he always has. We move off the dance floor and lean against the wall. I close my eyes as he kisses my ear.

I see us lying in Josh's bed, close, warm, the duvet wrapped tight round us.

I see Mum propped up in a hospital bed, Dad beside her, holding her hand.

I see Akash sprawled across his bed, headphones on, feet tapping to the beat of the music he's listening to, a smile plastered across his face.

Is Akash at home?

A razor-sharp pain buzzes through my temples. I open my eyes. Josh is holding my hands, smiling. When did we move away from the wall?

The club is brighter than it was earlier. Lights flash over the dance floor. The music's changed and is faster, lighter. Behind Josh, I see Fi dancing with Chris. I spot people I recognize from school dancing round Fi as she glides elegantly in and out of his arms.

My eyes ache. My head spins. I think I want to go home.

Mum. She's in hospital and the baby's coming. I need to know if she's OK. I need to call her. I pull my phone out of my bag.

'You OK?' Josh shouts above the music.

I shake my head. 'I need to call my mum.' But then I realize I can't call her because she'll know I'm out in town. She'll hear the music. They'll know I've lied. They'll find out about Josh. They'll take me to Pakistan immediately. I push the phone back into my bag. My hands are shaking. I'm trapped again.

'Neens?' Josh puts his arms round me.

'I'm OK.'

But I'm not OK. I'm sweating. Dizzy. It's all the lights. They're too bright. Too hot. I sweep my hair up and tilt my head back, trying to breathe, but what I see stifles my breath even more. We're standing under a CCTV camera.

I peer up at it and swallow. What if Mum and Dad are watching me through it? They might be checking up on me from hospital.

I stare at Josh. 'We need to get away from here,' I say, pulling him away from the dance floor. My heart's racing now. My chest is tight. There's not enough air.

We find an empty spot in a dark corner. 'You're shaking, Neens,' Josh says, anxious. 'What's wrong?'

I check for cameras, but can't see any here. I hold on to him tightly. 'Nothing. We're safe now.'

Something bumps into us. We turn to see an older Asian guy glaring at us. For a moment, I think it's Dad, but it's not. This guy has bad acne and he's much bigger than Dad.

'You all right there, mate?' Josh says, pulling me close to him. He seems suddenly taller, broader.

The guy stares at me. His eyes are like fire, rings of red round the white. His lips are almost black and he's wearing a red cap. He walks away, but he keeps glancing over his shoulder at me.

My skin burns all over. My chest is far too tight. I need to get out of here.

'Do you know him or something?' Josh asks.

'I don't know. I'm not sure. I . . . I need some air.' I try to walk but stumble instead.

Josh grabs my arm. 'Whoa there, steady. Let's get you some water.'

I shake my head. 'No. Air. I need air.' My chest is getting tighter and tighter.

That Asian guy is still looking at me. He's standing on the dance floor, staring. Not even hiding it. Just staring.

He knows Dad. He knows Dad. He knows Dad.

My scalp tingles. My fingertips go numb. My throat tightens. There's just not enough air.

'What's happening?' I say, grabbing Josh's arm. 'I can't breathe.'

24

We sway through the crowd. Josh's arm is round me. I lean into him, press my face against his soft cotton shirt.

Breathe. Breathe. Breathe.

But I can't breathe. I've got pins and needles in my feet. The music's too loud; my ears are ringing. My palms are sweaty, my back, my neck. I'm dripping with sweat. I glance up – the Asian guy's *still* staring at me.

I realize that it's Jay. Is it?

I step towards him, hoping he's come to tell me what he knows about where Akash might be. But his face is so cruel that I know that's not what's going on here. And I realize the truth: I kissed Jay. I cheated on Josh. Josh is going to find out.

I get it now. Fi has invited Jay here. She knows about the kiss and she wants Josh to find out too. I've fallen into her trap. My chest gets even tighter. Pain shoots through it and up into my neck. I grab hold of Josh.

Am I dying? Is this what it feels like? Because maybe I deserve to die.

I'm a cheat. Josh loves me but I cheated on him.

'What is it, Neens?' Josh says, shaking my arm.

I close my eyes. Concentrate on breathing. 'Scared,' I tell him. I'm going to die from not breathing.

'Don't be,' Josh says strongly. 'I'm here. I won't let anything happen to you.'

I open my eyes and gaze up into Josh's. I'm suddenly overwhelmed by my feelings for him, so thankful to have him by my side. 'I'm sorry I didn't say it back last night,' I blurt out. 'But I do love you. I love you too, Josh.'

Josh looks confused. 'Last night? Say it back?' He shakes his head. 'What are you talking about, Neens?'

I frown at him, the buzz of feelings in my belly fading. How could he have forgotten already? 'The picnic in the park?' I remind him. 'When you said you loved me? I should've said it back then – I think I was . . . I was afraid . . . of ruining the moment or something.'

Josh is staring at me like I've got four heads. 'What? We didn't go to the park last night! We didn't have a picnic . . .' His voice trails off and he continues to just stare at me like I'm an alien. 'You messaged me to meet you at the park, but I was asleep. I didn't see your message until this morning . . .'

Now it's my turn to stare at him. What he's saying doesn't make any sense. I can't quite figure out what's going on. I *know* we had a picnic last night. I *know* he said he loved me. I remember. I remember it all.

'We did meet – and you definitely said you loved me,' I tell him firmly.

Josh shakes his head again. 'No, we didn't, Neens. And I've never said that to you.'

Why's he lying? He's looking at me with pity in his eyes. Has he decided he doesn't love me after all, and so now he's denying the whole thing? Does he like Fi instead? If that's what's going on, I need to know. 'So you *don't* love me?' I ask, before I lose my nerve.

Josh puts his hands to his head. He looks genuinely confused. 'No, no, it's not that. I mean, I do . . . I do love you . . . I think . . . I've thought I have for a long time – years even – but I . . . The picnic, Neens. We didn't go. And I didn't say that last night.'

Now I'm *really* confused. The room spins around me. My thoughts whirl.

Josh loves me. He thinks he's loved me for *years*. But we didn't have a picnic in the park last night?

But I remember meeting him. I can recall how I felt when he kissed me under the moonlight. The taste of spice on his lips. And, this morning, the empty wicker basket was by my bedside. I'd pushed it under the bed when I was tidying up, because I was worried Mum or Dad might find it.

Nothing's making sense. Josh looks really worried now. And then it dawns on me.

Oh God. Was the basket actually still full? It was *quite heavy.*

No. It can't be. Can it? What does this mean? That I imagined it? Dreamed it? No. It was real. I remember. He said he loved me.

'You're lying!' I shout at Josh. 'I remember. I do!'

I'm shaking hard. Josh pulls me close and I let him because I don't know what else to do. I don't know what to believe.

If that was all a dream, what else was a dream? Is any of this real?

What about Akash? He's been helping me paint. Talking to me. Was *that* real?

Where is he? If he's real, where is he now?

Then over Josh's shoulder, through the swaying room, I see him. The back of him.

My brother.

All the remaining breath is sucked out of me.

White hoody. White trainers. Jeans. The same clothes he was wearing the last time I saw him. That night.

I grab hold of Josh's arm. 'I've found him,' I say. 'I've found my brother!'

'What? Let's get you some water.' Josh puts his arm round me again.

I pull away. 'No! I need to talk to him.' But I can't see him now. He's disappeared again.

I turn back to Josh. 'I've lost him. I've lost him and it's all your fault.' People move around us in every direction. I feel dizzy. Lost.

Someone bumps into me so hard that I bounce back against Josh.

'Ouch!' I say. 'Watch it.' The girl is twice my size. I touch my head, where her bottle of beer hit me.

Josh grabs my arm. 'Come on,' he says. 'Let's get some air.'

And then I catch a flash of Fi's red hair as she grabs my arm too and pulls me with Josh. She has one arm; he has the other. I smell Fi's flowery perfume. Her dress is silky against my arm. Their fingers dig into my skin.

'You're hurting me!' I shout at them, trying to pull away. Fi grabs me even harder.

Tears stir in my throat. 'Where is he?' I demand. 'Where's my brother?'

'What?' Fi says.

'Let's get her some water,' Josh replies.

I shake my head. 'No! I need to find Akash. I can't leave him this time.' I look around, but the place is too crowded. It's getting more and more crowded by the second.

'You'll never find him on your own,' Josh says. 'I'll help you.'

Fi shoots him a look but he glares back at her.

'I'll help her look,' he says, speaking slowly, looking at Fi very closely. 'If she drinks some water first. Right, Neens? That's the deal. Let's go to the bar and get some water. Where's Chris?'

'He's just gone to meet some friends,' Fi says, unsure. 'He'll be back in a bit.'

'OK, water first,' Josh says. 'Then we'll worry about anything else.'

They lead me to the bar, and I manage to gulp down a whole pint of water. Josh looks happy, but Fi's pacing in the tiny bit of free space around us.

'Good,' Josh says. 'Now let's get some fresh air?'

I shake my head. 'You said you'd help me look for Akash.'

Josh nods. 'Uh, yeah. OK. Let's look for him outside.'

'No way. I've had enough of this. I'm taking her home,' Fi says, looping her arm through mine.

I stagger back. 'Home? I don't want to go home!' *Why does no one else understand the urgency here? I have to find Akash!*

Fi squeezes my arm, gentle but firm. 'Neena,' she says. 'You're really wasted.'

Josh tries to take my arm, but Fi puts her hand on his. She and Josh share a look. Her hand grips his for a bit too long. Time slows down and sharp pain buzzes through my chest. I was right.

'I can see what's going on,' I say, looking at Fi.

'What?' she says, acting dumb.

'And you?' I say to Josh. 'How could you?'

Josh looks confused. But I understand everything very clearly now. Fi wants me to go home so she can have Josh to herself. She's sent Chris away too. And that's why she doesn't want me to find Akash: she doesn't want him to see her with Josh. And Josh seems to be helping her – denying he said he loves me, and trying to get me outside too. He must be under her spell.

'I trusted you,' I say to her, unable to keep it in any longer. And I think I might be shouting because the whooshing sound in my head is so loud that I can't hear myself think and my ears are really burning. 'You're the only one I trusted, for so long.'

'What are you talking about?' Fi says. 'You *can* trust me!'

How can she keep on lying? 'You told Josh to stay away from me! And you've been talking to the teachers about me behind my back too. You . . . you want him to yourself, don't you? That's why you invited Jay!'

Fi glances at Josh and then looks back at me. She thinks I can't see what's going on. 'You're very drunk, Neens,' she says.

'I . . . I did say that to Josh. But only because I was worried about you. And the teachers – they're worried too. We're trying to help. And Jay? Is he here? I haven't seen him. I have no idea what you're talking about. I'm honestly just trying to help.'

'Help?' I say. 'If you wanted to help, you'd find Akash. You wouldn't be cheating on him with Chris!'

Fi's eyes fill with tears. She looks really hurt. She's an excellent actress. That's when I see that she's holding Akash's cap. I snatch it back from her.

'Why have you got this?' I ask her. She's trying to steal it!

'What? You were wearing it, Neens! You just passed it to me a minute ago! You've been wearing it all day!'

I glare at her. She thinks I'm stupid. 'Why would I give it to you?'

Everything feels too painful and I can't stand it any more. Everyone's lying to me. I turn away from Fi and Josh.

I need to find Akash. He's the only one I can trust.

Suddenly I'm being tugged and pushed and pulled, and it's Josh and Fi. They've got one arm each again. I try to fight them off but they're too strong. They drag me out of the club. Into the darkness outside. Soft rain falls on us. The ground is wet but the air is warm.

'What are you doing?' I shout at them. They finally let go of me.

Fi gives Josh a poisonous stare. 'What the hell did she have to drink? Did you give her anything else?'

'Nothing! Just that wine. We were dancing . . .'

Fi rubs her hands over her face. 'We need to get her home,' she says. 'But she can't go home like this. Raheela will freak! And, if she tells Neena's parents, they'll kill her.'

I stare at Fi. 'That's it,' I say. 'My parents are trying to kill me.' That explains the cameras inside. And the baby that makes my chest hurt every time I think about him. Everything spins around me even faster now – it's getting hard to tell which way is up. 'I have to find my brother. He's come to save me! I need to find him.'

I try to get back inside, but a huge security guard with an angular face shakes his head at me. 'Sorry, love,' he says. 'You ain't going back in. You need to sober up.'

'Neena,' Fi says, taking my hands in hers. She wipes tears – I didn't know I was crying – from my cheeks. 'Look at me.'

I do look at her. At her glossy red hair and lipstick that matches. Her cheeks shimmer like an angel's though I know she's the devil. She squeezes my hands. 'Neena. I love you. Please. Listen to me.'

She's lying to me again. My brother is the only one who loves me.

I have the sudden urge to paint. I want to be in my room. In front of a blank canvas.

'But Akash is the one who's good at art,' I tell her. 'He's brilliant at drawing and painting. Not me.'

Fi's crying now too but I'm not sure why. Where has Josh gone? 'Listen to me,' she says again, sniffing. 'You're very drunk. Akash is not here, Neena. Akash is . . . Akash . . . he's gone forever.'

I tug my hands away from hers. 'Why would you say that? Why are you trying to hurt me?'

'Listen, Neena,' she says. 'Please.'

I shake my head. 'We went to the library together sometimes. He chose books for me, always ones about being strong. Now Mum's having a baby and the exams are coming and I'm going to the library to deliver the baby.'

Fi buries her face in her hands. 'You're not making any sense. I'm really worried about you.' She grabs me and hugs me hard.

I push her away. 'I just need to find Akash.'

'Akash is gone!' she says, and now it's her turn to shout.

But she's wrong. I see him again, at the end of the lane, leaving the pub on the corner. His jeans are so baggy. I always teased him about that. His thick-soled white trainers splash through puddles.

'There he is!' I scream. 'Akash!'

I run after him, down the dark cobbled lane, and along the alleyway that leads to the bus station. I'm out of breath by the time I get to the station and have to walk instead – I can't quite keep up with him, can't reach him. I catch a glimpse of his white trainers as he passes behind buses. Then he climbs the steps to the bridge over the river.

Of course!

I climb up after him. There's lots of traffic and he's already halfway across the bridge, but there are no other people, only him.

'Akash!' I call after him. 'Stop! Please!'

He spins round to face me. His face is soft and his eyes shine bright as always.

He has stubble on his cheeks.

My breath catches in my throat. 'It really is you,' I say. 'You came back!'

25

The traffic calms. The stars fade. The moon disappears.

The moon is full and bright, and I try to focus on that, try to distract myself, but it's not working. Nothing's working.

We're standing in the middle of the garden, Akash and me. Bare feet on crisp, dry grass. Akash has brought me out here because Mum and Dad are arguing inside. Their voices are getting louder.

I feel sick. I'm breathing fast, as fast as I can, because there's not enough air and I need more. My chest is tight. It hurts. My whole body hurts. I try not to cry.

Akash crouches down next to me. 'Breathe in deep,' he tells me, his voice low and calm. 'Like I showed you, yeah? Deep into your belly.' He presses his hands against his stomach.

I nod. Akash knows all about helping me breathe. He's fourteen and I'm eleven. We've done this before.

I close my eyes, ready to breathe into my belly. But everything — my chest, throat, my whole body — is too tight. Dad's still shouting but Mum's now quiet. Somehow that's even worse. Pain shoots across my chest, up my arms, my legs. 'I can't!' I tell Akash, my eyes flicking open.

There's a lump in my throat the size of the moon. The moon has fallen out of the sky and down my throat. That's impossible, I know, but this is how it feels. The tears I've been holding back drip down my cheeks.

Akash buries his hands deep into his jeans pockets, his eyes bright. 'You can. Try again. And think of somewhere nice this time. Remember?'

I nod. Dry my cheeks. Yes, somewhere nice. A happy place. I keep my eyes open this time; focus on Akash's wonky smile and straight teeth. I picture the seaside we go to in the summer. See Mum and Dad lying on the beach. I hear waves crashing against rocks. Feel my toes sink into warm sand. Smell salt and doughnuts.

And I breathe. Deep. Into my belly. Eventually, my chest stops hurting. My body feels looser. And, although my chest is still a bit tight, the moon is back in the sky, not in my throat.

'Do you think they're . . . getting a divorce?' I ask, remembering my best friend, Raheela. She cried for months when her dad left. Even in lessons.

'Nah. It's just a disagreement.' Akash shrugs. 'It happens.'

'Really? You're sure?'

He nods. 'Don't worry, OK?'

We sit down on the grass, facing away from the house, looking towards the shed at the back of the garden. Mum and Dad are now quiet. Maybe Akash is right.

'You're very wise,' I tell him, smiling now.

Akash laughs. He drapes his arm round my shoulders and I press my face into his soft, cosy hoody. He smells like he always smells: of deodorant, mints and cigarette smoke. 'Yeah, full of the wisdom, me! What would you do without me, eh?'

*

Akash walks across the bridge towards me. My legs are heavy and my throat aches. But I manage to step towards him too. And then we're so close we could touch. Rain falls on us, soft as snow.

'I knew you'd come back for me,' I whisper.

Akash tilts his head. 'Is it you?' he says. 'You . . . you look different.'

'Of course it's me!' My throat hurts. 'Have I changed *that* much?'

He scratches his chin. 'No, no . . .' he says. 'It's great to see you.'

'Yes,' I say, my breath as light as air. 'You too.' And then I reach out. I reach out to touch him.

Tick. Tock. Tick. Tock.

    Time.

        Slows.

            Down.

Like the beating of my heart.

A car beeps its horn. I catch my breath. I touch him. My brother. I touch my brother's arm. And his hoody is damp, but it's also soft, and I feel the warmth of him through it.

Light fills the sky. The sun comes out. A warm breeze blows over us.

I sink into his soft white hoody. It smells of smoke and deodorant and whisky and mint. I breathe him in. Hold him tight. My whole body shakes.

I've missed you, I want to say. *I love you.* But the words are stuck in my chest.

'Where did you go?' I manage to ask, the words scratching out of my throat.

Akash shrugs. 'I . . . I've been busy,' he says. 'But it's been good seeing you.'

I gaze into his shiny dark eyes. I want to stare into them forever.

'I've got to go,' he says.

The sky darkens. Stars peek through the darkness, half lit, shy. A moon, full and bright, appears, and then dies.

'No,' I say. 'Don't leave me. Please. Take me with you.'

Try to be happy, Neens. You deserve that. Be happy.

'Please,' I say again. 'Please don't leave me.'

Akash steps away. 'I'm sorry. But I really have to go.'

I lunge towards him and grasp hold of his arm. 'Take me with you,' I beg. 'I want to go with you.'

He tilts his head. Smiles his sweet, crooked smile. 'Yeah?' he asks. 'You sure?'

I nod, feeling suddenly calm. I let go of his arm.

'YEAH!' he shouts, punching his fist in the air.

Then he jumps up on to the ledge of the bridge; holds out his hand.

I take it. He grabs mine. And then I'm up, standing next to him, and we hold on to each other tight.

His fingers press against mine, and I feel light and strong. My heart is on fire. I'm half bird, half lion.

Akash roars at the darkness.

'I used to be afraid of heights,' I tell him, remembering the old me.

He squeezes my hand. 'Are you scared now?'

I smile. 'For once in my life, no.'

He grins. 'Don't let go of my hand, OK? We'll do it together.'

I nod. 'OK.'

I look out at the black water and the black sky. It's hard to tell where the water ends and the sky begins. It looks so peaceful out there, in all that still darkness; I want to plunge into the eternal quiet. Away from all the loud thoughts in my head. Away from Fi and Josh. Away from Mum and Dad. And any new brother.

I have a brother and he's *here*. Akash is here.

My heart races. 'What will it feel like?' I ask him.

'What do you want it to feel like?'

I spread out my arms, picturing a bird gliding in a windless sky. 'Flying. I want it to feel like flying.'

Akash smiles. 'It does,' he says, nodding. 'It feels like flying!'

The fire in my heart spreads. It bursts across my chest. Down to my stomach.

'I'm a bird,' I say. 'I'm free!'

'Yeah!' Akash says. 'YEAH!'

I lift my arms, and I grow wings. Akash raises his arms too. I look at him, at his spiky black hair and his smooth brown skin and his big, brown, shining eyes. The world swirls around us like hundreds of fireworks. Just like my sky-sea painting at home.

'This is the happiest I've ever been!' I say.

And Akash grins. 'You're happy!'

I nod. 'Yeah! Yeah, I am.'

The bridge sways. My feet lift slightly off the ledge.

'Ready?' Akash asks.

'Ready,' I say.

He grasps my hand again, squeezes it tight. 'One,' he says. 'Two . . .'

I close my eyes.

Together, we say: 'Three.'

26

But instead of falling forward, into the water, I slip backwards. The concrete smacks hard against my back. Someone screams. All the air is pulled out of my lungs.

There are voices. 'Neena! Neens!'

Car horns beep. Tyres screech. My back, arms, head – everything – throb.

'NEENA!'

I open my eyes. The sky is black. The moon is black. I can't see Akash. Rain is falling, making everything blurry. Is that why I can't see him?

I try to sit up, but something's holding my arms down. It's hard to breathe. I catch a glimpse of Josh's face. And then Fi's. I try to break free of whatever's holding me down, but the pressure gets stronger.

'Akash!' I shout.

But I can't see him and I can't smell him and I can't feel his hand in mine any more. I smell Fi's hair, sweet like grapefruit, wet against my face as she hugs me.

Akash isn't here.

Rain splashes around me. The weights on my arms loosen. Someone is propping me up. I rub the back of my head, where pain is swelling.

'Neens,' Josh says, grabbing my hand, kissing it. 'Jesus Christ, Neens.' He pulls me close. His arms are tight round me. I breathe him in, zest and sweetness. Tears roll down Fi's face, and I know why she's crying.

My chest aches.

I look around, all around, around, around.

But he's not there.

I scream into the darkness.

Akash is gone.

He's gone.

27

Fi, on the phone. Her cheeks wet, black from mascara. Traffic goes past: *whooooosh*. Josh. My Josh. His arm round my shoulders. Warm breath against my ear. A car screeches. Another voice. Chris. I'm being lifted. Cradled. I lie down. Back seat of the car. Head in Josh's lap. Voices – muffled, distant. Rain hammering the roof as we move.

Then we stop. Josh slips away. He returns, helps me sit up. Fi too. And then we're walking. Rain, puddles, splashing. A building. Hospital? Doors open. A gush of cool air. Snap shut behind us.

A man at a desk. No hair. Beard. Fi talking, crying, talking, crying. Josh talks too. Gentle. Calm. The man looks me up and down. Stands up. Calls someone across the waiting room. A woman. Glasses. She comes over and listens to them talking all at once. Leads me into a room. Fi. Fi. Josh has disappeared.

Woman with glasses checks my back, my neck, my head. 'Anything hurt?' she asks. The throbbing in my head seems to have stopped. I shake my head. 'I just want Akash,' I tell her. 'Mum's having a baby. But it's Akash I want.' Fi. Next to me. Sobbing again. The woman writes things down. Asks more questions. 'Akash,' I tell her. 'Akash.' My answer is always Akash.

Then there are two new women. One with a wide smile and eyes like black pebbles. The other woman is tall, hair the colour of lightning. The lightning woman is frowning; clutching a clipboard.

And then we're moving again. All of us together, but not the woman with glasses. Josh is back.

More doors open. Close. A long corridor. Narrow. Still hospital?

Mum's in hospital. Are they taking me to Mum? I don't want to see her, although I can't remember why.

Fi clutches my arm. Josh holds my hand. Josh's hand is sweaty. Nervous? We follow the women and the corridor goes on and on. I have a sinking feeling inside. I'm not sure the corridor will ever end. I stop walking.

'Where are we?' I ask. Chipped pale yellow walls and tiled floor surround us.

Fi and Josh are quiet.

'Why have you brought me here?' I ask.

The women usher us into a room. It's bright with peach-coloured walls and lots of blue chairs.

The women sit down. 'Take a seat,' the frowning woman says to us.

I look at Josh and Fi. Fi nods. Josh copies her. We sit in a row opposite the women. Everyone looks at me. What are they staring at? The frowning woman stares especially hard.

'Hello, Neena, I'm Dr Evans and this is Bethany, one of the psychiatric nurses,' she says. 'Your friends tell us your thoughts are very muddled. They think you're behaving unlike yourself and they're worried you may be a danger to yourself. We're trying to contact your parents, but we can't get hold of anyone at the moment. We'll keep trying.'

Thoughts . . . Muddled . . . Unlike yourself . . . Contact your parents . . . It all hits me, and I finally understand why they've brought me here.

'You're working with Mum and Dad, aren't you?' I say, standing up. 'All of you. You want to kill me!' I look at Josh. 'You too?' I ask, confused. But then I remember something; something about Josh and Fi that makes me wonder if I can trust them. But that something slips away again before the thought is fully formed.

'No one's trying to hurt you,' Dr Evans says. Her voice is deep and smooth and calm. 'We want to assess you. Help you get better. Please, sit down.'

Assess me? She means trap me. 'Get away from me!' I yell, backing towards the door.

Bethany stops smiling and also stands up. Her pebbly eyes seem to shrink. 'You're unwell. Do you recognize that, Neena? Until we get hold of your parents, are you willing to stay here voluntarily?'

I take another step back, but they all leap towards me. I try to grasp the door handle, try to escape, but Fi and Josh reach me first. Grab hold of me. I'm not sure if they're hugging me to protect me or if they're trying to push me down to hell. But then I smell Josh's apple breath, and I think I might be OK, that he might be safe.

*

A sky-blue room. I'm sitting on a chair. Josh crouching at my feet. Dr Evans towering in front of me. Her bright blue eyes. Piercing.

'We've spoken to your father,' Dr Evans says. 'He'll be here as soon as he can but he's held up. He's given his consent so we can give you medication.' She's talking really, really fast.

I shiver. 'No,' I say. 'They're trying to . . . to kill me.'

Josh holds both my hands. Presses his forehead against them. 'Trust me,' he says. 'No one is trying to kill you. Please, take the tablets.'

I look into his soft eyes. 'I don't know what's going on,' I say. 'Nothing's making sense.' I think I can trust him but I can't be absolutely sure.

'I know,' he says. 'But you know I love you, don't you?'

Josh has kind eyes; I know them so well. I know *him*. I love him. But does he love me? I thought he did, thought he said so, but then . . . What happened? Something happened that made me doubt that. Now I'm not so sure . . .

He wraps his arms round my waist. 'I do, Neens. I've *always* loved you.'

I want to believe his words. I think I do. I believe him. I lean into him. Soft hair. I smell lemon. Sweat.

'Take the tablets, Neens,' he whispers. 'You want to feel better, don't you?'

I nod. Better. Yes. That's what I want to feel.

'Then please, swallow the tablets and stay here. Just for tonight. Otherwise . . .' His voice trembles. 'Otherwise, I don't know what's going to happen.'

The image of a willow tree fills my head. It's confusing at first, but then I remember: it's the willow tree at the end of the school field. I remember kissing him. His soft lips. Josh's skin against mine. I *do* trust him. He's the only one I trust.

Dr Evans coughs and it makes me jump. I look up at her. Her yellow hair is too bright for her pale face. She holds out a tablet. A plastic cup filled with water.

I look at Josh. He takes a deep breath. Nods. I take the tablet; press it against my tongue.

'Good,' the woman says, handing me the water.

I sip. Swallow. She hands me another tablet.

'You'll feel better soon,' Josh says, squeezing my knees.

When I look down at him again, I see that he's shaking. His face is pale: he looks frightened. His phone rings and he pulls it out of his jeans pocket.

'Mum,' he says. 'Thank God! I . . . I need your help.' And then he's crying into the phone, talking about me. Sniffing and sniffing, trying to get his words out.

28

Heavy head. Lying in a bed. The sky-blue room again. Josh is next to me, sitting on a black chair. His hair's wild. Big tears drip down his face. Our eyes meet and he turns and looks up to where his mum's standing, her hands on his shoulders.

Mrs Stone smiles at me, but sadly. 'You've been sleeping,' she tells me, her voice soft and low. 'You're very tired. But you'll feel better soon.' She looks down at Josh; wipes the tears from his cheeks.

I want to ask them where we are. What I'm doing here. I want to know why Josh is crying. But my whole body feels heavy, even my tongue. I can't speak.

The door to the room opens. It's Fi. She's wearing a short dress, like she's going on a night out. But she's also crying. All her make-up is smudged: black liner and mascara all over her cheeks and red lipstick around her lips.

Why is everyone here, in this room? And why is everyone so upset?

Fi closes the door. 'They've managed to get hold of Neena's dad again,' she tells Josh. 'He'll be here soon, so you need to leave now.'

Josh shakes his head. 'I'm not leaving her side,' he says. He looks up at his mum again and she also nods.

'We'll stay,' she says. 'It's OK.'

'No way!' Fi's voice is raised now and she's bouncing from one foot to the other. She crosses her arms tight across her body. 'You need to go. I'm sorry, Mrs Stone. You don't understand. If Neena's dad sees Josh here, she'll be in trouble. And I . . . I mean, a *LOT* of trouble.'

Josh's mum looks down at him. 'This is what you were telling me about earlier?' she asks him. Josh nods.

'Then Fiona's right – we need to go.'

Fi sinks down on to the bed, next to my feet. She bites her nails.

'I'm sorry,' Josh says, reaching for my hand. 'I'll call you later?'

I still can't speak. My mouth won't work. Even my hand feels floppy, like it's not my hand at all. I try to squeeze his fingers to tell him I love him, but my fingers don't seem to work either. Nothing works. My eyes are too heavy to keep open.

I close my eyes; slip back into sleep. Back into my dream.

29

The church is quiet. The church is cold. It's winter in the church. We're in the front row: Mum and me.

I'm wrapped up in layers of black clothes: black dress and tights, jumper, coat, scarf, gloves, long black boots. But still my face is frozen from the cold. I can't blink. I can't move my lips to speak.

Around us, a sea of black. Heads bowed.

Out of the window, the actual sea. It's summer out there. The sky is bright and the sun is making everything shimmer. The church floats steadily on glimmering water.

Ding. Ding. Ding. The church bells ring.

I manage to move my neck enough to look up at Mum. I touch the thick black cardigan she's wearing over her black salwar kameez to get her attention. But she doesn't turn to look at me. She's frozen too.

Ding. Ding. Ding. The church bells ring.

Footsteps echo through the church. It takes a while, but slowly we all turn to face the aisle. It's Dad. He's dragging a huge casket towards the front of the church. His black suit is hanging off him, far too big; his heavy black coat drags along the floor. His face and body are thin and frail. Finally, he reaches the altar.

Ding. Ding. Ding. The church bells ring.

Dad falls to his knees and presses his head against the casket. There's movement around the church. Cries. Moans. Dad looks up. His hands are blue-black. His eyes are red and bulging.

Ding. Ding. Ding. The church bells ring.

Row by row, everyone visits the casket. They silently wipe tears from their faces. Then it's our turn. I hold on to Mum's arm as we walk to the front. Our legs are so stiff it takes a while. When we finally reach the front, we peer into the casket.

It's empty.

Mum falls to the floor. Her frozen face cracks all over and she lets out a wail. I shiver. I shake so hard that Mum takes my hand to calm me. Dad puts his arms round us both. We hold on to him as we stumble back to our seats.

Ding. Ding. Ding. The church bells ring.

The low hum of the organ vibrates through the air. Out of the window, waves crash and calm, crash and calm. And I spot Akash there, swimming in the ocean, his body strong against the tide. Alive! I press my palm against the window and try to open my mouth to call him. But my lips won't move.

Ding. Ding. Ding. The church bells ring.

The organ drones on. Through the ringing and the droning, we hear the piercing cries of a baby. The church sways. People stumble. Fall. The empty casket slides back and forth on the altar. Water drip, drip, drips through the ceiling. It pours through the windows. The baby cries and cries.

We grasp hold of the pews as everything – as we – slowly sink.

30

I open my eyes to the same small sky-blue room. But now Dad's here, standing next to the bed I'm lying in, his arms folded tight across his chest.

'You're not welcome here,' he's saying to someone. 'I've asked you three times now. Please leave.'

I follow his gaze. He's speaking to Fi, who's sitting at the end of the bed, next to where Dr Evans is writing something on a clipboard. Fi stands up and adjusts her dress. It looks like she's about to say something, but instead she nods, gives me a small smile, and leaves.

I glance around the room. Josh and his mum have also gone.

Dad sits down on the black chair next to me, and Dr Evans comes and stands next to him.

'How are you feeling?' she asks. 'You've been sleeping so well – Dad's been waiting patiently all morning to see you.'

'Neena, betee,' Dad says, touching my arm. His face looks thin and his eyes look sore.

The dream comes back to me. The empty casket. The baby's cries. 'Dad,' I say. 'Where's Akash? Is he gone?'

Dad looks so sad. He nods.

'And the baby?' I ask. 'Is the baby OK? And Mum?'

Dad's eyes fill with tears as he nods. 'The baby came last night. He's in intensive care – very small and we just have to hope he'll be OK.' He looks very, very lost. But then he smiles. 'Mum's doing OK though. She's still here, in the hospital, but very weak. She'll visit as soon as she can.'

I close my eyes and breathe deeply. The baby is OK. I want to sit up but I'm too exhausted.

'Time for your medication, Neena,' Dr Evans says.

'Medicine? Am I sick?'

She nods. 'Do you remember? You've been very ill, Neena. You're in hospital.' She helps me sit up and adjusts the pillows behind me. Dad stares at me like he's looking at a ghost. I don't know what she's talking about, but I do feel ill, weak and tired and confused. So I swallow the tablets and Dr Evans leaves. I want to talk to Dad, ask him about the baby. But my eyelids are too heavy; I can barely keep them open.

'Sleep,' Dad says. He presses his hand against mine. 'Don't worry about anything, betee. You're going to be OK. Everything will be OK.'

31

When I wake up again, Mum's next to the bed. *Mum!* Where has she been? She's stroking the back of my hand. The mattress I'm lying on is thin and hard. The sheets are rough. They smell of disinfectant. There's a black chair next to the bed and it's empty. Akash's cap is on the bedside table.

'Am I in Pakistan?' I ask, remembering the film I once saw with Raheela. Have Mum and Dad taken me there?

Mum frowns. 'No, my jaan! You're in hospital.'

'Oh!' I say, remembering now. 'Yes, of course.'

Images flash through my mind. The bridge. Dark sky. A car. A woman with a clipboard. Tablets. Josh's arms round me. A sign: PSYCHIATRIC UNIT.

'What's wrong with me?' I ask Mum.

She continues stroking my hand. A bit of rough skin on her fingertip catches on mine. 'You're ill, my jaan,' she says quietly. 'Just rest.'

'How long have I been here?'

Mum doesn't look too well herself. Dark shadows hang from her eyes like half-moons. Her hair's tied back messily, more grey than black, and she's wearing a dark purple salwar kameez that's too big for her. She peers at me like she's in pain. I see that she's in a wheelchair.

'Mum! Are you OK?' I ask.

She nods. 'It's OK, Neena. The baby, do you remember? He's here . . . I'm still recovering from the birth, that's why I've got a wheelchair.'

I nod. I vaguely remember about the baby. Dad said he's doing OK.

'You've been here since yesterday,' Mum says, brushing some strands of hair off my face. 'Resting mainly. I came to see you before, but you were very drowsy. They're giving you something to help you sleep. You're very tired. But I'm taking you home soon. I'll look after you there.'

'Home,' I say. 'That'll be nice.' I wish I was there right now.

Mum grasps my hand hard. Her eyes fill. 'Oh, my jaan! What happened? How did it get to this?'

'I don't know what's going on,' I tell her truthfully.

Her face is full of emotions that I don't quite understand. Her chest rises and falls heavily. 'When I had you, I felt like my life was complete. I thought I'd never want anything ever again,' she says. She lets out a small laugh. 'I know it sounds silly. But I had *everything*. My babies. You . . . and Akash.'

She stares into my eyes and my breath stops. I know she's waiting for me to say something, but I don't know what I should say.

'Maybe . . . Maybe a part of me *was* trying to replace Akash,' she whispers. 'It's a terrible thing to say, but I thought I wouldn't miss him as much if I had another child. That things might return to normal one day.' She shakes her head. 'I knew that wasn't true deep down, that it wouldn't bring him back. But I didn't know what else to do ... Can you understand that, Neena?'

I still don't know what to say, so I just say: 'Why *am* I here? What happened?'

'You tried to jump off a bridge, Neena.' Mum's voice is so tight, so desperate, that for a moment I wish I could change it all, the lying, the hiding, the bridge. Josh.

But at the same time I don't. 'I was with Akash,' I explain.

Mum looks away. Wipes tears from her cheeks. She doesn't say anything for a while. Then she holds my hand again.

'It was easier when you were younger,' she says. 'You always worried about things, but I knew how to reach you. And you talked – you always talked to me.' She swallows. 'I want to reach you now, Neena. Are you listening? Are you understanding me?'

I stare at her. I think I understand but I'm not sure. It's all so confusing. 'I don't know. I'm just really tired,' I say.

'Oh, Neena, my jaan,' she says. 'What I'm trying to say is that I'm sorry. And that I love you. I need you.'

32

Dr Evans smiles and crosses her legs. Mum and I are sitting opposite her, me on a blue chair and Mum in her wheelchair. We're in a room with peach-coloured walls and bright lights. It feels familiar. Mum's hand is on my back, gently rubbing. It's soothing.

'We've had a good talk with your mum,' Dr Evans says. 'And we're happy for you to go home; it's a much nicer environment for you, rather than joining the main ward, and we can see you'll get good support there.' She brushes a hand through her short hair. 'You've reacted well to the medication, so we're pleased about that, and please remember you're not alone. Our Home Treatment Team will visit you every day – we'll monitor your medication and make sure you're OK. And they will formulate a relapse plan with you.'

She looks at Mum. 'With good support, I'm confident she'll make excellent progress.'

Mum sighs. 'That all sounds good,' she says.

Looking back at me, Dr Evans smiles again. 'When you're ready, you'll be offered CBT – cognitive behavioural therapy –

where you'll learn to challenge your thoughts to take control of your anxieties. We'll also introduce you to relaxation methods and some talk therapy with our wonderful psychologist, Laura.' She takes a breath and peers at me. 'I know it's a lot to take in, but how does that all sound to you? We'll be available twenty-four hours a day. So if you feel anxious, and need to call us, you can at any time.'

I don't really understand all she's saying, but it seems to mean I can go home, so I nod.

'So you're happy to go ahead with that?' she asks.

'Yes,' I say.

'Thank you, Doctor,' Mum says. She kisses me on the cheek. 'Let's go home, my jaan.'

I push Mum's wheelchair as we follow Dr Evans down a long corridor with pale yellow walls. 'Dad's waiting in the car outside,' Mum tells me. She's carrying my overnight bag on her lap, which I didn't even know I had with me. And I notice I'm wearing black jogging bottoms and a sweatshirt that don't belong to me. They smell of Fi. 'We'll pick up some takeaway pizzas for dinner,' Mum goes on.

I feel in a daze, far away, somewhere outside my body, but I nod along to everything Mum says.

We pass a few nurses and then we reach some double doors. Dr Evans punches in a code and the doors slowly open. We step out into a cafeteria area. There are shiny steel chairs and tables attached to the floor and a single vending machine in the corner. Through the windows I can see the outside.

'So we'll see you tomorrow,' Dr Evans says, holding her hand out for Mum to shake. 'And please remember – if you start feeling unwell or anxious, call us.'

Outside, warm air hits my skin. The sky is blue and bright, and so comforting after being inside. It's a bit easier to breathe. Dad is waiting right outside the building, at the front of a huge car park, the car engine running. I climb into the back seat and Dad gives me a tired smile as he helps Mum get in next to me. She holds my hand tight. As we drive away from the hospital, I look back at the building like I'm in a dream.

I'm ill. That's what everyone keeps telling me. And although I don't want to believe them, I've got a horrible feeling they're right.

As we join the main road outside the hospital, I turn my back on the building and look ahead. The world slides past as the car drifts along the road. Trees. People. Traffic. I press my forehead against the window. It's all here, just as I left it, rows of shops and restaurants, people strolling in and out of them, the whole world continuing without me.

Nothing's changed. But, at the same time, everything's changed.

'Things have changed a bit at home,' Mum says, squeezing my hand.

I feel suddenly alert. 'Can you hear my thoughts?' I ask, panicked. *What if something about Josh pops into my head?*

'What?' Mum frowns. 'No, betee. It's just that . . .' She trails off. Dad glances over his shoulder, nodding at her in encouragement. 'Your little brother will hopefully be coming home soon, from hospital – just like you. So we had to prepare, make space for him. And Dad did that earlier today.'

'Oh.' I look into the distance. The noise of traffic grows louder. I'm still not really sure what she's getting at.

'We thought it'd be better to do it when you weren't there,' Mum says, but her voice is muffled. The noise of the traffic is drowning her out and taking up all the space in my head. My ears ring.

'We kept everything,' she continues. 'And all his artwork – that's for you. I'm going to put it all in the shed, safe, as soon as I get a chance. He loved doing his painting in there . . .'

The traffic gets quieter as I tune back in to Mum.

'They're all yours,' she says. 'Keep them in there, hang them up in your room, or maybe around the house. It's up to you.'

My throat aches.

Akash's room is gone.

Akash is gone.

The house smells of disinfectant and potpourri. I feel like I've been away for months. We take off our shoes in the hallway and Mum hugs me tight. She looks more like herself now that she's out of the wheelchair, even though she's weak.

'I'm so glad you're home,' she says. 'We can't wait for you to meet your baby brother, but Dr Evans thinks you should take your time and get a bit better first. OK?'

I nod. *Baby. I have a baby brother.* Everything really has changed.

'I'll put the kettle on,' Dad says, handing me my holdall.

Mum smiles at me. 'Are you hungry? I bought a carrot cake. Your favourite. Let's all have a cup of tea together and then we'll order pizza later. I need to go back to the hospital soon – I don't want to leave him alone too long, it's still early days . . .' She suddenly looks shy, and hopeful. 'Do you . . . do you want to know what we've called him?'

But my face must do something weird because she looks panicked and immediately backtracks.

'It's OK, Neena, don't worry – if it's all too much, we can just wait to introduce you properly.'

We walk up the hallway and I hover outside Akash's room. Which isn't Akash's room any more. The door is shut.

Mum rubs my back. 'You want to go in?' she asks, sounding nervous.

I shake my head.

'Whenever you're ready. Come, let's have tea.'

'I'll be there in a minute,' I say, looking at my bedroom door.

'Of course, betee.'

I slip into my bedroom and shut the door. My room's as it's always been, just neater. Did Dad tidy my room? My desk is clear. My shoes are lined neatly against the wall. The bed is perfectly made. I touch the books on my shelf, my paints, my easel.

Then I sit on my bed and open up my overnight bag. I pull out Akash's purple-and-yellow cap and press it against my face. It smells of cigarette smoke, and I wonder if it will always smell this way, of him. I think about putting it on but I don't. I bury it back in my dressing-table drawer.

And then, I don't know what makes me do it, but I look under my bed. I find a grey wicker basket full of containers of food. Oh God. I remember that I believed I went on a picnic with Josh. I thought we ate this food. That he said he loved me. But that didn't happen. All the food is here.

I don't know what has happened, or what hasn't. I can't trust my memory.

Everyone's right. I am ill.

I feel further along the bed. I find three empty bottles of whisky. I thought Akash was drinking them, but no. I now know that I drank these myself.

Akash is gone. My brother is gone. He's been gone for . . . for a long time.

I feel a familiar urge to pick up my paintbrush, let everything I'm feeling out. But I'm tired. So tired. I sit down on my bed instead, thankful for the comfortable mattress and soft sheets. I hear Mum outside my bedroom, the creaking of the floorboard. But then her footsteps fade as she wanders back towards the kitchen.

I'm glad to be home, but the reality of everything is hitting me.

I lie down on my bed. My whole body aches. I want Josh. I want him to hold me, and I want to hold him. To hear his gentle voice. Feel him next to me.

I want Raheela, wish she was sleeping on the floor next to me, like she used to when we were kids.

I want Fi. I want her to tell me that I can fight all this. That I'll be OK.

But, at the same time, I don't want to see anybody. What must they think of me?

A howl leaves my body, dragging itself out from somewhere deep inside.

I climb under my duvet and press my face into my soft pillow.

And I will sleep to come.

33

I sleep all day and all night. Mum goes to hospital and comes back. She brings me tablets and pizza, boiled eggs and creamy porridge. I'm not hungry, but I eat everything and swallow my medicine to get her to leave. I want to be alone. I want to sleep. I do not want to talk. I do not want to think. Days pass.

I hear Mum and Dad in the corridor. Whispering. Rushing around. Dad doesn't seem to be going to work. They talk about going to the hospital. He's doing OK, they say. Feeding. Putting on weight. Mum makes shopping lists and reads them to Dad: milk, eggs, ready meals for the freezer; garam masala and fresh ginger in case she has a chance to cook. Nuts. Neena needs almonds: they're good for the brain.

The front door opens and closes, opens and closes. But one of them is always here. The shower runs. The TV talks. The washing machine buzzes. Mum cleans my bedroom around me as I stare at the wall until I fall asleep again.

Even when it's quiet, there's no quiet in the house.

People come to see me every day. Strangers. *Home Treatment Team*. Different strangers every day. A tall lady with long dark hair and a deep, sleepy voice. A guy with no hair and a round stomach, who keeps telling me to smile ... Mum gently pulls me out of bed to see them. She wraps my dressing gown round me and leads me to the living room. They're always sitting on the sofa, sipping tea. 'You've been through a lot,' they all say. 'Just take it a day at a time.'

I nod. It seems the right thing to do.

They talk to me about illness, about broken legs and broken minds, and how they really aren't that different. Both take time to heal. They say I've had a 'psychotic episode' and tell me about the importance of positivity. I'm on the road to recovery, they say. They want me to talk. And they assure me that they're listening. But it's hard to talk when everything feels so heavy inside. My thoughts aren't racing any more. Instead, they're so slow they're almost still, barely thoughts at all. Nothing feels real. All I want is sleep.

Then, one day, I hear Mum and Dad talking in the kitchen. My bedroom door is open, and they're whispering loudly.

'I just don't understand!' Dad says. 'It's been days now – what's going on? All she does is sleep!'

'She's ill,' Mum says. 'It will take time.'

'What kind of illness *is* this?' Dad says. 'She needs to get up. Get dressed. She's not helping herself.'

'It's . . . it's an illness of the brain,' Mum says, and her voice is urgent now. 'These things happen! And please, keep your voice down!'

I block out their voices. I don't want to hear about how broken I am. I close my eyes tight.

In the seconds before sleep hits me, I think of Josh's warmth.

34

'You've been inside for four days,' Mum says, crouching next to my bed. She slides her hand under the duvet and grips my fingers tight. 'Come, sit in the garden with me. It's a lovely evening. Fresh air will help.'

She's left the bedroom door open and the smell of fresh paint is drifting in from the hallway. I try not to think about what it means, that sharp, new smell.

'Tired,' I tell her.

'Raheela rang again,' she says, her voice still upbeat. 'Why don't you let her visit? It will be good to see your friends.'

I get a waft of sweat as I pull the duvet tighter round me. I know it's not Mum. It's me. I've been here before. 'Not ready,' I say.

Mum is quiet. I wait for her to leave, but she keeps hold of my hand. After a few minutes, she squeezes my fingers so tight it hurts.

'Come on, betee,' she says, and her voice is desperate now. 'You have to find strength inside. Dig deep, bring your strength to the surface.'

I don't say anything. I don't have any strength. I don't have anything inside.

'You think I find it easy whenever I go outside now?' she continues. 'Well, I don't. Some days I want to hide in the house again. I want the world to continue without me. But I get up, get dressed and step out. Courage, betee. You must find your courage.'

I pull my hand away from Mum's grasp.

'Maybe . . . maybe we should get someone in to pray for you?' she says. 'Whatever this *thing* is, we can fight it together.'

'Tired,' I manage to say. I feel so drowsy. 'Rest. I need rest.' My body is heavy but I manage to turn over. I cover my head with the duvet. Close my eyes. I give in to the exhaustion. I let sleep take me.

I'm standing in our hallway at home, but it's long, narrow, too brightly lit. Like the hospital corridor. There are no family photos on the walls, no paintings, just chipped pale-yellow paint. I'm wearing an extravagant salwar kameez, the kind you'd wear to a wedding: a red silk dress embellished with jewels; shimmery gold trousers fitted at the ankles. My feet are bare. Live music is playing, thrumming through the house: the *tuck-tuck* of a tabla and the soft tinkle of a tambourine in the background.

People move around me but I'm perfectly still. Their mouths open and close as they talk and laugh, but I can't hear them. All I hear is the music, the beat of the drum. *Tuck-tuck-tuck*. Like my heartbeat.

My eyes are fixed on the doorway at the end of the corridor.

Josh. He's looking at me. Grinning. He stretches his arms and holds on to the top of the door frame. He lifts himself up, swings in the air, and I see his gold embroidered salwar kameez. The tabla beat gets louder, faster. My heart races.

I try to walk towards Josh but my feet are stuck. I try to call him but no voice comes out. I peer around, desperate for help, but no one's paying me any attention. I try to grab hold of Mum's friend, Aunty Roxanna, from our old neighbourhood. But my hands slip through her arms. She's a ghost.

Or am I?

I look back at Josh, but I can't see him properly any more – there are too many people in the way. I keep trying to move my legs, my feet. I try to call out to him. *Wait for me*, I want to say. *I'll find a way to reach you.*

Next to the doorway, Mum and Dad are shaking hands with people. Mum's slim, like she used to be, and she's dressed in an embroidered full-length pink skirt suit and heels. Round her neck is a silver dupatta. She glances at me but then quickly looks away. Dad's wearing a suit like he wears to work, but he has a pair of gold khussa on his feet, with tips that curl upwards.

The doorway sways. I catch a glimpse of Josh. He holds on to the frame and stumbles.

The music gets even louder, faster. *Tucktucktucktucktucktuck tucktucktuck.* The tambourine bashes against the sound of the drum.

And then Josh fades, ghost-like, translucent. He disappears.

The crowd turn to face me. Their outfits shimmer; their jewellery glistens. Gifts appear in their hands, wrapped in shiny paper and ribbon in red, green, blue.

The drumming stops.

Aunty Roxanna, who's much older than Mum, is holding a box of mithai. She presses her hand against my head – a blessing – and smiles her toothless smile. Then she opens the box and takes out a golden ball of the sweet dessert. Pushes it into my mouth. I bite into the soft, gooey sweet. It's sickly and stings my throat. Everyone cheers.

I realize that this *is* a wedding. And I'm the one getting married.

Where Josh stood minutes ago, a guy appears. He has golden brown skin, like mine, and he's wearing a man's version of my outfit. Red and gold. Long tunic over trousers. He has the same hair as Josh, curled up into a wave at the front, but his is black.

My clothes suddenly feel too heavy.

The *tuck-tuck* of drums starts again. Dad starts clapping. Everyone joins him. I stare at Mum, my chest bursting from all the things I want to say to her. *Help me*, I say with my eyes. *Please*. But she just smiles. There's a huge gush of wind and her dupatta flutters violently; it extends from her neck and waves like a flag, as if she herself is the pole.

'Josh,' I say, opening my eyes. I expect it to be dark outside – it feels like I've only been asleep for a little while. But it's light. Morning. The next day.

'Jaan?' Mum says. She's sitting on a dining chair next to my bed, wearing a nightie. Her duvet's wrapped round her legs. It looks like she's been there all night.

I cover my mouth with my hands and stare at her. *Did she hear me? Does she know?*

'What did you say?' she asks, her voice sleepy.

'I . . . I thought you'd be at the hospital . . .' I say, wishing I could be alone to call Josh.

She yawns. 'Dad's gone this morning. I'll go a bit later . . .' She closes her eyes again.

I relax a bit. I don't think she heard anything.

But now, like old times, all I can think about is Josh. His soft green eyes, his dark brown hair, his sweet smell. I remember our lunchtimes beneath the willow tree, his lips against my ear, the warmth of his breath, his touch. And I remember how tightly he held my hand when we were standing in that long yellow corridor at the hospital.

I've been avoiding seeing anyone, but I'm now desperate to talk to him. And, as I look at Mum, I know that I can't lie any more.

'I have to tell you something,' I say, before I lose my nerve. 'And you're not going to like it.'

Mum opens her eyes. Her gaze doesn't quite meet mine. 'Is this about your boy?' she says, and her voice is hard even though she's whispering.

My skin turns cold. I sit up. 'You know?'

'Of course I know! I'm your mother. I know my own daughter!'

My body feels weak. I pull my duvet tightly round me. 'I can't believe you know. When? How?'

Mum takes a deep breath. 'I've suspected for a while,' she says, looking down at her lap. 'I noticed a change in you.

Little bursts of joy, like I hadn't seen since . . . since before everything.' She looks up at me now. 'And I thought, "Oh dear. That girl is in love."'

I nod. Tears sting my eyes. 'His name's Josh,' I say, trying to hold on to my bravery. 'And you're right, I love him.'

Mum's lips tighten. A deep frown creases her forehead. My stomach goes hard, the anxiety making my body tense up. But I know I need to finish what I have to say.

'I know you and Dad want to take me to Pakistan this summer to get married,' I say, as calmly as I can. 'But that won't "fix" me. I'm not going to go.'

Mum looks shocked. 'Married? What?'

'You don't need to pretend, Mum. I heard you and Dad talking and I figured it out. I've watched the films. I've heard stories!' The tears come now and I can't stop them.

Mum covers her hand with her mouth. She comes to sit on the side of my bed, taking my hand in hers. 'You've got it all wrong, Neena,' she says, her eyes also filling now. 'We did want to take you to Pakistan,' she says. 'But for a holiday. Like we said. And I admit – we thought it might help you connect with our culture a bit more. We felt you were . . . lost . . . looking for answers in the wrong places. But marriage at such a young age? No, never, Neena!'

Mum seems so upset that I believe her. Have I got it all wrong? 'So you weren't going to trick me into getting married once we were there?'

Mum shakes her head. 'No! I can't believe you would think that. Have you been thinking this all the time?'

I nod and her face falls.

'Oh, Neena, I wish you'd talk to me!' Her face is full of so much pain. 'I know we've been more traditional since Akash passed, but you're too young to get married, and we want you to study first.' She touches my cheek. 'And to focus on getting better.'

I frown at Mum. 'First? No, Mum, I don't think you understand. What I'm saying is I *never* want an arranged marriage. It's not for me.'

She sniffs. 'It's this boy, isn't it?'

'No! I'm not saying I want to marry Josh either. Just that I want to choose. One day. That arranged marriage stuff, it's your culture, not mine.'

Mum's lips are tight but she nods. 'I understand.'

'I'm really not trying to hurt you. And of course it's *part* of my heritage. But I was born *here*. I should be allowed to choose what feels right for *me*.'

Mum nods again. 'I know. And I always thought that way too. I wanted you to have a choice over everything, Neena,' she says. 'But your brother, he was "in love" too. Sneaking out. Fighting with us. That's why we were arguing that night. He wanted to see her. She even came to the house – some nerve that girl's got! I sent her away, but not before your dad saw her.' Mum huffs. 'If he'd found a nice girl, that would be different. She's bad news. Took your brother down the wrong path. And I see that she's after you too!'

I pull my hand away from hers. 'Nothing is Fi's fault, Mum. Any path Akash or I went down has been our own choice.'

Mum's quiet now.

'She loved Akash!' I continue. 'And he loved her. Maybe if you'd listened to him . . .' It's all coming out now and I don't think I can stop it. 'Maybe if you'd let him go he wouldn't have been so upset that night, wouldn't have got so drunk, and he wouldn't have done it, he wouldn't have —'

Mum lets out a deep, long wail. I gulp in air and cover my mouth with my hands. Tears drip down Mum's cheeks, and mine too.

'I'm so sorry,' I mumble through my tears.

But Mum looks down at her lap and nods. 'No, no. You're right. I think about that every day. If only . . . if only we hadn't argued that night . . . But it was the drugs, all the drugs — we just wanted him to stop before something happened!'

She looks up and we stare at each other.

'But he hadn't taken anything that night, Mum. The . . . the report showed that. He'd been trying to change,' I add, remembering Jay's words.

But Mum shakes her head. 'I don't know. I just don't know what to believe any more. Things were very bad at one point.'

I look down at my feet. 'I didn't know that,' I say, but it makes sense now. It's why Mum and Dad were so strict with him.

If only I'd gone to the party with him. If only I'd answered the phone later. If I'd been there to stop him getting so wasted, to stop him on the bridge . . .

Mum rubs her temples. 'No, we wanted to protect you from all that, Neena. But we were beside ourselves with him. We . . . we'd tried everything. And I guess it seemed he changed when that girl came into his life. But you're right. It was always there – we just didn't see it, didn't want to see it.'

We're silent for a while. All this time, I've been angry with Mum and Dad. But now I see that there was so much I didn't know, or understand. I lean forward and hug Mum. She hugs me back tightly.

'Anyway . . .' she says, when we finally stop hugging. 'What do *you* want, betee? I don't understand.'

'Didn't you ever have a crush, Mum? Someone you liked before Dad?' It feels like a weird thing to say, but I need to make her understand.

'Of course I did, Neena. All teenagers do. But you grow up, and you realize there's so much more to love than "crushes". We're just trying to protect you.'

I press my hand against my heart. 'I know, Mum. But you don't need to protect me any more. I need to find my own way.'

My eyes fill now because I'm realizing the truth of what I've just said. Mum's eyes dart around my face. She looks very worried. 'Shhhhh,' she says. 'It's OK.' And her eyes soften and she reaches out and touches my arm. 'I want you to be happy more than anything, my jaan. And healthy.'

I take some deep breaths. I just want her to hug me again.

'No one's going to force you into anything. Let's forget about the marriage stuff, until you want to get married one day? And then we can talk and I promise I'll listen. Does that sound OK?'

I nod. Mum looks as relieved as I am.

'One more thing,' I say, ignoring the nerves making my stomach flip. 'I want to meet Josh over the next few days. But I don't want to lie any more. I don't want to hide.'

Mum frowns a bit. But she nods. 'OK. But don't tell your dad.'

My heart sinks. 'More secrets? Is that really the answer?'

'No, my jaan, it's not. But this . . . this would be too much for him right now. These things, they take time. I'll work on him. Until then, this is *my* secret, not yours – you don't need to worry. Understand?'

I'm still not convinced this is the answer, but I do feel a bit lighter. And it means I can see Josh. 'Yes. Thanks, Mum.'

She manages a smile. 'Be careful,' she says. 'The heart is a fragile thing.'

35

After our talk Mum gives me my morning medication and goes to the kitchen to make breakfast. I hear her singing hymns and praying for me loudly. Ignoring her, I look for my phone, finally finding it in my bedside drawer. I haven't messaged Josh or spoken to him for days – I've been too embarrassed and haven't felt myself. Plus I'm still trying to make sense of everything. But I need to speak to him, I realize now. Need to know what he's thinking and feeling.

I turn on the phone but it's out of juice, so I plug it into the charger and try again. After a few minutes, it turns on and the messages come in. A few from Raheela, about five hundred from Fi, the rest from Josh. I scroll through his, reading the oldest first.

> You OK Neens? Want to see you – your parents at hospital? Call when you can. X

> Trying to call you but don't think you got your phone?? J x

Let me know when safe to visit you –
really want to see you. x

How are you today? Worried about you. Sorry keep
messaging. Don't know what else to do. Tried
emailing too. Love, J x

Hi, Neens, really want to talk. You getting my
messages? x

School's crap without you. Teachers stressed. So
much revision. Had lunch under willow tree on my
own today. The tree misses you & so do I. J x

Josh's messages make me smile and cry at the same time.
He loves me. He's missing me. I quickly message him to
explain that I haven't had my phone but that I'm OK and will
call as soon as I can.

Mum comes back into the room with toast just as I send the
message. She sits on the edge of the bed and watches me eat.
'You'll be up and about soon,' she says. 'You look a bit better today.'

I suddenly feel sweaty, sticky. When did I last wash? I push the
empty plate into Mum's hands. 'I'm going to shower,' I tell her,
pushing my phone under my pillow and pulling the duvet off me.

Mum's face brightens. 'Oh, Neena,' she says, smiling. She
draws me in for a hug. 'That's wonderful, my jaan. Wonderful!'

I roll my eyes. 'Calm down! It's just a shower, Mum.'

But she grins back at me and I think maybe she's right. I do
feel a tiny bit of my old self fighting to come through. I do feel
a bit better.

I hurry past Akash's room without looking at the door. I ignore the sharp smell of paint that stings my throat. In the bathroom, I peel off my pyjamas and get straight into the shower. Then I relax as warm water glides over my skin.

It feels like a huge weight has been lifted, telling Mum about Josh.

I close my eyes and imagine lying next to him on his bed, his body pressing against mine. But what does he think about what happened, I wonder? I shampoo my hair; the smell of orange and cinnamon comforts me. I lather myself in too much shower gel and imagine the soap washing my illness away.

My tears merge with the water and my heart skips beats, as if it's forgotten how to work.

Psychosis. It's such a big word. Amid all the noise of that word, how will I ever find myself again?

Then I think about Akash. My brother. He was my rock. Losing him is the worst thing that's ever happened to me. But somehow I need to piece myself back together. I understand that now.

The skin on my fingertips is wrinkled by the time I get out of the shower. I wrap a soft towel round me and walk over to the mirror. I can't see myself because it's misted over. But I press my fingertips against the glass and draw circles for faces, dots for eyes, curves for smiles. I swallow. I want to be happy but maybe Mum's right. Perhaps I've been searching in all the wrong places.

Neena Gill, I write in the middle of all the smiles. Sometimes you need to remind yourself who you are, don't you?

My bedcovers have been changed when I return from the bathroom. It's like Mum was just waiting to pounce on them! The window's open, a fresh breeze blowing in. My phone's charging on my bedside table. I pull on the jeans and T-shirt that Mum's put out for me on the bed, wrap my hair up in a towel and check my phone.

I have a message from Josh. My heart races.

So glad you're OK! Can't wait to speak to you! x

My heart races as I message him back.

Just waiting for some privacy . . .

When I look up, Mum is standing in my doorway. Talking of privacy . . . But, instead of sighing, I smile. How can I be angry with her, after everything we've all been through?

'Dad's back and I've made halva,' she says. 'Have a little, huh? Almonds. Good for your brain.'

I laugh, and it feels so good. I can't remember the last time I laughed. Mum looks at me in surprise.

'What's so funny?' she asks.

I shrug. 'Just strange how some things never change,' I try to explain. 'Even when everything else does.'

She looks at me blankly. 'So you'll have some halva?'

I laugh again. 'Yes, yes! I'm coming!'

Dad's already sitting at the dining table, staring out into the garden. He's shaved and he's wearing his work suit. Although he looks smart, his face is thin and his eyes are puffy. The pungent scent of his aftershave has mixed with the smell of fried almonds and sultanas. He glances at me, and smiles.

'You're looking stronger, betee,' he says. 'Come, sit. I'll make tea.' He gets up and fills a teapot.

When he returns, he sits next to me instead of in his usual place. He fills three mugs with steaming tea, tops them with milk, hands me one. There's something different about his body language. He seems looser, more open. Every time I glance at him, he smiles at me kindly.

Mum serves up the halva in big bowls. I'm not hungry, but I force myself to eat. The halva is smooth and buttery; Mum's drizzled honey on top and it melts into the semolina. I feel hungrier as I eat, and it warms me. This seems like the most normal thing I've done in a while, sitting here with my mum and dad, drinking tea, and it feels really good. But it still feels like there's a glass screen separating me from the rest of the world.

After a few minutes, Mum fiddles with the honey pot. She looks at me nervously. 'Dad has to go back to work today,' she says. 'And I need to visit the hospital to drop off some milk and clean clothes.'

'I'm sorry, Neena,' Dad says. 'I've had a lot of time off. But, if you need anything, you can call me.'

I look from Mum to Dad, back at Mum again. Why are they treating me like a baby? 'I don't need to be watched twenty-four hours a day!' I say. 'Please. Go to work. Go to the hospital. I'm tired anyway. I'm going to rest.' I also realize this is my chance to finally call Josh.

'But will you . . . be OK? On your own?' Mum asks. 'I thought about asking Jasmine to come over. I should have. I can still ask her – she won't mind . . .'

'No! I don't need a babysitter!'

Mum reaches across the table and squeezes my hand. She takes a deep breath. 'OK. If you're sure? And it does give you a chance to speak to your psychologist openly.' She glances at her watch. 'She'll be here in half an hour.'

Psychologist. Ah. I'd forgotten she was coming, though Mum mentioned it yesterday. The Home Treatment Team are stepping back a bit as they're happy with my progress; a psychologist called Laura is taking over. We'll have a few sessions at the house and then I'll go to the hospital to see her. But I don't want to see her at all; I just want to speak to Josh, to see him, although I know that's not possible right now. And I do know that I need some professional help.

'I promise you I'll be OK, Mum.'

She nods. 'Right. I really need to get back to the hospital. The baby will be hungry soon.'

I try to picture this baby, imagine him in Mum's arms. It doesn't feel real.

'Is he . . . OK?' I ask. I know I haven't asked about him since I've been home, and I've tried so hard to ignore him, but suddenly it's really important that I know he's OK. *He's my brother.*

'Stronger every day,' Mum says, welling up. 'He's in the right place.'

'And . . . what's his name?'

Mum's wiping her tears. It's Dad who speaks, softer than air.

'We've been calling him something, but we want to know what you think. We want to call him Raja – Raj for short. It means radiance. And in Arabic it means hope, which I really like. What do you think?'

Raj. Hope.

I picture this tiny thing the size of my hand; imagine him curling up in my arms, against my chest. I imagine the silky feel of his skin. Will he smell of soap and talc? All fresh and new? Will he have a whole head of black hair, like Akash had when he was born? Will his face be shaped like a heart, like mine was?

Raj.

'Yes,' I say. 'That sounds . . . OK.'

Once Mum and Dad are gone, I plan to phone Josh, but I find myself standing outside Akash's room instead. My heart's racing. My eyes are fixed on the closed door; it's like a whiteboard that's been rubbed clean. Anxiety is creeping up my neck. I do my deep breathing.

Raj.

I have a brother called Raj.

But to me this will always be Akash's room. Won't it?

I take a very deep breath, press down the handle and push open the door.

I'm not prepared for the brightness. It winds me. Fresh white paint. Cream carpet. White crib and lampshade with tiny grey stars all over it. The brand-new, empty bookshelves.

Where is all of Akash's stuff? I slam the door shut.

I rush to the kitchen, trying to catch my breath. I open the back door, run out into the garden and fling open the door to the shed. There they all are. His paintings. Just like Mum said they'd be. They're neatly stowed in a huge portfolio.

I step into the shed and close the door. I carefully flick through the paintings and stop at my favourite one – of a man's face. It's abstract, harsh triangles spreading from the man's head in bright colours. Akash loved Andy Warhol and he loved Picasso, and the painting has influences of them both. But, although the face itself is angular, the eyes – and that's the bit that gets me the most – are bright and soft and sleepy at the same time.

They are Akash's eyes.

I sit on the floor and lean into the painting. I close my eyes and remember him in his bedroom, in front of his easel. I loved watching him paint. The way every stroke of the brush mattered. He'd get paint in his hair, on his cheeks, his arms. But he didn't care. All that mattered was the picture, the curve of a petal, the exact colour of a leaf. And I loved the look on his face when he finished painting. Like he'd travelled round the world and come home again, as he always planned to do.

I vaguely remember Mum saying something in the hospital about realizing that Raj can never replace Akash. And, while I want to believe that, I'm still scared.

I worry that everyone will forget my brother. I worry that his memories will fade if I don't grip hold of them extra tight.

My phone buzzes, pulling me away from my thoughts. I take it out of my pocket, expecting it to be Josh, but it's Fi. I haven't spoken to her since the hospital.

'I'm glad you called,' I say. 'I was just thinking about Akash. He's really gone, isn't he?'

Fi takes a sharp breath in. 'Yeah,' she says. 'Yeah, he is. You OK?'

I swallow. I'm not ready to talk about the psychosis yet, so I try to concentrate on Akash. 'I don't know. I just . . . I don't want to forget him. Ever.' I'm trying to make sense of everything I'm feeling, but it's overwhelming again. Will it always be this way?

'I've been thinking though, Neens. And . . . he'd want you to live *your* life. Not his. You know?'

We're quiet and I keep staring at the painting. 'I know,' I say. 'I think I just needed to live his before figuring out my own.'

'Yeah, I know. I know, Neens . . . Listen, I . . . I actually need to talk to you about something. Your mum and dad too. So I'm going to come over this evening. I just wanted to warn you. But I'll . . . I'll see you then.'

'Is that a good idea?' I ask, thinking about my earlier conversation with Mum.

But the phone is dead. Fi's already gone.

I stare at my phone. I want to call her back, but I haven't got time right now. A burst of nerves flutters through my chest. It's time for my session with the psychologist.

36

Laura, my psychologist, looks like an actress. She has clear pale skin and thick black hair that falls around her face and shoulders in shimmery waves. Her eyes are golden brown flecked with yellow and her cheeks are rosy. She smiles and tilts her head a lot. Her voice is soothing.

She seems really nice, but I pace the living room, up and down by the window, like Mum does. Well, like Mum used to do; she seems much calmer lately. Laura watches quietly for a few minutes before indicating the sofa beside her.

'Why don't you sit down, Neena,' she says. 'It's not easy, but try to relax. This should feel like an informal, helpful chat. I'm not here to judge. I'm here to support you.'

I force myself to sit.

'Neena,' she continues. 'You had a psychotic episode. You got very ill. Do you understand that?'

I pull my legs up on to the sofa and hug them. I picture the bridge at the end of town. I remember climbing up on to it. Looking out at the endless darkness.

'I saw my brother,' I say, my voice weak. I close my eyes and fight the tears. I press my face into my knees.

'Yes,' Laura says. 'It was a hallucination. That can happen during a psychotic episode.'

I keep my head on my knees. My heart's beating so fast. 'It felt so real,' I tell her.

'Would you like to talk about how you're feeling?' she asks.

I squeeze my eyes shut tighter. 'Scared. Weak. Hopeless. I can't believe this has happened; I'm so embarrassed.'

'Open your eyes, Neena,' Laura says. 'Look at me.'

I open them a little. The room is so bright. Her hair and face are so bright. But all I feel inside is darkness.

'Everything you're feeling is normal, I promise you,' she says. 'So don't be embarrassed. One in four people suffer from some form of mental illness. It can happen to any one of us.'

I peer at her. She's so beautiful and happy. She doesn't look like the type of person who could possibly suffer from any sort of mental anguish.

'It's an illness, Neena. Things go wrong with our body; they can also go wrong with our minds. And I'm here to help you get better. We're going to overcome this together.'

Help. Better. Overcome. I shake my head. It all sounds impossible. 'I've always worried more than other people,' I explain. 'I don't think I can be fixed.'

She tilts her head. 'I promise you you're not the only one who worries – we all do. Some people worry less, and some much more than you. But it's hard feeling this way so be kind to yourself, OK?'

I take a deep breath and nod.

'Are you feeling anxious now?' Laura asks.

'Yes. No. I mean, not really, not like I was. But I still feel like there's something stuck in my throat. And everything feels . . . difficult. And distant.'

Laura nods. 'That feeling of something being stuck in your throat is anxiety. So, as well as talk therapy, we'll look at relaxation techniques, cognitive behavioural therapy and mindfulness. We all get anxious from time to time – the important thing is learning to manage it. Does that sound OK?'

I nod.

'Would you like to tell me a bit about your relationship with your brother?' she says.

Now my throat really tightens. I wasn't expecting to talk about him so soon. Laura gently presses her fingers over her notes as she waits. She looks so perfect, so *together*. I'm not sure she'll get it.

After Akash disappeared – no, he didn't disappear, he died . . . After Akash died, Mum told me the world is divided. There are those who have lost someone they love and then there's everyone else. And 'everyone else' will never understand those who have lost someone, however hard they try.

'Do you have a brother?' I ask her.

She smiles. 'Yes.'

'Have you ever lost anyone?'

She nods. 'I was especially close to my grandmother.'

OK, so maybe she understands. 'He looked out for me,' I say. 'I mean, he *really* cared. And he just got me. I didn't need to explain things to him.'

Laura nods. 'You miss that?'

I try to swallow the hard lump in my throat. 'Yeah.'

'Do you feel like anyone cares about you now, Neena?'

'I've got Mum and Dad. And a couple of friends from school. But it was different with him. Like I said, he just got me. We were going through everything together.'

'Is there anyone who understands you now?' Laura's voice is as gentle as a lullaby.

And yet a razor-sharp pain shoots across my chest. 'Maybe one person,' I say, thinking about Josh. 'But it's complicated.'

There's silence for what feels like the longest time. Laura doesn't write anything on her notepad. She just sits, and so do I.

After a while, Laura says, 'Tell me more about your brother. What was he like?'

Where do I begin? 'He was generous. And kind. He never judged anyone, you know? I loved that about him. He used to buy me little presents to help me – art books and books about being calm. That sort of thing. And he was funny.' I smile. 'Everyone wanted to be his friend. And he wasn't afraid to speak up for what he thought was right.' I take a deep breath, realizing my cheeks are wet. 'He really was everything to me.'

Laura has a small crease along her forehead.

'We still don't know what happened to him,' I say. 'Not really.'

'I didn't know that,' Laura says, glancing down at her notes.

'They said he might have slipped into the river. Fallen. Or that he could've been pushed.' I dig my nails into my thighs through my jeans. 'Or . . .' I whisper. My skin crawls. 'That he jumped.' It feels such a relief to finally say that to someone. 'I couldn't believe any of it though . . . I never saw his body after the police found it, though Mum and Dad said I should. I . . . I didn't want to believe it.'

Laura nods. 'That's understandable.'

'I didn't even go to his wake. I . . . I couldn't handle the thought of him jumping.'

Her eyes are soft. 'You were close. That must be a very difficult thing to imagine.'

'I just wish I'd gone with him that night,' I say, my voice breaking. My throat and chest tighten so much I can barely breathe.

Laura looks confused.

'He . . . he wanted me to go to the party with him. If I'd gone, if I'd been there, I could've . . . stopped it all happening. I could've stopped him drinking so much. I could've stopped him climbing on to the bridge. I could've talked to him if he wanted to jump . . . I could've brought him home . . .' My throat is so tight it hurts. I try to breathe through all the pain, speak through it. 'He wanted me to go with him. If I'd just gone . . .'

Tears pour out of me. They drip on to my jeans like fat raindrops.

Laura moves a little closer to me on the sofa. Her perfume smells of roses and peaches. 'It's not your fault, Neena,' she says.

'But if I'd been there . . . If I'd just . . .' I cry and cry.

'Look at me,' she says after a while. 'Listen to me.'

I look at her. There are tears in her eyes too. 'It's *not* your fault,' she says.

I close my eyes. Let more tears come.

'Look at me again,' she says. This time, I look her in the eye.

'It's *not* your fault, Neena,' she says. 'It really isn't.'

And, for the first time, I begin to believe it.

37

Josh calls me before I have a chance to call him. 'Can you talk?' he asks. His voice is low and serious. 'I'm on lunch.'

I've been asleep – the session with Laura exhausted me. It was strange: I felt dizzy and drowsy and literally stumbled to my bed the moment she left. With the phone pressed to my ear now, I sit up. It's so good to hear his voice, but I'm also really nervous.

'Yes,' I say. 'I'm here.' I'm still spaced out, but I know that's also partly the meds.

Josh sighs. 'Oh, thank God, Neens. Are you . . . you know, OK?'

'I guess it depends on your definition of OK,' I say, trying to be a bit jokey. 'I'm not psychotic any more, if that's what you mean.'

'That's not what I meant!'

'No, I know, I know. I'm sorry.' I don't know what's wrong with me. I've been dying to speak to him, but it's like I've forgotten how. 'I'm feeling really groggy – from the meds,' I try to explain. 'And I had this intense counselling session which wiped me out.'

'You've got a lot going on.'

'Yeah. I'm sorry.'

'No, no, don't be sorry. I . . . I love you, Neens.'

I manage a smile. It's so good to hear him say that. 'I love you too.'

There's silence. It seems he's forgotten how to talk to me too. My insides twist. Why did things have to change?

He gives an awkward cough. 'So you're . . . all right?'

'Sort of . . . Does everyone at school know about me?' I hadn't realized how much that's been bothering me. I want to know. I don't want to know. I hold my breath.

'No one knows anything. They think you've got really, really bad flu.'

'Oh . . .' Relief washes over me. 'Good.' I don't want to hide but I'm also not ready to talk about this yet. I guess I need time to get used to everything myself first.

'Josh,' I say, feeling a sudden burst of warmth in my chest. He's my very, very good friend. He's known me most of my life. He's seen me in my bra. And held me while I've cried. 'I've missed you,' I tell him, as I imagine hugging him. I can almost feel the warmth of his body.

'Can I come and see you?' Josh says. 'I didn't know what to do when I couldn't get hold of you. I thought about coming to your garden or something. Can you sneak out?'

'No!' I say, a bit too abruptly. But I'm picturing the impossibly dark circles round Mum and Dad's eyes. Anxiety flares up in my throat like fire. 'Please don't come here, Josh. My parents – my dad . . .'

He doesn't say anything. I take a slow, deep breath. I know Josh isn't going to do anything I don't want him to – I just need to talk to him.

'I want to see you,' I tell him, 'but let's meet up somewhere else.'

'Yeah, OK. I'm sorry, I wasn't sure you were up to leaving the house . . .'

The panic subsides and I close my eyes. I imagine being under the willow tree with him, my head resting against his chest, listening to the strength of his heartbeat.

'I'm still weak,' I tell him honestly. 'But maybe in a few days?'

'Whatever you need, Neens.'

We're quiet again.

'Have you been stargazing?' I ask, suddenly wanting to know everything I've missed.

He laughs. 'Of course! And I've been thinking of you . . .'

I smile. And I think he's smiling too.

'Neens?'

'Yeah?'

'Was it my fault?' he says. 'What happened to you. Did I do that to you?'

'What?'

'If I hadn't pressured you to go out with me . . . If you hadn't had to deal with all that lying, all that guilt . . . And then I practically *made* you come out that night . . .' Josh sounds like he's crying now. 'I'm so sorry, Neens.'

My heart is bursting. I wish so much that I could hug him right now. 'No, Josh,' I say to him. 'You didn't force me into anything! You're the best thing in my life. How can you think that?'

He's quiet. Sniffs.

'Josh?'

'It's just . . . If I wasn't in your life, things would be a lot simpler for you, wouldn't they?' he says.

I breathe in deeply. 'Maybe. But I don't want that, OK?'

'I just want things back to normal,' he says.

'And they will be,' I tell him. 'Soon.'

But, even as I say it, I know it's not true. Everything, absolutely everything, has changed.

38

I message Fi after I speak to Josh, telling her not to visit the house. She turns up anyway, exactly twenty minutes later. We all sit in the living room, politely sipping tea. Dad is staring at his feet; Mum looks teary and tired. But they both try to smile. Fi's holding a piece of paper, which she keeps glancing at nervously.

'I need to tell you all something,' she says, and her voice is quiet and shaky. 'It's to do with Akash. And . . . and I'd really appreciate it if I could just talk. And then I'll leave you in peace.'

Mum and Dad don't say anything.

'It's OK, Fi,' I say.

She nods. Keeps her eyes on mine. 'Akash and I, we had a fight the night it happened.' She glances at Mum and Dad, and they look at each other. My heart beats hard against my chest.

'That's why he left mine and went over to a friend's house – Jay's . . .' She glances at Mum and Dad.

'Jay?' Dad says. 'Who's Jay?'

'He's . . . an old friend of Akash's,' Fi says, looking back at me.

I nod, encouraging her to go on. I'm feeling a huge surge of love for Fi; she promised me she'd find out what he knows and she has.

She breathes in deeply. 'Anyway, I've been speaking to him and trying to find out more details. He's finally admitted that he *was* with Akash when it happened.'

She looks down at her notes. 'I'm sorry, I . . . I don't want to forget anything . . .' Her hand's shaking a bit. She swallows and looks up at me again.

'I thought . . . I thought it would be good for us all to get some closure. Especially you, Neens. And I felt so guilty about the fight . . . Anyway . . . We all needed to know the truth about whether he –' her voice is shaking – 'was pushed. Or maybe even *jumped*.' She looks at me with her big, kind eyes. 'I know you worry about that, Neens.' She's staring at me, but I don't know what I'm thinking or feeling, or if I even want to hear what she's going to say. 'The report being inconclusive,' she continues, 'I found it so confusing and up-setting. I wanted them to investigate further, like we all did. Anyway . . . Jay – he says they were both messing around, balancing along the wall of the bridge. They'd been drinking a lot. But it was an accident.' Fi bursts into tears now. 'He slipped. He didn't jump.'

Mum and Dad begin to cry now too. And so do I. We all cry for what feels like a very long time.

Fi takes a deep breath and wipes her cheeks. 'I'm so sorry,' she says. 'For everything. Neena . . . if I just helped her live her life . . . I could maybe make everything better. But I . . . I can see now that I wasn't helping. I'm sorry, Neens.'

I go over to Fi and hug her. 'But you did help,' I say through my tears. 'You've been a really good friend.'

'I don't know about that, Neens,' Fi says.

'You really have,' I say, hugging her harder.

We all sit in silence for a while, until Fi gets up to leave. I see her out.

'Wait,' Mum says, and we turn back round to face Mum and Dad. They're clutching each other's hands really tightly.

'Thank you, Fiona,' Dad says, and Mum nods too, crying again.

At the front door, I step out with Fi, shutting it behind me so that I can say goodbye to her properly.

'Thanks for getting that out of Jay. Was it . . . OK?' I ask, thinking about that day in his room. I've made some bad choices over the past year, and I know that Fi has too, but I really hope that isn't one of them for her.

She shrugs. 'Yeah. I don't think he would've told me, but I accidently ran into his mum at his house and I explained the situation. She literally held him by the ear until he told me what happened!'

We both laugh at the image. Fi hugs me tight. When I let go, I look her in the eyes. 'Akash asked me to go to your party that night,' I say. 'If I'd been with him, I could've . . . stopped him falling.' My chest feels like a brick is crushing it as I stare at Fi.

She looks at me hard. 'Jay couldn't stop him,' she says firmly. 'No one could.'

I concentrate on breathing.

'You know that really, don't you, Neens?'

'I . . . I think so.'

She takes my hand and squeezes it until my chest loosens and I can breathe properly again. 'You know that really,' she repeats. I nod. I know she's right. Just like Laura said. It's not my fault. I couldn't have stopped it. It's not Fi's fault either.

'OK?' Fi asks.

I nod. 'OK.'

'Listen, I . . . I've also got a confession. I'm so sorry for flirting with Josh,' she says. 'But it never meant anything. And it was always one-sided – I don't think he even noticed!'

'What?' I can't believe what I'm hearing. 'I thought I'd imagined all that?'

She shakes her head. 'I would never have actually *done* anything. I promise. But I think my therapist will probably have something to say about it . . .'

I take a minute to let it all sink in. It's actually a relief to know I didn't make it all up. I knew it in my gut, or at least I thought I did.

'Hang on!' I say. 'Therapist?'

Fi sighs. 'I should've been honest with you about that too. I've been seeing one ever since Akash died. I guess I haven't been dealing with it all too well myself . . . I'm sorry. I really do care about you. I hope you know that. You're amazing. And brave and strong. If you can forgive me, I'd like to be here for you now. Or at least try . . .'

I smile at Fi. 'I'd like that,' I tell her.

'What are you doing Friday night?' she asks.

'Fi, I'm not, I won't be . . .'

'No, no, no more parties!' she says. 'Not for me either! I think I was trying to escape things too . . . But how about the cinema? We can catch up over dinner first?'

I nod. 'That sounds really wonderful.'

Fi looks relieved. Then she looks down at the ground. 'It was really scary seeing you like that, Neens. I thought . . . I thought I was going to lose you too. Look after yourself, OK? And if you ever want to talk . . .' She looks up now. 'They said you might not remember things?'

'Yeah,' I say, feeling just a bit brighter. 'Who are you again?'

We laugh, and it feels like the old us. But better. Truer.

39

It's a week later. Saturday morning. Almost 10 a.m. I'm waiting for another session with Laura, and Mum and Dad have gone to the hospital to see Raj. I sit on my bed, staring at my phone. I'm dying to message Josh, but instead I bury my mobile in the bedside drawer. We haven't talked much since last week's conversation and it keeps playing on my mind.

I wonder if Josh was right, a bit? Did the pressure of all the lying contribute to making me ill? With everything else of course.

The sound of a car pulling into the driveway interrupts my thoughts. The doorbell rings and I walk out into the hallway to answer it.

'Any chance of a cup of tea?' Laura says, shrugging off her leather jacket as she steps through the door. Her black hair is tied up in a bun today and she's wearing all white – white skinny trousers, white blouse and white sandals. She looks as elegant as a ballerina. Her eyes shimmer.

'Of course,' I say, still a bit distracted, thinking about Josh.

The kettle boils while Laura pulls out her notes and places them neatly on the dining table. I make two cups of tea and pass one to her as I sit down opposite.

'You star!' she says, pulling the mug towards her and taking a couple of sips. She glances at her notes. 'How are you feeling today?'

'I'm not sure,' I tell her honestly. 'I feel . . . worn out.'

Laura nods sympathetically. 'Counselling can be quite emotionally draining at first; make sure you get plenty of rest.'

I look into my mug. I do want to rest, but I can't stop thinking about Josh. *I just want things back to normal* – that's what Josh said to me last week. But were things ever normal for us? For me?

'I'd like to talk about when your anxiety started,' Laura says.

I nod. 'I mean, I was an anxious kid. But my brother helped keep it at bay, when I was little. And then he left, and I felt anxious all the time.'

Laura tilts her head. 'And was there anything you were particularly anxious about, leading up to your episode?'

'I'm not sure . . .' I say, fibbing a bit. 'I've been trying to figure it all out. Why does this sort of thing happen?'

Laura breathes in slowly. 'Well, it can happen for a number of reasons. Stress. Environmental or biological factors. Sometimes drugs . . . Often the exact cause isn't clear, and it can be a combination of factors.'

I nod. It makes sense for it to be more than one thing. That's life, isn't it? Hits you from all directions at once.

'Do I . . . maybe have an anxiety disorder?' I ask.

'At the moment, we're just trying to understand why it *might* have happened – to stop it happening again. Let's not put any labels on anything. OK?'

'Oh God. Will it happen again?'

'Hopefully not,' Laura says firmly. 'It can – it's important you take your medication and use the help offered. But you're on the right track, Neena. This could absolutely be a one-off.' She smiles at me.

'But it *could* happen again?'

'Well, yes. Some people have multiple episodes. They might need medication for life. Every single person's experience of psychosis is different, just like everyone's experience of anxiety is different. But just try not to worry, Neena. OK?'

It's a lot to take in, but I nod.

'So, we were talking about things you were particularly anxious about in the lead-up to you getting ill . . .'

I swallow. 'You asked me the other day if there's anyone who understands me like Akash did. Well, there's this guy. Josh. He does. Sometimes I even think he understands me better than I understand myself.'

Laura smiles. 'That sounds really special.'

'It is. But I've never been allowed a boyfriend so I've kept it hidden. And I think it's having an impact on us. And maybe on me . . . on my mental health. Or maybe my mental health has had an impact on us. I don't know, it's confusing . . .'

'That sounds hard. Is that pressure . . . cultural?' Laura asks carefully, and writes something down on her notepad.

I nod. 'I feel guilty a lot of the time. And torn. Like I can't just be myself without upsetting someone. I want to be in a relationship with him, but I also don't want to disappoint my parents. But then if I just do what they say all the time, it's like my feelings don't matter. *I* don't matter.' I shake my head. I'm not sure I'm making much sense. 'In many ways, they're really modern.' I laugh a bit. I hate that word 'modern'. It seems old-fashioned in itself. 'They don't make me wear salwar kameez at home, like some people I know,' I try to explain. 'But they have all these rules – they've been really overbearing since Akash. And all these cultural restrictions are just too much for me!'

Laura looks thoughtful. 'It sounds like there are some real pressures there,' she says. 'And we'll look at how you can address them. But there's also one other thing to consider.' She pulls out a 'Thought Challenging Chart' from her clipboard. She introduced them to me before she left the other day. 'Have you ever separated what is *actual* cultural pressure from your parents, and what is *perceived*? You might be projecting some of your own fears of letting them down on to them, and you could be viewing their rules as tight cultural boundaries when actually they're not about that.'

I cross my arms. 'Hmm . . . I don't know.' It's always felt pretty clear to me.

Laura pushes the Thought Challenging Chart towards me. 'You mentioned they became extra strict when Akash died. Could it be just about that? Their need to keep you safe? I suspect parents from any culture might do the same in response to a tragedy.'

As I look at the chart, I remember the whole incident with them wanting to take me on holiday to Pakistan. How I jumped to conclusions. And I remember Mum saying so many times, and Dad too, that they're just scared, that's all. Now it's like I'm hearing them for the very first time, and I finally understand.

'Will you give it a go?' Laura asks. 'It can really help challenge anxieties.'

'Yes,' I say, realizing that I've been running to Josh each time I've been anxious, relying on him to make me feel better, just like Akash used to. Now, it's time for me to rely on myself.

'Great,' says Laura. 'Let's try it now.' She smiles, but my cheeks are wet.

I'm understanding that Josh has been my safe space. He's been the only thing that calms me down for a while now. But that's not healthy. Not in the long term. Not for me but also not for him. For *us*.

40

Mum opens my curtains when she comes to give me my medicine the next morning, but I'm already awake. Light streams in, stinging my eyes. She kneels down beside my bed. She's wearing all black.

I look into her eyes. 'A whole year . . .' I say. She nods and strokes my cheek.

'What now?' I ask.

Mum takes a deep breath. 'Now we celebrate his life. We live, like he would want us to.' She tries to smile.

I put my arms round Mum and we hold each other tight.

After a while, Mum stands up. 'We're in the kitchen; come when you're ready.'

I nod but I don't move. After she's gone, I stare out of the window, at the bright sky and the drifting clouds. The sun slowly brightens. It's fierce on my face. I turn away from it and climb out of bed.

I want to be with Mum and Dad; I feel suddenly desperate for them.

They both look up at me when I walk into the kitchen. On the table is a cake big enough to feed five families. Three tiers of sponge with thick, frosty icing.

'What's this?' I ask, sitting down.

'I couldn't sleep last night,' Mum says. 'And he deserved a celebration. We never properly celebrated him. The wake . . . it was so grim . . . and you . . .' She glances at me. 'You weren't even there.'

I feel bad, and Mum must see it, because she shakes her head.

'It was the right thing at the time, Neena. You mustn't feel sorry. But now – *now* we celebrate him. And I was thinking we could scatter his ashes somewhere, once everything's a bit calmer. They've been in our bedroom for so long, hidden away . . .'

I'd been ignoring the urn, had almost forgotten they had it. But now it seems only right to set Akash free. 'Yes,' I say, nodding. 'That would be good.'

Mum cuts us slabs of cake and pushes plates towards us. The sponge is buttery and light and the icing is sweet and tangy. She pours us mugs of tea.

'I was bursting with pride the day he was born,' Dad says. 'I wanted to be a better person, to show him what a good man could be.'

I look at Dad. It's the first time he's talked about Akash like this. He's wearing black jogging bottoms and a black T-shirt and, although he's wearing those clothes because they're black, because of what today is, I remember Dad used to love running and playing football with his friends. He used to do a lot of that, before everything happened. I'd forgotten.

He shakes his head. 'But *he* was always teaching *me*. He had such an appetite for life, such gusto. He taught me to see what's around me.'

Mum rubs Dad's arm. 'He was always telling me he wanted to see the world,' she says. 'But he'd always say, "I'll come back to you, Ummi, don't you worry. I'll look after you when you're old."' She presses her hand against her heart. 'He was always trying to explain new things to me.'

Mum and Dad look at me. I realize they're waiting for me to say something too, but I don't know what to say. *Always trying to explain things? Teaching them? Really?* All they did for years was fight. With them, I realize, Akash was harsh and erratic and uncompromising. I feel a surge of anger towards him as I remember the pressure I felt to go to parties with him.

Then, and I don't know where it comes from, I laugh. 'I loved him,' I say, 'but didn't he give us all hell sometimes?'

Mum and Dad look shocked. Then Dad laughs too, and Mum joins in.

'Oh yes,' Dad says. 'Impossible, when he felt like it.'

'Couldn't get any sense out of him about his future,' Mum adds.

We all laugh and, when we stop, we're all crying. It's like now we've finally acknowledged his death it makes it so much easier to talk about him – flaws and all. It's easier to remember Akash, rather than the memory of Akash.

'He was loud and annoying and stubborn, but he could definitely make us laugh,' I say, sniffling. 'He'd do something to cheer us up if he was here.'

Dad nods.

'He'd make some comment about this cake for a start,' I say. 'What were you thinking, Mum? You could serve that at a wedding!'

'Don't you worry, your wedding cake will be three times this size,' Mum says, her face brightening a bit. 'Vanilla sponge, cream icing, strawberry jam. Classic. It will melt in people's mouth like butter.'

'Not *my* wedding,' I say, rolling my eyes. I can't help briefly thinking about Josh though. '*A* wedding, Mum.'

'Come on, stop all this talk of weddings and let's eat more of this cake,' Dad says, chuckling.

Mum cuts more slices. 'We're going to the hospital in a while. There's food in the fridge for lunch,' she says. 'I made chicken with aubergine. And there's naan bread. I didn't have time to make roti – you just need to heat it all in the microwave.'

She looks nervous suddenly, fingering her dupatta. 'Or maybe Dad should stay with you today.'

'It's OK,' I say. Tomorrow is Monday and then . . . 'The exams start on Thursday – I've got plenty to do.'

'Art first?' Dad says.

'Yeah. I could do with some practice – I haven't painted for ages.'

Dad nods. 'But I want you to know that there's no pressure, OK? You don't have to sit your exams if you don't want to.

Only do them if you're ready. I've been acting like . . . like the whole of our future depends on it.' He shakes his head. 'I shouldn't have put you under so much pressure. I just didn't want you to miss out on anything; I thought I was helping you focus, but I realize now that . . . I'm sorry, Neena.' He leans across and kisses me on the forehead.

I stare at Dad, and then at Mum, and take in a long, deep breath. Their eyes are swollen and red. They're worn out. My throat hurts as I realize – really realize – how much I've put them through. How much we've all been through. And, although I haven't had this conversation with them before, something about it is familiar. The way they're looking at me. Their gentle voices.

It's how it always was when I was a kid. Before Akash was a teenager and started drinking, and before they started fighting. Before he encouraged me to do the same and I began to hide things from them, stopped talking to anyone.

'Thanks, Dad,' I say, remembering that this – actually talking about things – is a better way. 'But I think I'm ready.' And, as annoying as Dad's been at times, I now wonder if I'd still be ready if he hadn't obsessed about my schoolwork. Even if it was another pressure, another possible trigger, to making me ill.

Mum looks suddenly uncomfortable. She wraps the corner of her dupatta round her little finger. 'I don't know – maybe *I* should stay with you today?'

I roll my eyes. 'Really, I'll be OK!'

Dad pushes a spoonful of cake into his mouth and leans over to pat Mum's arm. 'Listen to your daughter. She'll be OK,' he says. 'Give her some space.'

It's such an unexpected thing for Dad to say that we all laugh.

'Actually,' Mum says when we stop, 'we . . . we've also been talking, Neena. About counselling . . .'

'Yes, Mum,' I say. 'I know I need it. I'm doing well.'

She nods. 'Yes, but there's something else . . . We were wondering . . . If . . . if it's OK with you, we'd like to get some as a family.'

'Counselling?' I ask, shocked.

Mum nods. 'We've all been struggling. And I still am – it's difficult every time I leave the house . . .'

I look at Dad. 'You too?' I ask. Somehow I can't imagine him sitting in a room and talking openly about his feelings.

But Dad nods. 'I think it would be a very good idea,' he says.

'I thought you were both thinking we could pray this away,' I say, only half joking.

Dad smiles. 'We will still pray!' he says.

'But we've seen the difference that medicine and therapy has made to you already,' Mum adds. 'And we realize that we *all* need it.' She laughs. 'Better late than never?'

'It's a great idea,' I agree, my chest filling with so much relief that they're finally beginning to get it. And, as I look at Mum and Dad, I already feel a bit closer to them. Weird, but this will be the first time we're doing something as a family, even if it is therapy sessions! And that makes me feel . . . well, a bit less alone . . . and a bit more together. It feels like a fresh start.

'Right,' Mum says, standing up and clearing the dishes. 'I

need to get some clean clothes together for Raj,' she says to Dad. 'I'll pack a bag, and then we'll go.'

Raj. *Hope*. I'm beginning to feel more than just a bit of it. And suddenly I realize that art preparation can wait.

'Can I come too?' I ask. My heart is racing. 'I'm ready.'

41

The Neonatal Intensive Care Unit has white walls and grey tiled floors. It's clinical and serious, and the blue patterned curtains do nothing to hide that. I'm not sure what I expected. Those wicker baskets you sometimes see babies in? Maybe even nursery rhymes playing in the background? Instead, in every direction I look, there are machines, tubes, leads and tiny babies. I clutch Mum's arm.

'Why are they in those boxes?' I ask.

'They're incubators,' she says. 'They're like heated cots, to help them maintain their body temperature.'

I think I knew that really, but it's still weird seeing all the incubators lined up, with all the little babies inside. I don't know why but it makes me nervous. I guess because they seem so fragile. I take deep breaths as I follow Mum and Dad to the far end of the room.

There, a nurse in a white uniform is cradling a baby in her arms. She peers at us through her black-rimmed glasses. She looks efficient and tough. I get a good feeling from her.

'Morning, Mr and Mrs Gill. I've just changed his nappy and checked his temperature,' she says, her voice low. 'Good news – I think we'll be moving him from ICU to Ward 76 very soon!'

'Oh!' Mum says, smiling widely, and Dad makes a little noise of delight too. 'That's wonderful news!'

I'm not exactly sure what this means, but it's clearly good so I smile too.

Mum squirts some antibacterial gel on to her hands and passes me the tube. We're all standing round the efficient-looking nurse and the baby.

I realize that this baby is THE baby. It's Raj. Though I can't really see much of him from here, my heart beats fast, in a good way. After all the dreading and all the waiting, I'm truly excited to see him.

Mum takes tiny Raj from the nurse, holds him close to her chest; she plants soft kisses on his forehead. 'Look, Neena, betee,' she says. She turns, and I get my first proper look at him.

I stare at Raj's wrinkled skin and tiny arms. His small nose. He has a white knitted blanket round him. And long eyelashes. My breath catches in my throat.

My brother.

'Do you want to hold him?' Mum asks.

I nod.

The nurse indicates an armchair next to the incubator. 'You can sit down. Make yourself comfortable.'

I sink into the chair.

'Meet your sister, Raj,' Mum says, very carefully placing him in my arms.

I look down at him. He's so small. And light. So fragile. I cradle him against my chest. Everything around me fades away.

I stare at his little ears, the size of pennies, at his fingernails, not much bigger than grains of rice.

He turns his face towards me, presses it into my chest. Then he yawns, his little mouth forming a perfect 'O'.

Mum and Dad are talking, but I don't hear what they say.

'Hi, Raj,' I whisper.

He opens his eyes and they glint at me, tiny dark pools. And then close again.

Oh, Raj! He's perfect.

There's a painting by Gustav Klimt called *The Three Ages of Woman*. It has a woman with long, flowing blonde hair, with flowers in it, and she's leaning her head on her baby, who is tucked in close to her. They've both got their eyes closed and they look so content in each other's arms. They fit together, completing each other. Whenever I've looked at that painting, I've felt a warm glow inside.

But now, thinking about that picture while cradling Raj, fire burns in my stomach. Like the woman and her child, we are also our own world. He's my brother and I'm his sister.

Just like Akash is my brother, and I am his sister.

And nothing will ever change that.

42

A few days later, I call Raheela and ask her if she'd like to come over. She says she's really glad I called – study leave has started and there's no school, so she'll come right away. I lie on my bed and stare at the ceiling while I wait for her. I think about Raj. I've been visiting him every day and I still can't believe how tiny and perfect and beautiful he is. I picture his bright eyes, and I feel light and warm.

There's a knock on the door.

'Come in,' I say, sitting up and swinging my legs over the side of the bed.

Raheela edges in hesitantly, clutching a huge carrier bag. 'Your mum let me in,' she says. 'I hope that's OK.' She's dressed all in black: skinny jeans, vest top, hijab and lots of black eyeliner. Plus tons of silver jewellery. I notice a tremor in her hands.

'Of course! And don't look so worried,' I say, laughing. Now that she's here, I can't remember why I was so anxious about seeing her.

She smiles. 'How are you feeling? Oh God, that's probably a really insensitive thing to ask. Is it? Sorry . . .' She puts down the bag and sits on the edge of the bed next to me.

'No, no – I'm doing . . . OK. A lot better than I was.'

She plays with one of the millions of bracelets on her wrist. 'I'm sorry I . . . I haven't been there for you,' she says. 'I should've noticed something was wrong. I mean, I knew something was up, but I had no idea how bad . . .' She looks down at her lap. 'I've been a terrible friend.'

'No, no one could've known. Don't feel bad. And anyway I'm a lot better . . .'

She smiles. 'I've actually got a get-well present for you.' She picks up the carrier bag and puts it in my lap. 'My books so you can catch up. I'm done with revision, so you can have them.'

I laugh. 'Wow, you really know how to cheer a girl up.'

'I know, I know. You can thank me later. Oh, and I saw Mr Butler the other day. He said he's really pleased you're sitting the exam. Is it tomorrow?'

I nod.

She nods too. 'And he said to use your experience. Draw from life and inject it into your work! Or something deep like that. Oh, and that you're a lot more talented than you let yourself know.'

I hug Raheela. 'Thank you. I've missed you so much.'

'I've really missed you too,' she says, hugging me back.

After Raheela leaves, I've still got a couple of hours until my session with Laura. Mum and Dad have gone back to the hospital to see Raj, so I try calling Josh, but I get his voicemail. I leave him a message asking how he is, and saying it would be good to chat soon. Maybe even meet up? I'm feeling much more like my old self today, I tell him, and I can't wait to see him.

I lie on my bed and think about what I want to discuss with Laura today. She says I'm making good progress and that I should think of anything I haven't yet talked about to get the most out of our time together. But I'm not sure what I want to chat about today.

I'm a bit nervous about exams starting tomorrow, but I know that's normal. And I realize the world's not going to end if I do mess up.

I still miss Akash, but that's normal too.

Josh and I aren't chatting much and I don't know what to make of it. I miss him but I'm not panicking. I'm not having any racing thoughts. I'm controlling my flutters of anxiety. And I'm learning to challenge my thoughts using CBT when something irrational or worrisome pops into my head.

I think maybe Josh and I just need a bit of space after everything that's happened. I wanted him to fix me so much – but I now realize that you can't rely on other people for that. It doesn't mean we don't care about each other. I do care. And I know he does too.

I'm feeling positive. I know I'll be on meds for a while yet, to make sure I don't get ill again, but that's OK. I'm learning that mental health is always a continuing journey anyway.

Wow – I've learned, and am learning, a lot.

I take a deep breath and listen to the quiet. The house is silent. I wonder what it will be like when Raj is home; I try to imagine his gurgle noises filling the house. His sweet, hiccupy cry. Raj. My brother. He makes me want to be better, to look after myself so I can look after him too.

I get up and walk over to my dressing table. Looking up, I see that my sky-sea poster is missing. I frown, and look around. I check under my bed, but there's nothing at all there – I cleared out all the empty alcohol bottles the other day. I look in my wardrobe, but it's not there either. I find it behind my dressing table and I have a vague memory of either me or someone else putting it there, though I have no idea why. After I've hung it back up, I look at it for a while.

It really does capture how I feel in the world. A bit wobbly at times, but often beautiful, and that really is OK.

I walk out into the hallway and press my palm against Akash's bedroom door, but instead of going in I slide my fingers along the wall until I reach the kitchen. I look around the room. I've told Mum and Dad so many lies in here, just trying to be myself. But I'm going to try to be more honest with them from now on.

In my mind, I see Josh's kind face. I taste his fierce kiss. Then I picture the dark circles under Mum and Dad's eyes, and Mum sitting beside my bed night after night when I was ill. I think of Raj again and his smell, sweet and soft, like milk and honey.

I tie my hair up off my face and open the back door. Warm air blows into the kitchen and I breathe it in as I peer out at the grass and the trees and the blue sky. Slipping off my sandals, I step out on to the patio. The stone is warm beneath my bare feet. The air's thick. The sun glides over my bare arms as I step on to the lawn; warm strands of grass tickle between my toes.

Sinking to the ground, I stretch my face up to the sky. I listen to the gentle breeze rustling leaves in the trees, the noise of distant traffic passing on the road. The sun warms my face.

I smile.

Josh is waiting on the Ridgeway as we've planned. He's sitting on the grass, peering out at the rolling hills with his legs stretched in front of him. The sun is setting, its orange glow fierce against the lilac sky. Our eyes meet as I walk towards him. I want to run into his arms – it's all I want – but I stop myself.

'Neens,' he says, standing up and pulling me in for a hug.

His soft yellow hoody smells of soap and coffee and his eyes are almost luminous green in the strange evening light. He has stubble on his cheeks – when did that happen? – and his hair is long, down to his chin. We sit on the grass and he looks at my face, waiting for me to say something.

I've missed you, I want to say. *Can we go back to the way things were?*

But the words are stuck somewhere deep inside, and really I know that there's no going back to how everything was.

Things have changed. We've changed.

The silence seems too much for Josh. He looks out into the distance again.

'I love coming up here,' he says.

'You do?' I've never seen him here before.

'Yeah, I used to come a lot. Early mornings, before school. Helps me put things into perspective. Reminds me how big the world is, you know?'

'Yeah,' I say, wanting to grab hold of his hand. 'That's exactly it.'

We suddenly turn to face each other again.

'I've missed you,' Josh says.

'I'm sorry,' I say.

We laugh because we've both spoken at the same time and then Josh asks, 'Sorry for what?'

'Everything? I don't know . . . It's all been so intense, hasn't it?' I notice dark shadows under his eyes and my heart sinks. I wish I'd been able to spare him all the heartache of the past few weeks. 'I'm sorry for dragging you into it all.'

'You didn't drag me into anything, Neens. I love you.'

I manage to smile at him. 'I know. And I love you too.'

Josh smiles back. 'So what now?' he asks nervously.

I take a deep breath. *What now?* It's a good question.

'Well, I finally told my mum about you.'

'What?' He smiles. 'You told her? Wow! What did she say?' He stops smiling. 'But what does it mean? Will she let you see me? I don't want to lose you, Neens.'

He reaches for my hand and squeezes my fingers. I let him. It feels so good to hold his hand again.

'It's OK,' I tell him. 'It's going to be OK. It'll take time for her to come round to the idea properly. But I just couldn't do it any more, you know, all that lying, all that guilt.'

Josh nods. 'It was so hard. I can't imagine how it was for you . . . And then everything with your brother . . .'

'Yeah . . .'

Josh puts his arm round me and I lean into him.

'Why do people have to die?' I say, more to myself, and the world, than to Josh.

'My mum used to say it's to make space for new people in the world.'

'Do you believe that?' I ask.

'I don't know. But I believe that someone new can walk into your life and remind you what it means to live. As cheesy as that sounds!'

My throat aches. 'No, it's not cheesy. It's true. But I also think . . . I don't know . . . that you also sort of have to remind yourself?'

Josh nods. 'You're right. But I love you, Neens. And you *have* reminded me of how great things can be, despite all the crap that life can throw at you.'

I force myself to pull away from his embrace, just for a moment. 'And that's great, and I love you too,' I say. 'But I was thinking it might be a good idea to tone things down a bit? I mean, we're only fifteen and I've – we've – been through a lot. I need to take some time to focus on me . . . And perhaps you should do the same?'

I hold my breath and watch Josh's face. I want him to tell me he understands, that he maybe even feels the same, but he doesn't say anything. He looks out at the hills for what feels like ages. I try to hold myself together. I know this is the right thing to do, however painful it is.

He finally looks at me. And, as we look into each other's eyes, I know that this isn't what either of us really wants, but it's what we both need. I bury my face in his hoody again; breathe in his sweet, soapy smell.

Then he presses his lips against mine. And we have one last kiss.

Two Months Later

I'm sitting on our bench. Mine and Akash's. The morning's just beginning, but it's already warm. I close my eyes and feel the soft sun on my face. I breathe in slowly, deeply, and look out across the Ridgeway; my eyes glide over the gentle slopes of the hills in the distance. I listen to the silence. Finally, I look down at the envelope I'm clutching.

My GCSE results.

It's a moment that I always thought I'd share with him – Akash, my brilliant, amazing, troubled big brother. But I'm alone, and that's OK.

Whatever happens, I'll be OK.

My hands are steady as I tear open the envelope and scan the page. My shoulders relax. I smile. Breathe in the warm air.

Our worst misfortunes never happen, and most miseries lie in anticipation.

I can't remember who said that, but Laura gave me the quote during one of our sessions and I think it's true. I get out my phone to message Raheela and Josh. And then I dial home.

*

Mr Butler grins when he sees me. He stands up and leans across his desk to shake my hand. 'You star!' he says. 'You like to keep me on my toes, but I knew you could do it!'

I look for my painting among the others spread out around the room. I spot it in the corner.

I've painted a waiting room in a psychiatric ward. In the middle of the room, two people in love are dancing. The waiting room has white walls and white chairs, but the man and woman are dressed in red. Around them, the world is a hazy swirl – the seats meld into people, into lamps, into the stained-glass window, into the single painting of flowers on the wall.

But the couple, they are solid, clear, bright. Untouched by the chaos around them.

My heart had hammered against my chest as I painted.

There's no ceiling to the room. Just the sky, dark navy, bursting with bright golden stars. It's as if the outside has come inside, or the inside out, intertwining. It looks like it could be any waiting room, and I like that. It could be an A & E, or a maternity ward. I've called it *Love in a Waiting Room*.

'It's a beauty,' Mr Butler says. 'Original and technically very solid. I knew it was top marks as soon as I saw it and the examiner agreed. You were inspired!'

I stare at the painting. I love the way it pulls you towards this couple in red, the way the waiting room swirls around them like a dream. It feels like something only I could have drawn.

I look back at Mr Butler. 'It's one of the best paintings I've seen this year,' he tells me. 'You should be very proud of everything you've achieved.'

'Thank you,' I say. And I am. I am proud.

My phone buzzes. It's a message from Josh, asking me if I want to meet for a celebratory coffee. I smile. I'm so glad we're still friends.

Later, after coffee with Josh and lots of chats with Raheela and Fi, me, Mum and Dad celebrate everything with a Chinese takeaway. Then we sing nursery rhymes to Raj and once he's asleep we all take a nap in the living room ourselves. It's dark again when I wake up. Mum and Dad are still draped across the sofa, fast asleep. Dad's snoring; Mum has a half-eaten spring roll in her lap and mugs of cold tea sit on the coffee table. Raj likes to wake at night, which has been tiring them out. I sleep through anything these days.

I move the spring roll off Mum's lap and sit watching them for a moment. Dad went to play tennis with his friend this afternoon, and is still in shorts and trainers. Mum's been going to a mother-and-baby group, so she makes an effort to get dressed every day. She's lost some weight and she smiles a lot. Things are returning to normal. Well, our version of normal.

The house is quiet. Still, I tiptoe down the hallway and slip into Raj's room.

The bright white room looks magical in the soft glow of the lamp. It smells of paint. All new, all fresh. There's a small white shelf with some children's books on it. A blue-and-white mobile hangs above the crib with stars and a moon dangling from it.

I crouch down next to the crib and peer through the bars. My heart skips a beat.

Raj is so tiny. His head the size of an apple. Hands curled into fists no bigger than Maltesers. He's beautiful.

'I'm your sister,' I whisper. 'And you're my brother.' My eyes fill. 'I'm going to look after you.'

He stirs, yawns. His tiny hands uncurl, spreading out like beautiful starfish, and then curl up again. He whimpers and my throat aches.

'Shh,' I say. 'Don't cry.' I slip my arm through the bars of the crib and rest my hand on his stomach, the way I've seen Mum do. I gently rub my palm against his tummy.

His breathing steadies. The ache in my throat eases. I rest my forehead against the bars. I can't stop staring at him.

I wonder what he'll be like. Will he be quiet or loud? Serious? Adventurous? Will he like art? What will we do together? Where will we go? What will we see?

I stand up and wander around the room. The carpet is soft beneath my bare feet as I stroke my hand over the new furniture. The white curved chest of drawers. The bookshelf. The single white wardrobe.

Akash is gone. All of his stuff is gone.

But he's still here. I can feel him.

I look out of the window and touch my fingertips against the cool pane of glass. I listen to the noise of the traffic. I watch a couple walking hand in hand down the road. Street lights shine against the darkness. Raj's gentle snuffling fills the room.

Life goes on. You try to stop it but it has to. Even when you have a huge, gaping hole in your heart, it must. In the end, all you can do is give in to its flow, however scared you are, however lost. Let it take you forward, back, then forward again – to where you need to be, where you need to go.

For the first time I can remember, I feel whole, like I've managed to glue the million pieces of myself back together. And I feel free. Really free. For so long, I've been looking for something or someone to help me breathe – but now, now I can breathe alone.

I tie my hair back off my face and take a long, deep breath.

You have a picture of how your life will be when you're older. A dream, I guess you could call it. Lots of dreams – some big, some small. All important. Those dreams, the belief that you will live them, propel you forward from day to day, week to week, month to month – and sometimes from minute to minute. When part of that picture shatters, slips through your fingers like ice-cold water, you can lose yourself within that loss. All your plans sink away.

But whether your dream is intact, or broken, you have to be brave. You have to take leaps of faith from day to day. You might worry about things but that's OK. You just have to be strong and let people and dreams find you again.

You have to piece yourself back together.

I grip the windowsill and press my forehead against the glass. I peer up at the dark sky.

The stars are twinkling, like tiny seeds of hope, and the moon has appeared. It's full and bursting with brightness.

Like my beating heart.

Dear Reader,

I wrote *The Million Pieces of Neena Gill* after someone very close to me suffered a psychotic breakdown. I was there. I looked after them. I cared for them afterwards. We were a team: there was the illness and then there was us, and we weren't going to let it win. It was scary, and it was hard, but we survived. And we eventually came out the other end stronger.

But one of the things I found hardest was watching the recovery afterwards. The lack of understanding from people who had no experience of mental illness, but did have plenty of opinions on it, most of them very negative. Battling that stigma day after day was unbelievably tough – as if fighting the illness itself wasn't hard enough.

I knew that stigma.

I had experienced it myself.

Although this book is fictional, there is a large part of me in Neena. I suffered from a long period of extreme anxiety many years ago. I've been to the dark place. I understand the darkness. The feeling that it's swallowing you up and that you're losing yourself to the illness. I didn't really talk to anyone about it because I wasn't sure they would understand. And with that secrecy came shame.

What's wrong with me? Why can't I be 'normal'?

I felt completely alone.

But I'm here to tell you that there is no 'normal'. And there is nothing 'wrong' with someone who is suffering: mental illness can happen to *anyone*. Neena is just an ordinary teenager going through a difficult time in her life. She is anxious, like so many of us. But she's also so much more than that. She is brave and kind, creative and intelligent, and she has courage and strength that she didn't know she had. This illness is not her whole story: it does not define her.

So if you take anything away from this novel, let it be this: it's not abnormal to struggle sometimes; you are not alone; you are stronger than even you know.

When Neena finally accepts her illness and loss, she says this:

Sometimes you need to remind yourself who you are, don't you?

If you are suffering, or even if you're not, take time to remind yourself of who *you* are. It's so easy to lose yourself in this busy, noisy world. Find yourself, and your dreams, and keep them close. If you know someone who is struggling, please tell them: *You are more than this thing that you are going through.* And if you are struggling, then dig deep within yourself and start fighting.

Fight for a better, brighter day. A day where those million pieces of your heart and life, the million pieces of you, can slowly but surely start coming back together.

I believe you are strong enough.

I believe in you.

With love,
Emma xxxx

Getting Help

If you or someone you know has been affected by any of the issues raised in this book, please remember you're not alone.

The following organizations might help:

The Samaritans (www.samaritans.org) are there if you need someone to talk to. Completely confidential and supportive, the Samaritans are available to listen twenty-four hours a day. Call free, any time, from any phone: 116 123.

You could also call Childline on 0800 1111.

YoungMinds (www.youngminds.org.uk) supports young people's mental health and has a good section on understanding your feelings and how to get help.

Mind (www.mind.org.uk) has an A–Z of mental health with information on a wide range of conditions and details of various treatment options. There are also lots of case studies, plus self-care tips.

If you'd like to find a counsellor, the following links to associations of accredited counsellors in your area might help:

UK Council for Psychotherapy –
https://www.psychotherapy.org.uk

British Psychological Society – www.bps.org.uk

The British Association for Counselling and Psychotherapy – https://www.bacp.co.uk

You might also consider approaching your GP, who may be able to tell you about local services that can help.

For more resources, including useful books and things that I've found helpful for anxiety, please visit my website.

Acknowledgements

I was very young when I discovered the power of stories. How they allow us to travel without moving our feet. How they can transform us, and make us feel less alone. How they can save us. So it's such a privilege to be able to tell one of my own, and I'm truly thankful to the wonderful people who have helped make that happen.

First and foremost, my heartfelt thanks to editor extraordinaire Naomi Colthurst. You have made my journey to publication so special. Thank you for your love for this book from the very start. Thank you for handling Neena (and me!) with such care and attention. Thank you for believing in us. This book is what it is thanks to you.

And a very big thank-you to my super agent, the incredible Jo Unwin. Your enthusiasm for Neena's story – and your endless support and wisdom – means so much. There's no one I'd rather have in my corner.

To the whole team at Penguin Random House Children's, but especially: Andrea Kearney, you designed the perfect cover for Neena and I can't thank you enough; Shreeta Shah, you have been a dream copy-editor, thank you for your careful notes and suggestions; Jasmine and Michael, my very own dream team, I am so lucky to have you two by my side through publication. Special thanks to Siena Parker and everyone involved in the brilliant WriteNow scheme. To my fellow mentees: what a privilege to share this journey with such a talented bunch! Nazneen Ahmed, thank you for reading an early copy and for your kind words. And an extra big thank-you to Ruth Knowles: this journey began with you, and I honestly couldn't think of a better home for Neena than PRH Children's.

I have many ridiculously talented writer friends who have supported me: I'm grateful to you all. But I have to say a special thank-you to a few. Dr Sharon Lewis, I can't quite express how special your friendship is and how much it means to me. Thank you for reading, for your endless support, for your professional advice and for your constant generosity. I'd be lost without you. And Abi Lown, I could not wish for a kinder writing buddy: thank you for all the last-minute reading, the pep talks and your brilliant insights. More than anything, thank you for always being there. To my small but wonderful writing group, Sanjida Kay and Claire Snook, for all your encouragement, feedback and wisdom, especially in the early days. You ladies helped me stop procrastinating and get Neena's story down on paper in the best way that I could. Thank you. And to Ali Reynolds, thank you for believing so fiercely that I could do this. Sometimes people come into your life at just the right time; this was one of those times.

Thank you, dear Dr Bekki Stone, for reading (more than once!), for understanding so completely, for supporting me so generously and for giving me your professional thoughts. Any mistakes are my own. Your passion for this book has meant so much – and your friendship has kept me going through my own tough times, for which I'll always be thankful.

To my brilliant Bristol writing group: Tannith, Harriet, Ken, Kate and everyone else, thank you for always being there and for championing the early chapters of this book. You are all wildly talented and I look forward to sharing bookshelves with you.

Over the years, I've been incredibly lucky to have some outstanding writing teachers. Thank you, all of you. But special thanks to David Morley for being the first to tell me I was a writer and setting me on this path, and to Maureen Freely for the words that made all the difference at a time when I needed them. Richard Kerridge, Mimi Thebo, Lucy English and Glenn Carmichael – your encouragement has meant so much.

It's been such a pleasure to have met the Nineteen Newbies on this journey. Aisha Bushby, thank you for sharing my excitement when the good things began happening and for all your advice in the early days. And a very special thank-you to Yasmin Rahman for being my sounding board when I barely knew you, and for your generous sensitivity-read and boundless enthusiasm for this book. I'm so glad Neena found her way to you, and that I did too.

To my wonderful family: where do I start? Thank you for your unwavering belief in me and for all your support. Son and Sim, for all the endless chats, the coffees, and for dreaming with me. Kit, for all your thoughts and excitement at every stage. Dad, thank you for filling the house with poetry and your stories when we were growing up, and not even realizing the impact they had. Thank you, dear Mum, for helping us believe that anything is possible, and for showing us that too.

And to my Nano, who is no longer here – but who lives on, fiercely and wildly, in all of us. I will be forever grateful for everything you taught me simply by being you. My very own Akash – with me wherever I go. My dear family, thank you for having such big hearts, and for teaching me to grow mine again after things were hard. You are, all of you, an inspiration.

And, last but not least, to my loves Oli and Benji. Thank you, thank you, thank you. Oli, you have shared my dreams and joined me on this adventure, and it's been such a privilege to share it with you. And thank you, my darling Benji, for making my dreams bigger. You are so strong and unbelievably kind, and you inspire me every day. You are both my world.

About the Author

Emma Smith-Barton was born in South Wales to Pakistani parents. Growing up between cultures has heavily influenced her writing, and she is especially interested in exploring themes of identity and belonging. Before writing, she taught in secondary schools for six years and is passionate about increasing awareness of mental health in young people. Her short stories have appeared in various publications, such as *Mslexia* and the Bristol Short Story Prize 2016 anthology (under her pseudonym for adult fiction, Amna Khokher). *The Million Pieces of Neena Gill* is Emma's first novel for young adults.

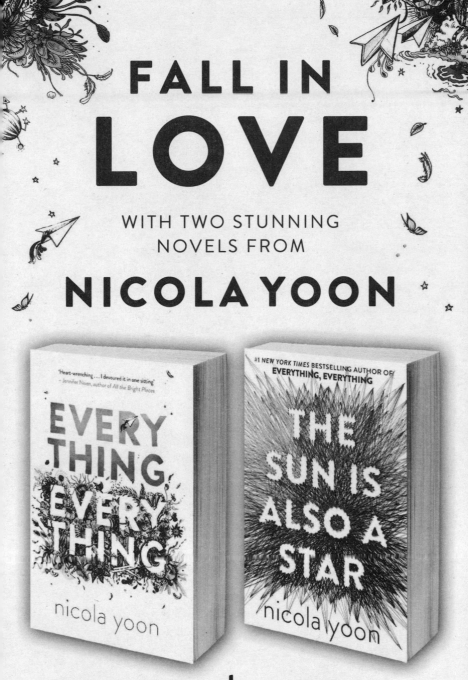

HAVE YOU READ
Jennifer Niven's
STUNNING
YA STORIES?

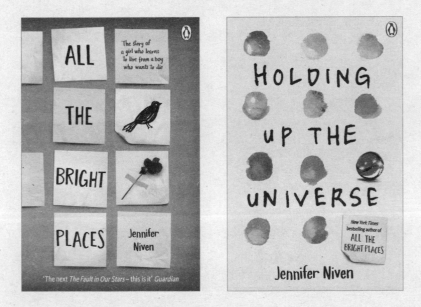